# EVENINGS
## AT THE
# TANGO PALACE

Also by Alan Schwartz —

No Country for Old Men
*New American Library, New York, 1980*

# EVENINGS
## AT THE
# TANGO PALACE

◆

Alan Schwartz

XYZ Associates LLC

EVENING AT THE TANGO PALACE
XYZ Associates LLC
Atlanta, Georgia

*Cover design, book design, page layout and editing*
Marian Haley Beil

◆

ISBN-978-0692485323

May 2016

*For Joan*
*"for keeps"*

# CAST OF CHARACTERS

*In order of appearance:*

Max Bergman (1950– ) — the protagonist

Ben Bergman (1920–1990) — Max's father

Rita Peretz Bergman (1925–1977) — Max's mother

Arlene Bergman Stein (1946– ) — Max's sister

Ursula Miller (1950– ) — Max's romantic companion

Eddy Stein (1944– ) — Arlene's former husband

Ellen Bergman Stein (1971– ) — Arlene and Eddy's daughter

Charlotte Bergman Baum (1932– ) — Ben's sister

Phil Peretz (1928– ) — Rita's brother

Nachman Peretz (1895–1950) — Rita's father

Adelle Balanescu Peretz (1901–1942) — Rita's mother

Meyer Bergman (1910–1970) — Ben's cousin

Viola Balanescu Frank (1926– ) — Rita's cousin

Mike Frank (1924– ) — Viola's husband

Jules Gordon (1950– ) — friend of Max

Theo Theophrastes (1947– ) — friend of Max

Angela Battaglia (1947– ) — friend of Max

## Ben's side of the family

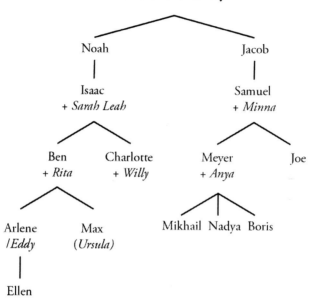

## Rita's side of the family

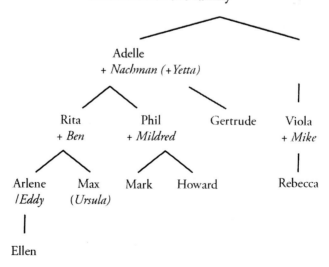

# GLOSSARY

*Babka* A dense, yeasty, cinnamon coffee cake.

*Ess und gedenk* Eat and remember.

*Gentile* A non-Jewish person.

*Gonif* A cheater, crook, or thief.

*Goy* A gentile

*Goyish* Gentile-like.

*Gut Shabbos* Good Sabbath, a greeting

*Gymnasium* A secondary school in Germany, Russia, or Eastern Europe.

*Hassidim* An ultra-orthodox Jewish sect.

*Kaddish* A Hebrew prayer for the dead.

*Kaddishl* A son or daughter who says kaddish for a parent.

*Kibitzer* A joker or teaser; one who gives unsolicited advice.

*Kvetch* To complain *v.*; A complainer *n.*

*Landesman* Relative, or person from the same country, compatriot.

*Macher* An important person, as in "big macher" ("big deal")

*Mensch* A decent, honorable person.

*Meshugenah* Crazy person.

*Minyan* A quorum of ten persons gathered for prayer.

*Nachis* Joy, good luck.

*Narishkeit* Foolishness.

*Ne plus ultra* The ultimate. (Latin)

*Nudge* To bother or pester.

*Oy* An exclamation of grief or pleasure depending on context.

*Pishiker* Literally "a little pisser." Affectionately applied to a child, contemptuous to an adult.

*Pishke* An alms collection box, usually a small can with a slotted top for coins.

*Plotz* To drop dead.

*Rauch nicht* A request: "Don't smoke."

*Schmagegge* A jerk, fool.

*Schmuck* Literally "prick." Usually a heavy-duty jerk, fool.

*Schnorrer* Literally "beggar." Usually a person who is always looking for whatever is free.

*Shabbos* The Sabbath; Saturday for Jews

*Shiksa* A gentile woman.

*Shiva* Literally the number 7. Generally used to mean the seven days of formal mourning.

*Shonda* Shame.

*Shtarker* A strong, tough, resilient person: "She's a real shtarker, she beat the cancer."

*Shtetl* A rustic Eastern European village where Jews were permitted to live.

*Shtick* Literally, "piece." Used figuratively to describe people offensively e.g. "shtick pferde"(a piece of a horse i.e "dumb") or "shtik drek" (a piece of shit), or quirks.

*Shul* Literally, "school." Used mostly to refer to the Synagogue (where worshippers study sacred texts).

*Shys* NYC slang, an abbreviation for "shyster."

*Taliener* An Italian.

*Tam* Taste.

*Tz'drehter oigen* Literally "crossed eyes." Cockeyed.

*Verkakteh* Shitty.

*Yenta* A busybody or gossip.

# EVENINGS
## AT THE
# TANGO PALACE

# 1

THE SMELL OF BURNING LEAVES drifted through the October air, and Max lifted his eyes from the grave in front of him to look around for the smoke. In the garden of a house on the other side of the cemetery fence, a guy shoveled leaves into a smoldering oil drum. Beyond, a huge jetliner dropping slowly toward Kennedy, hardly moving, as though the invisible hand of a child held up a toy in the hazy, morning sky.

The burial had said nothing to him, no drama at the open pit. Just memory. The last cars left the cemetery, hugs done, cheeks kissed, hands shaken, tongues tutted, and he stood alone watching the gravediggers toss the brown dirt onto his father's coffin. The ghost would come . . .

◆

"You'll break my heart," his father said, holding Max's hand as they crossed the street.

It was a Saturday afternoon and Max had gone to his father's office after going to the movies with his friends. He liked visiting the office with its shiny brass plaque, "Benjamin Bergman, Chiropodist," on the door, the smells of the medicines, the sharp cutting instruments in the sterilizer tray, and the large, clean, steel-lidded

1

glass jars of cotton and gauze and swabs. The room was paneled in dark wood and he felt safe there, secure.

When his father was ready they walked toward Grandma's house for the regular Sabbath visit. If his father had what he called a "good week," Max knew that the four of them, his sister Arlene, his mother, Rita, his father, Ben, and he would go out to eat. Max hoped it was a "good week." He could already taste the pastrami, the sour pickles, the cream soda.

"And what if I don't want to be a doctor?" Max asked as he had before.

"I've already told you," Ben Bergman said to his son, "it would break my heart."

Was his father's heart like a box of Valentine candies that spilled all over the street when somebody pulled the top off too quickly and broke it?

"I want you to be a doctor," he continued. "You'll like it. You'll be an important person and make a lot of money. Did you ever see a poor doctor?"

Max never had. At 10 years old, he had seen very few doctors. Dr. Felner, the huge man who visited the house when Max or Arlene was sick, was the only one he ever came close to, and Dr. Felner scared him. He was so tall he ducked his bald head under doorways, and he talked too fast. Max felt that the doctor didn't like him because of something he had done.

He also knew that his father was called "Doc" by a lot of people, but he wasn't really a doctor. He fixed their feet, and he wore a white coat, but he really wasn't a doctor, and he wanted Max to be like Dr. Felner. Max didn't want to be bald and to have to duck his head under doorways.

"Are we poor, Daddy?" Max asked.

"No, but I have to work too hard not to be poor the way we once were, and I don't want that for you. Be a doctor."

◆

2

Max did become a musician, and his sister became a physician. He was forty now and their father never forgave either one of them. There were rules about what boys and girls should do.

He stepped back from the graveside and sat down on a concrete bench, letting his eyes wander over the headstones. He was surrounded by the past — by the graves of his mother, grandparents, aunts and uncles, friends of his parents, and even one of his cousins, Rebecca Nevins, the daughter of his mother's cousin, Viola.

Rebecca was one day older than Max and used to play with him when his family visited her parents' house in Flatbush. She teased him and ignored him, and once hid in the closet with him and let him feel under her brassiere the little lumps hardly larger than his own.

"What's the big deal?" he asked, and she kicked his shin. Then he socked her in the stomach and she cried. His mother slapped him and then he cried.

"You must never, never hit a girl again," his mother said, "especially in the stomach. Promise." He promised.

Eight years later Rebecca died giving birth, and now she lay here, a few graves away from his parents, almost completing his childhood. Everyone came here sooner or later. A process of accounting.

The gravediggers finished, leaving a mound of pale soil piled a foot higher than the ground level. One of them stuck a little signpost into the edge of the mound. "Benjamin Bergman," it said, with the date of his death. For them it was just a job, all in a day's work. They climbed into their pick-up truck and drove away, taking no notice of Max. Deference to grief? Indifference? For them only the dead existed.

◆

The last part of the rehearsal worried him the most because he'd scored some changes to his opera, and he would hear them played by the orchestra for the first time. Accompanying the final aria, "My life locked out, I hid, children heard the whispers . . ." — the death scene — the woodwinds were scored with the Argentine motif that he wanted to be plaintive, not syrupy.

Over the weeks he rescored the part several times because the clarinet didn't sound right. It was too woody, too mellow. So this time he tried giving the part to a bassoon, but the range was wrong against the soprano's voice and it made her sound nasal. The reedy tone of the instrument also didn't work. Dropping an octave made it clownish.

After coming home that evening, tired of trying to get the orchestra to do what he wanted, Max thought of rewriting the part yet again.

He poured a drink, flopped into the leather chair, flipped the switch of the stereo, too tired to even look at the disk Ursula had been playing while she worked earlier. Coltrane soared into "My Favorite Things" as Max closed his eyes, and tried to let go into the music. Halfway through the long track, the scotch beginning to unwind him, he heard the sound he was looking for. The reedy lyric bite of Coltrane's saxophone was close to it. *Could the clarinet player play soprano sax? Probably.*

He would love to have a jazz musician come in to do it, someone who could lay back in the phrasing, just behind the beat, but he knew that the orchestra's starchy management would never allow that, and he didn't have enough reputation to call all the shots.

That would come later.

He'd have to get the woodwind section of the Symphonica to do as best as they could, and put up with the result. The soprano sax had the tonal suggestion of the Argentine bandoneon, the small accordion of Astor Piazzolla. He wished he could use that instrument, but he would have the same hassle about hiring an extra musician. No, the soprano sax would do the trick. He'd work with what he had until he got the sound he wanted.

He went to his piano at the opposite end of the loft, and began to rescore the woodwind parts, transposing for the soprano sax and revoicing the other winds to accommodate.

Later that evening Ursula found him asleep at the desk and dragged him to bed.

At the dress rehearsal, the clarinet player on soprano sax got it — finally — after endless nagging. It wasn't just the tone, it was the slight hesitation, the laying back behind the beat the way a jazzman would. Cajoling, scolding and *kibitzing* finally did their parts and the aria really worked.

Max had scored all the woodwinds an octave lower, and now it did sound like a bandoneon to him, and the soprano sax worked well with the singer. The reedy biting edge to it, with the rounder, almost brass, sound the clarinetist coaxed out enriched the singer's voice and gave Max just the right tone color for the ending of *Number Our Days* —

> . . . and a man shall be a refuge
> from the wind
> and a shelter from the tempest,
> or like runnels of water
> in dry ground,
> like the shadow of a great rock
> in a thirsty land.
> The eyes that can see
> will not be clouded,
> and the ears that can hear
> will listen;
> the anxious heart
> will understand and know . . .

she sang, and then threw a Bible she was holding in her hand, and screamed: "DAMNED TO HELL" into the hush of darkness of the theater.

There was no sound from the orchestra.

She stepped back to the austere hospital bed in which she had slept away her exile from life, and picked up the diary she wrote in every night. Suddenly clutching her hands to her heart she fell over, half on, half off the bed, dead.

Cymbals crashed, horns roared, bows scraped. Across a twelve tone cacophony that decreed final chaos, an apocalypse of sound raked five octaves, hammered with drums, and a lone spotlight played on the family picture on the nightstand. It then came up enlarged thousands of times with on a back projection screen at the rear of the stage. It brightened in intensity until it became a blur of screaming white light, while the tympani thumped one measure of a tango rhythm, then sudden blackness, final silence. The curtain fell.

There was long and sustained applause from the dozen or so people in the auditorium, and as Max turned to face them, acknowledging their appreciation, he saw Ursula coming toward him, her pale face luminous, ghostlike in the dim light of the opera house. He knew something was wrong, and when she spoke the words he knew them in advance as she said, "Max, your father is dead."

Ben Bergman was dead, and there was no point in stopping the rehearsal, she said.

*It wouldn't help*, Max thought, remembering his father's crude joke about the death of a great star of the old Yiddish theatre:

> When the manager tells the audience that Thomashefsky is dead and that the show will not be performed as scheduled, a voice from the rear cries out, "Give him an enema!"
>
> Through the awed hush, the manager, appalled at the suggestion, responds, "Madame, Thomashefsky is DEAD. An enema wouldn't help!"
>
> "It wouldn't hurt either," returns the heckler.

Max heard the sound of his father's laughter as he told the joke for the thousandth time, put his baton down on the podium and leaned on Ursula, who had thrown her arms around him and was crying. It was as if it was her loss, not his, and he wanted to take it back from her, keep it for himself, his hole in the pocket, not hers, his place to drop a hand into, seeking a key or a coin, to find nothing, emptiness, a void of shredded cloth. But he held her as she sobbed, patting her on the back.

No tears came for him. *It was unexpected*, was all he could think. *Give him an enema.*

Later he called Arlene, and she described how she discovered their father just sitting in the living room of the house she shared with him, reading the afternoon paper, as she often found him when she got back from her hospital rounds. But this time he was dead. Arlene said it was a massive heart attack and over instantaneously. He'd probably blacked out and that was it. No pain.

*Good to have a doctor in the family*, Max thought, as he put the telephone down. What, he wondered, was going to happen now? Would the empty place fill in, the pocket be sewn? Would he feel better, or be able to rationalize the remembrance that he hadn't spoken to his father for several weeks prior to his death?

Ben Bergman had annoyed him the last time Max telephoned. He wanted Ben to hear the opera, witness his triumph, say, "That's my son, the great . . . .."

"So . . . how's Toscanini?" Ben asked .

"Toscanini's dead, Poppa, but Max Bergman's fine."

"That's good to hear. It's a shame about Toscanini," his father said. "When did he die?"

"Years ago, Poppa . . . .."

"Years ago you were also fine," Ben said, "until you got this *narishkeit* into your head about being a musician instead of a doctor. So look how you live!"

"How I live is fine, Poppa, I make out okay."

The game was on.

*Batter up.*

*Wily Ben shifted his stance at bat; Max could almost see him eyeing the ball about to be pitched. It was the sport of the week. Nail Max with a line drive to his gut.* Let him know that you didn't even dream that your son would become a composer, and would support himself all the years he studied with Boulanger in Paris, with Overton in New York, by playing in jazz clubs, a sideman, not a star. Then the breaks, the string quartet performed at Tanglewood, the guitar concerto commissioned and recorded by Julian Bream, the grant from the National Endowment for the Arts, faculty appointment at Juilliard, the Ph.D from Columbia, and now, finally the opera premiering at Lincoln Center, and somehow his father wasn't satisfied. But if he had been a doctor, even an indifferent one, a neighborhood hack, as long as he had the M.D. and drove a Cadillac, his father would have crowed.

"So how's Ursula?" Ben asked. *Would he bunt?*

"She's okay, working very hard on some new canvases for her show next month."

"You'll get married?"

"No. I don't think so, Poppa, not yet."

"What are you waiting for," Ben asked, "until you're too old?"

"Too old for what?"

"To have kids. What else?"

"Even if we would get married, I don't think we want kids."

"Baloney," Ben scoffed. "Every woman wants kids, so if you marry her, instead of living with her — and you know I don't think that's right — you'll see how quickly she'll change her mind."

"I really doubt that, Poppa, and maybe I don't want kids."

"So there'll be no more Bergmans? You'd let the family name die out?" Ben sounded hurt, betrayed. *Would he strike out, walk, hit?*

"I really don't know about that, Poppa. All I know is that Ursula has her career, I have mine, and we're happy together right now. I can't see the future."

"If you don't plan for it, there won't be any," Ben answered, *eyeing the man on third.*

"You'll come to the opening night, Poppa, won't you? It's in three weeks."

"You'll give me a ticket, I'll come. Arlene too?"

"Of course," Max answered. "Best seats in the house."

"To see the story that your mother, may she rest in peace, pleaded with you not to use, because she was so ashamed."

Max had heard it all before, but he always allowed himself to be put on the defensive. There was no way to avoid it with this subject. *Bases loaded. Careful on the pitch.*

"Poppa, I used the outline of the story, the idea. Most of it is made up, fiction."

Max wasn't allowed to finish.

"She agonized over it, you know that? But you could do no wrong as far as she was concerned, so she never said anything to you after the first time that you told her and she asked you not to do it. But let me tell you, Max, she ate her heart out over the whole thing. Killed her."

*Max pitched his fast ball hard:* "Operas don't promote the spread of cancer. Ask Arlene."

"But Arlene also specifically asked you not to make use of Rita's mother's diary, and you went ahead and did it anyway. It ate her heart out too. But did you care? Your art comes first, then everything and everybody else." *Thwack! And the ball was heading for the foul zone.*

"I can't make you understand, can I, Poppa? You don't want to. You get some kind of pleasure from trying to make me feel guilty, and I don't feel it. So give up. I'll send the tickets and look forward to seeing you on opening night. Stay well," Max said, and got off the telephone *before Ben could a hit a long one and they both saw the ball land among the scrambling fans. Game over.*

◆

"You lousy bastard!" Max screamed at the pile of dirt at his feet. "Why did you have to go and die? Just for spite? Just so you wouldn't have to applaud at the performance of my opera, so you wouldn't have to begrudge me some recognition, some of your golden approval? To have to say that I accomplished something?"

He wanted Ben to hear the opera, witness his triumph, say, "That's my son, the great . . . .."

He toed the dirt with his polished black shoe, kicking at a small stone so that it went flying over the mound. "Why couldn't you wait?" Max muttered, the tears he had not been able to summon earlier rising to his eyes and dripping freely down his cheeks. He rummaged in his back pocket for the handkerchief he remembered placing there this morning. "Without a handkerchief and a pocket knife, a man's not dressed," Ben used to tell him. Max had both now, so he dried his eyes, blew his nose. He could also whittle a stick or cut a string to show Ben that some parental advice had been taken, but that seemed over the top.

Max felt alone in the universe, an observer from outer space, standing there under the warm October sun, the planes passing in their descent toward the airport every minute or so. He wanted to go to the airport and take the first plane anywhere, just to keep moving, to get away from this moment, from this pile of earth covering his father, from the trimmed dwarf yews covering his mother's adjacent grave. He felt as helpless as an orphan — abandoned. His sister Arlene was there, it was true, but still, they were not very close over the years, and Max always felt that she and his father had formed a family cabal of disapproval, a pair of tsk-tsking, sideways-shaking heads over the prodigal unregenerate who insisted on breaking out of the mold his father had cast, and into which his father's daughter slipped. There was something about artistic expression that appalled them, especially when it was dredged from the silt of a family's past. Would it have been any worse had he been a writer, if he told stories that were only thinly disguised episodes of his youth?

◆

"Thou shalt not embarrass the family" was the Bergmans' eleventh commandment. "Nobody should know what goes on behind our doors," his mother used to say. Once Max had broken that commandment.

One evening, when there was no school the next day, his mother let him go out after supper. It was a welcome escape into the quiet darkness of the Brooklyn street. Under the light of the lamppost a few kids were playing skelly with soda bottle caps. His friend Jules stood watching the game, waiting his turn.

"Ya wanna play, Maxie?" Jules asked. "We could make another court. I got some chalk."

"Nah, I don't have a checker," Max answered.

Not put off so easily, Jules said, "I got some extras in my pocket. Aw, c'mon, Maxie."

"No. I just don't wanna, and don't call me Maxie. My mother doesn't like it."

"Whatcha' wanna' do?" Jules asked.

"Let's go to the candy store and get an egg cream."

Max and Jules sat in a booth at Cohen's Soda Fountain with their drinks, flicking a nickel across the Formica tabletop. Three shots, chances to make the coin protrude over the opposite edge without falling off, and win a point. Seven points and your opponent lost a nickel, or half of his egg cream.

It was then that Max told Jules about a fight between Arlene and his mother, something to do with Arlene wanting to go away to college, which his mother said they couldn't afford. It went on for days — silence and glaring at the dinner table, Arlene getting up in tears and running into her room.

Later that evening Jules told his mother about the fight at the Bergman's, and the very next day she saw Rita Bergman in the A&P. She said she'd heard that Arlene was giving her parents grief. Annoyed with Max, Rita said to him when she came home: "You forget an argument with your family quickly, but you tell a stranger and they never forget." Max could still hear his mother's voice.

It always rankled him, the idea of keeping grief to yourself, of assuming that all the power to heal and be healed came from within the family and that wounds inflicted by parents and children must never be shown to the outside world. But the interdiction was laid on him and though he often wanted to talk to a friend about his father, he couldn't. It violated a law, and underneath the law lay a doctrine of exclusive confidence in the family.

◆

Before Max decided not to be a doctor, nothing he did was wrong as far as his father was concerned; afterward, nothing he did was right. "You wouldn't let me show you," he said to Ben's grave, "you wouldn't just let me be. You closed your mind to me because I didn't live out your dream of my glory, but I had my own dream. And now I can't show it to you. It's too late."

He toed the dirt again, walked the length of the path toward the gate, then turned back, passed the grave, went toward the cyclone fence and looked at the modest brick houses on the other side. The smoke continued to rise from the oil drum, and the man was raking together another pile of leaves to burn. He looked up from his work, noticed Max looking at him and the smoke drifting toward the graves, and lifting his hand in a gesture of acknowledgment shouted, "Sorry!"

*What was he sorry for?* Max wondered. The death of Ben? The grief of a mourner, any mourner? He must have seen a lot of them across the fence. Or for the acrid drift of gray smoke across the clutter of monuments. Max waved back as if to say it's all right, and then he stood and watched for a minute as the man heaped several more arm-loads of leaves into the drum and poked them around to insure that they caught on fire. The guy then turned and saw Max still looking at him. Max walked toward the fence.

"Sorry about the smoke, man, but I tried to wait until your funeral was over before I lit up. Didn't know you were going to hang around."

"It's okay," Max reassured him. "You have every right to burn your leaves. It was nice of you to wait anyway. Thanks."

Max turned to walk away.

"Who was buried?" the man called after him.

"My father," Max said over his shoulder, stopping.

"That's rough, man. I been through that myself." He pulled a

Marlboro pack from his pocket, came closer to the fence, and offered one to Max, who took it. "Not against your religion to smoke in the graveyard, is it?"

"I don't think so," Max said, taking the matches the man handed through the fence. "Besides, they don't know," motioning toward the cemetery at his back.

"I lost my daddy when I was fourteen, and let me tell you, that was rough, growing up without an old man to clout you in the head if you got out of line."

"Well, I had more time than that," Max said, then hesitated. He wanted to say that Ben never stopped clouting him on the head, but then Rita's law intervened, although Max knew that he could say what he wanted to now. There was no one watching anymore, and this man's mother wasn't going to see his mother at the supermarket tomorrow. But he said nothing.

"Helps to talk about it," the man said, leaning on the springy leaf rake.

"It's still too raw," Max answered.

"You want a cup of coffee?" the man asked. "I was just about to get me one."

"No, thanks. I really should get going. My family will be waiting for me. I should have gone with them. Just wanted time here alone."

The man smiled. "You can get a bus right there in front the main gate. You sure about that coffee?"

Max said he was, thanked the man for the cigarette, and turned to walk down the path toward the exit. He didn't stop to look at the grave again. Despite the warm sunlight Max shivered involuntarily.

He glanced over his shoulder when he reached the gate, but the man must have gone inside to get his coffee. No one was there and the smoke was drifting straight up in the air. He couldn't see a bus coming along Springfield Boulevard, so he decided to walk toward Forest Hills, and take a cab when he got tired. They'd have to manage at Arlene's house without him for a while.

# 2

THE DAY OF THE FUNERAL should have been cold and blustery to fulfill Max's need for the world to reflect his own drama. But it wasn't.

And ideally, he didn't want to turn and see Uncle Phil picking his nose while the rabbi recited the formulas sanctioned by time, or his sister glowing in the show of family unity because Eddy, her former husband whom she loved to hate, came to the funeral out of respect for Ben, who always liked him, and now stood with his ex-wife and nineteen-year-old daughter, Ellen, down from Vassar.

There should have been thunderclaps, driving rain, a tympani of sounds, a tempest in the sky, a fitting backdrop for the sufferings of the children of Israel at a great milestone in their history. Drums and trumpets announcing heaven's opening; *that* was how it should have been. But there was no drama. He would have to do something with it later, play it out on his own stage, let his imagination riot.

Max walked fast, and soon he was perspiring. He loosened his tie and slung the dark blue jacket of his suit over his shoulder. Trucks and cars slipped by along Springfield Boulevard as he cleared the last cluster of cemeteries and stonemasons' yards where the clichés of death and remembrance were carved into marble for eternity.

The day had an undecided quality that looked backward toward spring and summer: there was a shimmer, a yellowish quality to the light, which against the sky paled almost to white. Yet there was autumn too. Drifts of leaves spread out along the curbstones, and here and there an enterprising householder had piled them up in mounds. Irresistible to small children on their way to and from school, most of the piles were scattered about. Rows of attached brick one- and two-family houses lined the wide street. Clean, orderly little boxes, some with tiny gardens and flower pots. Sturdy, anonymous defenses against the wolf of "house of straw . . . house of sticks . . . huff-puff . . . and blow the house down." Not these. The neighborhood was still as it was eight years ago when his mother was buried. He hadn't been out here since then, but nothing had changed. It was still an African-American, middle-class area of households.

He imagined what the insides of the houses were like. Newish furniture bought from inexpensive stores in coordinated sets, with plastic slip covers over the sofa and chairs. A dinette off the kitchen where a Formica table served the family during the week and was covered for weekend meals by a tablecloth. Green carpets with sculpted patterns. A large television set the focal point of the living room. Like apartments he knew in Brooklyn when he was a kid. But he knew so much about the appearance of things, and so little about their meaning. What did these homes represent to the owners? To their children? A quantum leap from the South, from ancestors' plantation slavery? A way of distancing Harlem, or the closer squalor of South Jamaica? Later would their children leave the neighborhood and disperse into America beyond the Hudson? Did they want to escape from the confines of these boxes where daily working, sleeping and feeding was relieved only by hours in front of the tube, where life was watched, like a spectator sport? Or was he projecting his own feelings once again onto an unwilling screen, peopling the abstractions of his fantasy and coloring the figures black?

◆

His parents had discussions about being "outward bound." After sixteen years of Max's life in Williamsburg, where the Bergmans lived on the top floor of a brownstone, Ben and Rita — mostly Ben — wanted to move up in the world. By then Arlene was in medical school and living in the dorms in Manhattan.

At dinner one evening Ben said he wanted to move to a better neighborhood in Queens because he could afford it now.

"I wouldn't mind as long as we stay in Brooklyn," Rita said, folding and unfolding the reading glasses that hung from a chain around her neck, "There's some very nice areas here. Why Queens?"

"It's the coming thing," Ben told her. "Forest Hills, Kew Gardens. Brooklyn is on the way downhill. There are more and more blacks and Puerto Ricans every day, and a lot of our kind are moving out."

"It's expensive!"

"I can afford it now. Business is good."

"But your office!" Rita objected.

"I'll drive in. Maybe I'll open only three days a week, and try to start a small practice out there on the other days."

His father explained to his mother that he would like living where he could see a bit of grass and trees, and that he would actually enjoy driving into Brooklyn since at that point he hardly used the car. It just stood on the street in front of their house most of the week, a shining announcement of Ben's prosperity. Sundays they usually drove to visit family and friends who *had* left Williamsburg. Fridays during the summer, when Max wasn't in school, his father took the day off and they drove to Prospect Park to row, to a Dodgers game in Ebbets field, to the beach at Coney Island.

◆

"Listen, Maxelleh . . . you'll grow up, be a doctor . . . you won't have to drive a Buick like me, strictly Lincolns and Cadillacs for you. That's what it'll be."

They were at Coney Island and Ben was teaching him to swim. Waist deep in the calm, full, morning tide, Ben held Max under his stomach and chest while the boy kicked and stroked as his father showed him. "You'll have it good, my son, better than me. Like I said, only classy Lincolns and Caddies; I wouldn't kid you . . .." Then Ben was hard to hear over the loud splashing and stroking as Max tried to follow instructions: head in, stroke, head out, stroke, head in, stroke, head out, stroke, turn to one side only, kick hard, legs together, keep them stiff, flatten the feet. He felt himself moving along. It worked. It worked! His father wasn't telling him about cars, and he looked over to the other side to see why. When he saw that Ben wasn't there holding him up, Max remembered that he hadn't felt his father's arms under him for a minute. He was so busy kicking and concentrating on putting his head in and out and stroking that he wasn't conscious of the upward pressure. Ben was standing thirty feet back applauding.

"You can swim now, Maxie. You can do it yourself. Hooray!"

"I can swim, hooray!" Max shouted, raising his arms.

"I can swim myself . . .." he shouted and swallowed a mouthful of ocean, which choked him, blinding him as the coughing brought tears into his eyes. Kicking, screaming, finding that he was going under the water again and couldn't see, couldn't touch the bottom. Then Ben was lifting him up, carrying Max out of the water toward the beach.

"It's all right, all right, Maxie . . . nothing happened. You just swallowed some water because you were so happy to be swimming by yourself, that you forgot you were in deep water and stopped swimming. That's all!"

Max sobbed a little, wanted to get down from his father's arms. He was eight, wasn't a baby any more and didn't have to be carried in the water. He could swim now.

◆

"BEEEEEEP BEEEP" blasted an automobile horn into his reverie and Max turned to see a large, bright-blue car swerve suddenly to avoid crashing into a garbage truck that had just pulled out from the curb where the crew loaded the hopper. The truck was trying to get around a parked car to the garbage cans in front of the next house. The blue car screeched to a halt and the smoke of burned rubber rose from the black skid marks on the roadway, as the driver of the sanitation truck hit the air brakes and lurched the slow moving mammoth to a standstill.

"What the fuck you doin', drivin' like a crazy bastard?" the sanitation man yelled from the cab of the truck. The other two garbagemen put down the metal cans they had just lifted, and moved toward the truck, and the car stopped in the middle of the road.

The driver of the car, a Puerto Rican in his early twenties dressed in a bright blue suit exactly like the color of the car, jumped out, furious: "You doan look how you goin' neither," said the Puerto Rican. "It's your fault . . .."

"Nothin' happened, José, so keep your shirt on."

"You very lucky nothin' happen because if something did to my *coche* I make you sorry."

"You and who else, ya' little greaseball?" shouted the driver who had opened the truck door and stood on the running board. He was a huge Sicilian who looked as though he could turn over the shiny blue car with one meaty hand.

"My brother and me," blue suit said. "We kill you and throw you in your fuckin' garbage where you should be"

The car's passenger door opened and another Puerto Rican got out. He was older, taller, and broken nosed. He stuck his hands in the pockets of his tight fitting beige suit, pulling back the open jacket so that the handle of a pistol showed sticking up from the waistband.

"You tink I'm afraida dat water gun? Pull it out and I'll shove it up your ass!" The garbageman stood on the running board of the white truck, towering over the two Puerto Ricans.

Max saw the other two garbagemen grab heavy shovels from the front rack of the truck and move around toward the blue car.

"My mother's in the car, so you a lucky man," said the gunslinger. "Otherwise, you be dead like a *cucaracha* if you mess with el Pacito."

An old woman in black with a matching kerchief tied around her gray head opened a window and shouted something in Spanish to her sons. Reluctant and in sneering lordship over their honor, they got back into the blue car and with a screech of tires shot away.

"Your mother eats shit," shouted one of the shovel wielding garbagemen, but the sound of his voice was lost in the roaring acceleration and the passing of a stream of cars and trucks that had been held up, beeping horns, behind the stalemated warriors.

"Motherfuckin' spics," shouted the third garbageman, a black man. "Go back where you came from."

"Fuck 'em all," the driver said to the shovel bearers as they put their weapons back in the rack and returned to the steel cans on the curb.

The driver waited until all the traffic passed, eased the truck around the parked car, and then stopped moving while his comrades in arms fed the grinding hopper.

Max shifted his jacket to the other shoulder and walked on.

Halfway down the street the garbage truck was idling in the middle of the roadway. Only a few parked cars on the street and there was room to pass on either side of the truck. The garbagemen stepped to opposite curbs, hefted the heavy metal cans to their shoulders, returned to the center where the truck waited, and dumped their loads into the grinding mouth of the hopper. Then one of the men would yell, "Yyeeoh" and the truck moved forward several yards to await its next feeding. The collectors carried the empties to the curb where they were dropped or tossed with a rasping clatter, skittering and thumping across the sidewalk. Then the men moved to the next house to repeat the performance. Surging anger gave a rhythm to their work, as they cursed the cans, the garbage, trucks waiting to pass, and each other.

◆

"Nah! You'll never do it," Marvin, always the skeptic, had said to him long ago.

Freed from the classroom by Easter vacation and the Passover holy days, the boys sat on Max's stoop. The sycamore trees lining the Williamsburg street already was covered with leaves, and the day was warm, sunny and humid, a hint of summer indolence thrown out by a school-less universe.

Joey had just won everybody's filberts in a nut rolling playoff, a traditional Passover street game. A walnut is set up as a target and prize, then each player rolls or tosses a filbert until one of them hits the walnut and wins it. The winner then becomes the new game keeper, and collects and keeps all the filberts that missed the target as a reward for his marksmanship.

The walnut was now in Marvin's hands, his last lucky filbert had conked it, but he didn't want to play any more, and said he was going to eat the walnut, a clear violation of the unwritten rules of the street. The game was over, therefore, until someone would go upstairs and grab another walnut from the bowl on every family's dining table, but no one was willing to confront his mother lest he be sent on an errand or forced to stay indoors on this beautiful day.

Then Joey orchestrated a playoff without Marvin's walnut, on ten to one odds against hitting a filbert, and the challenge to the boys' prowess resulted in Joey now having a corner on the filbert market. He offered Marvin five little nuts, then ten for the walnut, but Marvin said no, so Joey began to give the little round ones away. But they had to eat them, he said, handing one at a time to the group, a smirk of lordly benevolence on his hawk-like face. "*Noblesse oblige*," he said, but he wouldn't give any to Marvin.

Max, bored with cajoling Marvin as well as with the mockery of Lord Joey's grace, had been watching the garbagemen work their way up the street getting nearer and nearer the brownstone stoop.

"What if I yelled 'Yyeeoh?'" he asked his friends. "Would the truck move?"

"If it sounded like the garbagemen it would," Joey answered, placing a filbert in his handkerchief so he could crack it by swinging it hard against the step.

"But boy, would they be mad," Jules said, "they'd moider ya' dead . . . ."

"I'd be a block away before they came after me," Max boasted. He was a fast runner, always winning the street races.

"Nah, you'll never do it," Marvin repeated and, throwing out the epithet every boy who grew up on the streets of New York was honor-bound to deny, he added: "You're chicken!"

The heat was off Marvin — and on Max. He had to pick up the challenge now or suffer eternal chickenhood. Immediately filberts and walnuts ceased to be interesting to the boys, and they concentrated on the garbage truck that was approaching the front of the stoop — and on what Max would do.

"You'd better get ready to get out of here," Max told his friends as they watched the men dump the cans of the adjacent house. Joey was already at the bottom steps, and Max moved down to lounge as nonchalantly as he could against the gatepost.

"I'm staying put because you ain't gonna do it. You'll chicken out," said Marvin. Snug in his corner at the top step he examined the shell of his walnut, studying it as if it were a precious stone. The truck passed them, was fed, grunted and moved on at the shout of the scowling men in their green fatigues.

"Ya see? I told you Max would chicken out!" Marvin said from his perch.

Just as he spoke the men started to dump their two can loads into the hopper and Max cupped his hands to his mouth and yelled: "Yyyyeeeee . . . ohh . . .!"

The driver moved the truck forward and the garbage from the upended cans continued to pour out onto the middle of the roadway.

"WHAT THE HELL YOU DOIN'?" screamed one garbageman. They were so surprised that they stood poised in the same position, without remembering to put the garbage cans upright, and the loads of bones, bottles, potato peelings, coffee grinds and sodden newspaper clattered and dripped and splattered at their feet.

"You fuckin' kids!" one of the men yelled. "I'll kill youse." He

22

dropped the now empty can onto the mess in the middle of the roadway and leaped toward the group of boys who were roaring with laughter at the slapstick prank Max had devised.

Max sprinted toward the end of the street with Joey. He heard Marvin yelling, "I didn't do it! They did." And then scream, "MA — MA — MA!!"

Max turned his head to see the driver of the truck leaping up the steps to grab the screaming Marvin. One of the dumpers was chasing Max and Joey, while the other was running after Jules in the opposite direction.

"Little sheenie sons of bitches!" shouted the garbageman who was chasing Max and Hawk (Joey's nickname that you couldn't call him when you wanted to, only when he wanted you to), but not gaining any distance. They had about a fifty yard lead and weren't running full speed yet. Hawk, two years older than the others, was fast, already in high school and on the track team. He just seemed to glide along, his long legs lifting him effortlessly through the air. Paced by the older runner, Max thought he could run for miles. But the garbageman seemed to be gaining.

"Faster, Hawk, faster . . . he's catching up," Max said when he saw the squat, furious guy getting closer. When Max turned to look back again, the man brandished a fist and shouted something. Hawk increased the pace slightly and the distance widened.

"If we just keep it up like this," the older boy said, "he'll tire out and stop chasing us."

"But shouldn't we run faster, lose him, and then hide?" Max asked.

His breath was beginning to come quicker and he knew that he didn't have Hawk's cross-country team endurance. Max was a sprinter, untutored.

"Do what you want," Hawk practically sneered. "I'm going to keep this up until he gets tired and stops chasing."

"Maybe we'll go different ways at the corner," Max said, "then, if he chases you, I can stop."

"What if he chases you?" Hawk asked.

"Either way, I've got to stop before you do. I'm getting winded!" His chest was beginning to pound and he could feel a stitch in his side as they neared the end of the long block of Hewes Street, where they both lived, and approached Nostrand Avenue. "I'm turning right up the hill," Hawk said.

Max's confidence in keeping up waned along with his ability to breathe easily. The hill would stop him for sure. "I'll go left down toward Penn Street; he can't chase us both!" They hesitated at the corner for a moment to see the swarthy man in green still running hard toward them. Hawk grinned and darted right up Nostrand as Max leaped to the left across the street, the pressure on his chest feeling like when all the players piled on top in a football game.

He was halfway down the short block, gaining some speed from the slope, zigzagging around the women with shopping carts.

"Watch where you're going, *meshugenah*," a fat woman shouted as he dodged around her, banging into her grocery bag. An old man raised his cane as though to strike Max and he dodged again, then turned to look for his pursuer, hoping that the swarthy Italian chased Hawk. He wasn't there! Not believing he'd escaped, Max stopped to scan the sidewalk for the green man, and then spotted him, running hard down the street facing into the traffic. Terror froze him to the sidewalk for a second. Should he turn, slip by the man and follow Hawk up the hill? His body decided what his mind couldn't, and he jumped forward in the direction he had first chosen and screeched left around the corner onto Penn Street, almost knocking down a kid coming out at Kramer's Bakery.

"U.S. Keds, save me now!" he said to no one, remembering how that plea worked in the comic book advertisements. The pounding in his chest threatening to break through his ribs, he sprinted as hard as he could along the almost empty side street passing identical brownstones.

The garbageman dropped back a little then, and Max pressed his legs harder, harder, his heart pounding like a drum, his breath shorter and more painful every step.

"I'll get ya — ya litle Jew bastard!" the garbageman yelled, "if I have to chase ya all day."

When Max glanced back again, he saw that the man had slowed to a trot and was dropping further behind. Suddenly there was a sharp, searing, burning in Max's chest as a rush of air seemed to enter his lungs and he didn't feel the shortness of breath any longer, although the stitch in his side was still there. *This was "second wind"!* He had never felt it happen before, only read about it in books. He ran faster and reached the corner of Penn Street and Marcy Avenue while the man was only halfway down the block behind him.

If Max turned left, he would be back at Hewes Street again, and maybe — just maybe — the other garbagemen would still be chasing his friends and he could duck into his house before he was seen. *But what if they weren't?* And he didn't have the key. He'd have to ring the bell and wait on the stoop until his mother answered. *What if she was in the toilet or something?* The men might see him and then know where he lived. That would be worse because they'd always be able to get him, maybe even tell his parents. He thought of running down Marcy Avenue to his right, but in two blocks he'd be in the Irish neighborhood, and if the kids there saw him running from the garbageman, they'd trip him, or catch him and hold him for the man to beat up. Join in maybe, laughing. That was no good either.

On the opposite corner of Marcy Avenue and Penn Street was an apartment house, one of the few in this brownstone neighborhood, the building where Barry Rosen lived. They used to play tag up and down the steps and the alleys sometimes, and ride the elevator, stopping it between floors by sliding back the folding gate. Max knew all the tricks in this apartment house, and remembering the alleyway on the Marcy Avenue side, turned right and leaped down the three steps into the dark stone alley among barrels filled with ashes and blackened tin cans from the incinerator. The door to the basement was usually open during the day. When Max reached it, he pushed hard. The metal door swung open with a grating sound and he stepped inside quickly, slamming home the inside bolt.

The boiler room was next, and he tiptoed so as not to disturb the big Polack janitor who often dozed there in the afternoon, sitting like a hairy bear in his undershirt, half drunk on a flat bottle of whiskey that always stuck out of his back pocket.

Chest pounding so that he was sure everyone could hear it, Max made his way past the noisy boiler, across the laundry room where some women were talking, to the elevator, which he hoped would be stopped in the basement. Otherwise he would have to spring up the stairs two at a time, and he wasn't sure he could do it. He was beginning to think that getting hit by the garbageman couldn't be worse than the pain in his chest, and almost turned around to walk into the arms of the vengeance seeker. But the elevator was there and Max pulled open the gray door and stepped into the brass cage that always smelled of insecticide.

He pressed the worn button with number seven etched on it and leaned back on the side of the cage, watching the bricks of the shaft pass the gate until the machine stopped on the seventh floor. He pushed the accordion gate back swiftly and stepped into the tiled hall, but no one was there.

Sprinting up the stairs to the roof, he unlatched the large hook holding the door closed, and stepped out onto the tarry roof. Some clothes on lines flapped in the breeze. He walked to the edge and leaned over the high wall to look down at the street eight stories below. That always made him a little queasy, but now he needed to see where the garbageman was. If he couldn't see him from up here that meant he had come into the building and Max would have to make his escape another way. During the boys' tag games he learned to use the fire escape. He would climb down the steps to the second floor, release the hook holding the ladder one story up from the ground, and then climb down the ladder to make his way out through the alleyways and back yards he knew so well. Yet he was still breathing heavily, and hoped that he wouldn't have to make his way down the fire escape. Even though he had done it many times before, the open gratings still scared him, and he imagined the whole metal structure

26

falling as he had once seen in a movie. Then he flushed with relief. No fire escape was necessary.

There below him at the corner of Marcy Avenue and Penn Street the garbageman stood, scratching his head. His chest heaved in and out as he looked around, up and down Marcy Avenue, back and forth scanning Penn Street for a sign of his quarry. Max was safe! He smiled to himself and pulled his head back from the edge, just in case the man looked up, leaned against the brick chimney and gasped great gulps of sweet air. Perspiration poured off his forehead, and he pulled the freshly-ironed hankie his mother had handed him that morning out of his back pocket and mopped his face. He looked over the edge again to see the garbageman, his bloodlust unfulfilled, walking back up Marcy Avenue toward Hewes Street, still looking around him — for a sight of the boy whose bones he wanted to break. Max felt pleased with himself.

"The quick brown fox jumps over the lazy dog," he repeated over and over, half aloud, until it sounded silly to him and his breath returned. Then he began to laugh uncontrollably, his eyes filling with tears; he felt this was a sweet triumph. But he'd have to remember to go inside the next few weeks every time he saw the garbage truck working its way up Hewes Street. He sat in the corner by the chimney in the warm sun until he thought the garbage would be picked up from the street and the men gone, closing his eyes in the glare.

◆

But that wasn't what happened, Max knew, as he walked along Springfield Boulevard almost thirty years later.

The garbageman caught him halfway down Hewes Street, gave him a hard clap in the face and went on to chase Joey, who got away. Max went upstairs to his house crying. His mother was making lunch. He didn't pass through the kitchen, but went and lay down on his bed, dimly aware of the noise in the street as the three-man crew quickly shoveled up what he caused them to spill, and then rode away.

They never caught any of the others. Max and his friends were afraid for weeks afterward that the men would come after them or tell their parents. But nothing was ever said. Many times Max imagined how he would have liked it to be, and, by now, the escape into Barry Rosen's apartment house and the victory of watching the befuddled, green uniformed man below had as much reality as the truth. He preferred the dramatic version.

◆

A McDonald's on the corner of the next cross street caught Max's attention and he walked toward it purposefully. A cup of coffee now seemed like a good idea. *Plastic in plastic on top of plastic surrounded by plastic*, he thought, as he stirred the artificial cream into the Styrofoam cup with a plastic stirrer. He sat on a fiberglass seat at a Formica table next to a wall that was paneled in plastic imitation wood grain. He wondered if the coffee was real. Actually, it didn't taste bad. Maybe, if he had walked a few blocks farther, he would have come to a place he'd like better; maybe there wasn't anything else. And he had settled for the expedient over the ideal, but what was ideal? *Would he have found the Cafe Deux Magots or Les Tres Amis?* Not likely. *A Greek diner with thick white china cups, a green stripe around the rim? Or an old 1930s-style place, like the one in Hopper's "Nighthawks" with U-shaped bays and revolving stools covered in red leatherette?* Also not likely and less possible. What pleased him? "*Keine sach gefahlt im nicht,*" his mother used to say. It was true. Nothing pleased him. Not really. Only what he imagined. Reality was too often disappointing.

Sipping at the coffee he wondered, *How could this break for a pick-me-up been better?*

Well, it could have been at the station buffet in the old Penn Station, before they tore down the Great Hall to make room for a nondescript office tower, a sports arena that was as flavorless as a McDonald's and a railroad waiting room and departure area that did for rail travel what Kennedy Airport did for flying. Remove the

28

romance. Replace marble facings, pillared halls and neoclassical columns with plastic walls and the cheap blue haze of fluorescent lights, disperse any lingering sense of class or elegance with homogenizing, level everyone with the same common tool. Ah, the virtues of democracy.

It was no wonder that Ben was so prejudiced. Max used to argue with his father at great length, calling him a bigot, racist and every other fashionable put-down, but inwardly he understood, in recent years especially, what his father objected to. Lots of credit and a market flooded with easy-to-buy consumer goods made life more pleasant for the average person. But that also made the pleasure in quality more difficult to find. What Max wanted was a marble counter, gleaming nickel urns, a white coated attendant who would smile and draw a cup of real coffee, not brewed from premeasured packets, but loose in a muslin filter at the top of the steaming urn, tasted by somebody who knew what good coffee was, and re-poured through the filter if it wasn't just so. He wanted this served up to him on the gray marble counter in a thick ivory-colored china mug, slightly hourglass in shape, and alongside it a small matching pitcher of real light cream, or, if you asked, hot milk. Even the old Automats were gone, where a nickel bought you the famous coffee from the spigot on the vending wall.

◆

One Friday during summer vacation Ben took Max to Penn Station just to eat at the buffet.

"Best pancakes in New York," Ben said, and Max believed him. He was too young then for coffee, but he had milk, he remembered: two men lifted the largest milk can he'd ever seen into a gleaming nickel dispenser. Max had never seen milk freshly drawn by a counterman in starched whites. Served in a thick fluted glass, the milk tasted fresh, and was frothy, creamy, the best milk Max ever had. They both ate griddlecakes, and Ben enjoyed the coffee so much that he drank a second cup.

"Coffee stunts your growth," his father said, when Max asked if he could have some. "There's plenty of time to drink it when you grow up."

Max knew then that when he was a grownup, he would come to Penn Station all the time, because when he was a rich doctor he would always take trips on trains; maybe somewhere on the Twentieth Century Limited and have a little sleeping cabin all to himself, like Ben had told him. Then he would be able to drink all the coffee he wanted, like Ben told him, and he might get a second helping of pancakes.

"I could eat that now," Max told his father, and Ben smiled and ordered another helping "for my son, the doctor," he said to the counterman, who smiled and showed big, sparkling teeth in his dark, friendly face.

"He be a fine lad you got there, suh," said the man, stacking the plate again. "Yo' sho got some appetite, son. Now doan you let yo' daddy down." Max couldn't finish the pancakes; Ben did.

◆

Max left MacDonald's and walked again under a sky that was obscured by high clouds with the sun only a glare penetrating the haze. He continued his walk north along Springfield Boulevard.

He had needed to stay at Ben's grave after the others left, needed to let his own feelings come through without others around him, without seeing what looked to him like counterfeit grief on their faces. But the moment passed and now he knew he was only indulging his whim to be by himself. Walking here through the utter monotony of southern Queens had absolutely nothing to do with his father, grief and mourning. There were so many questions, so few answers, and he wouldn't resolve them now.

At Arlene's house, they were probably wondering about him, maybe even worrying. Not that they need worry; he was quite all right, but nonetheless, maybe he should find a taxi.

He kept walking.

Sounds filled his head, a diapason to the rhythms of the passing traffic. The sounds were colors to him. There was a red and orange sound of the road and a deep blue for the houses shading to black. Clusters of notes passed before his eyes and he heard them all as big, thick globs of color in closed voicings, a discordant chorale melody played by a full orchestra. He heard the chord sustained by five trombones and then added to the overtone series with the French horns. It was ominous, and a moment of dread. No sentimentalism would ruin the mood, no sudden brightness like a cloud opening, and no sweet violin's ray of light would shine through. No, the mood was final here. *Was it an aftermath to* Number Our Days? *The music when the lights went out? Or was it something new, orchestral only, a sort of requiem for his father?* He had to wrte it down.

In a small stationery and card shop he bought a pad of paper; they didn't have any music paper, but sitting on a bench in a playground he quickly sketched in some rough lines for the staves. A few young mothers watching over children in the sandbox eyed him suspiciously, this bearded guy in a suit scribbling music on a pad was out of place here, but they lost interest in him quickly as he sat and covered several sheets with notations.

Peacocks fanned a range of colors across the pages as Max sketched the sounds in his head, a stately pavane, in four square chorale blocks of sound, a procession with steady motion. High above in the musical sky there was a single voice in bel canto descant, but though he could catch gleanings of the sound he couldn't get it right.

He needed a piano to make sure that the voice part wasn't too luminous. Half a dozen pages later he stopped, unable to go further. Arlene had a piano in the basement playroom. He'd go there now and use it.

# 3

WHEN ARLENE HAD MADE the house ready the night before, she disconnected the neon sign from the electric outlet and "Tango Palace — 10 cents a dance" no longer flashed on and off in the corner of her living room. The green and purple sign was quieted to sullen gray fluorescent tubes of block letters. Max had found the sign at a "going out of business" sale at an old dance hall on 48th Street in Manhattan's music district, and brought it as a house warming present when she and Eddy moved in. Eddy used to put a dime on her night table when he wanted to get together. She needed some "get together" now. Maybe after the *shiva*.

Should she cover the sign as she had covered the mirrors in the entrance foyer and the one over the couch? Uncle Philly said that she should, but how could she do it in the dining room where mirrors filled the walls, floor to ceiling as her decorator insisted? Eddy always hated the dining room: "I don't like to watch myself eat supper," he said. But he loved the Tango Palace sign and always said that Max was full of great ideas. *She* always thought of her brother as an annoying brat, even as an adult.

Now Eddy was eating from the buffet lunch she ordered from the local delicatessen as though he hadn't seen food in weeks, and his appetite wasn't deterred by the mirrored walls. She didn't call to tell him that his ex-father-in-law had died, but their daughter Ellen must have done it. When he showed at the funeral she was secretly pleased, although she didn't do anything more than accept his condolences and give him a polite peck on the cheek he offered. Nevertheless, she liked it when he sat in the first row of the chapel next to her and made a show of unity for the sake of appearances. Ellen sat on her other side, and Arlene felt some small comfort in the illusion that they were once more a family against adversity, even though she knew that she was riding the coat tails of death's formal dress stroll through her life.

Before Eddy moved out, the three of them were not getting along. Afterward it was worse: Ellen blamed Arlene for the breakup and was either sullen or absent most of the time. By the time their daughter went off to college, Arlene was glad to see the back of her, although Ben missed her a lot. A deep affection had grown between the grandfather and the granddaughter from which Arlene felt excluded. A secret cabal of need in both of them. The aging widower and the "fatherless" child filled the vacuums in their lives with each other. Arlene was happy to be off the hook, and could look after her practice and career more easily because she didn't feel as though she was abandoning either her father or her daughter; however, she often felt jealous of their relationship. If Ben was as attentive to her when she was a teenager as he was to Ellen, things might have turned out differently.

"Is there any coffee?" Eddy asked her, as he stuffed some more potato salad into his mouth.

"Yeah, I'd like some too. Very light," said Uncle Philly, a length behind Eddy, but also galloping his mouth.

"I'll go see if it's ready," Arlene answered, trying to keep an even voice. She wasn't going to let this week of mourning rattle her, at least not so soon. The demand that she look after the needs of guests when she should be tending her own wounds was an irritation, but it was too early to let it get the better of her. Besides, she was more annoyed with Max for staying behind at the cemetery despite her plea that he get into the limousine with her and the family, and go back to the grave later if he wanted to.

"You're not supposed to come back to the graveside during the shiva period," Uncle Philly said to her in the car, "so let him stay for a while. What's the difference? He'll get to your house by himself. He's a big boy now."

Aunt Charlotte nodded agreement, then looked to Ursula for support, but there was none .

"Try not to tell him what to do," Ursula said. "It only leads to an argument."

Arlene expected no more from Ursula. That one was brought up not with a silver, but a platinum, spoon, and never needed to meet anyone's demands but her own. Yet she and Max lived together for these past dozen years without getting married. Maybe Ursula didn't consider it her right to insist. Was that any way to run a relationship? Arlene thought about how Max and Ursula managed living together, independent and strong-willed as they both were, as she transferred brewed coffee from the electric urn to a serving pot, and arranged cream and sugar on a tray.

When Max arrived, Uncle Philly was standing near the dead, gray, neon tubing of the Tango Palace sign, absent-mindedly rubbing his fingers across the letters while he sipped at a cup of coffee. The large mirror behind the art deco couch that Arlene bought at the Roxy auction was covered with a sheet. She sat on a wood-grained cardboard box with her shoes off. Another of the boxes supplied by the funeral home stood empty next to hers: Max's official seat for the shiva, he supposed.

Arlene frowned.

"So glad you could make it," she said sarcastically.

Max wanted to parry, but a warning look in Ursula's eyes made him hold his tongue. "It was hard to get a cab," he said, offhandedly.

35

"Do you want something to eat?" Ursula asked. "There's still plenty."

"I'll get it," Arlene cut her off. "Bagel and cream cheese okay?"

He nodded.

"Coffee?"

Another nod. It wouldn't be served in a plastic cup, either.

"What were you doing, Maxie?" Uncle Philly asked, turning from the neon sign in the corner the of the room.

Max saw Ursula wince at the diminutive that reduced him to a kid on the street once again, but he knew that his uncle could only see him that way and still appreciated the small avuncular touch that made him feel safe for a moment.

"I stayed there for a while, walked a little, then found a cab. You thought I went dancing?"

Uncle Phil looked surprised: "There's no dancing this week, Maxie, you know that?"

Then he averted his eyes and asked: "You're going to say *Kaddish*, aren't you?"

Max didn't know; he hadn't thought about saying the ritual prayer in his father's memory.

"Here, sure, when they have an evening *minyan*," he answered Phil, "but afterward, for a year, I don't know."

"I think you owe it to your father, Maxie. You did it for your mother, didn't you?"

Max's mother was Philly's older and beloved sister and he would have been upset by a negative response, so Max answered yes.

"Well, so equal time is what God demands."

"Then equal time is what he/she/it will get," Max said.

"Maxie; don't talk like that. It's not nice," his uncle said.

Not nice! The exaltation of a conscience not his own. Whose?

◆

At a family council held in Arlene's living room, Max's father told him that it was "not nice" that he was going to Paris to study with

Boulanger after they learned that his mother was ill with cancer and it was terminal.

"What good will I do for her if I stay here in New York?"

"You'll be able to see her regularly," Ben said, "so at least she'll have some pleasure from you before she goes, a little bit of *naches*. You owe her that!"

In their collective wisdom, Arlene and Ben had decided that the reality of Rita's illness should be concealed from her, and they had thought out all of the details. It was a bad case of hepatitis, they told her. The superficial symptoms were the same as cancer of the liver: the weakness, the jaundice, the digestion problems. She would take medicine, rest, and, although it was to be a long recuperation, she'd be better again soon. Max had little choice but to go along with the mythmakers.

"When she knows that I have canceled my plans so that I could be at her side, she's going to know that you've lied to her, and that it's more serious than hepatitis," Max said to them.

"Tell her that you decided to continue your studies here," Arlene suggested.

"You can't say that you changed your mind, or that Mrs. Bullango got sick or something?"

"Madame Boulanger, BOO – LAN – ZHAY," and Max repeated the phonetic pronunciation for his father, who always insisted on mangling the name, just as Max always corrected him, "is not ill, and I have a Carnegie Endowment Grant to study with her. If I don't go, I don't get the grant and besides, if you two hadn't acted like assholes and preempted any part I might have in making a decision about what to tell Mom, maybe I wouldn't be forced into such an untenable position. She's no dope. However you lie to her, she's going to know the truth, and you'll be forced to tell bigger and bigger lies. Jerks!"

"A nice way to talk to your father and sister!" Ben said, appealing once again to the code of "nice" and "not nice" that governed his life more than the Mosaic Laws.

"You think I haven't seen a lot of patients like this?"Arlene asked. "They don't want to know; they want to have faith."

"In what?" Max shouted, "In miracles where a 'nice' God steps out of his mythical heaven and makes the nastiness go away? In some cure another medical quack dreamed up as a way to torture the dying and fleece their families? Like eating mashed prune pits or shit like that?"

"You were always selfish and you'll always be selfish!" Ben snarled. "Your mother is dying and all you can think of is your own pleasure."

"Pleasure? I'm studying my life's work with one of the world's greatest teachers. It would be the same if Arlene wanted to study some specialty and wanted to go somewhere else to do it. You heard of Mohammed and the mountain?"

"Some comparison — music and medicine: how can you be so obtuse?" Arlene asked.

"I can compare my choice of profession with anybody else's," Max answered hotly, "and it's not your place, either of you, to draw up value judgments for me. Stuff it!"

"Once again," Ben said, "the cultured and refined artist speaks. How come you are only sensitive to yourself? What about your mother?"

Max realized that whatever he said would be wrong to them and sound defensive; he couldn't make it stick. As far as Ben and Arlene were concerned they were protecting Rita, and Max was running away from his responsibility. He could even step across the court and see the whole thing from their point of view — one of the shortcomings he always felt in himself — that he lacked sufficient conviction to wholly believe in what he felt and did, and was always driven to doubt and re-examination by somebody's challenge.

Could he think of a reason not to go? Probably. And make it sound convincing to his mother so that she wouldn't think he was just marking time until the end? Possibly. Was he going to do it? No, not if he could help it. His father and sister edged him out of decision making; why should he be forced to lie, to go along with the fabrication that suited their convenience, or their rationalized cowardice?

"No," Max said. "It's enough with the 'not nice' routine. I'm going to Paris, but I'll come over to New York more frequently, every month or six weeks, and I'll call weekly, and write a lot of letters. That's all I can do."

"You really don't care about what's happening to your mother, do you?" Arlene asked, "When push comes to shove, you really are only for yourself."

"Are the two of you quitting your work?" he screamed at them, and without waiting for an answer, continued: "Well, my work is in Paris with Boulanger, and if you don't like that, too bad. It doesn't rate on your scale of values? Also too bad! Next time you want to make a family decision, remember that I'm part of the family. I vote too. Make it without consulting me and you have no right to expect my compliance."

That said, he turned and stalked from the room, past the flickering green and purple Tango Palace sign and out into the street, leaving the clucking of tongues behind him.

Max delayed his trip to Paris until Rita was home from the hospital.

He sat by her bedside the day of his departure talking of his plans — the concerto he was working on, the opera he dreamed of composing, his search for a story idea.

"Open the second drawer of my desk," his mother said, "and take out the book on top. A red leather notebook."

Max brought the scuffed and crackling volume to her.

She grasped it with thin arthritic fingers, a bird's claw.

"In case something happens to me, Max . . .," and she waved aside the beginning of his objection to her fatalism, ". . . I want you to have this. It belonged to my mother. It is the diary she kept when she was in the institution. I don't know whether it will explain a lot or nothing, . . . and I'm not sure that I even understand it myself. But I'm certain that your father and sister don't and won't. I want to know that you have it, and that it won't disappear into oblivion, like . . ."

Suddenly she broke off talking, handed him the book, turned her head away from him, and begun to sob quietly. Max was chilled with fear by his mother's tears. He felt helpless, awkward.

"What's the matter, Ma, what is it, tell me!" He leaned forward and put his arm across the bed, holding her thin shoulder.

He had never held his mother like this, never had the idea occurred to him that she would need comforting, and never had he known her to be sick. He remembered her doing the same for him many times — comforting and consoling the feverish child in bed with the flu or the dozens of other ailments that kept him home from school; now, suddenly, it was his job. How thin her arm and shoulder were. The well-fleshed woman who was his mother was melting away.

She kept her head averted and, feeling he failed in the feeble effort of consolation, Max took his hand away and sat by the bedside, waiting. When she turned, her face was dark and streaked with tears.

"I wish I could talk to someone," Rita said, eyes boring through his skull miles beyond him.

Max knew right then that his dire view of the futility with which Arlene and his father distorted reality was being borne out. Rita would now have to lie in order to protect those cowards against the possibility of their discovering that she saw through their charade.

And that was just what his mother would do, thus adding the loneliness of not being able to speak freely to the torture and fear of the death growing within her. In her love, she forgave them, understood, and accepted the burden of suffering alone. But Max's hate for the rationalized evasions and manipulations of his sister and father overwhelmed any vestiges of love for them. He didn't care about those two now, only Rita, who would have to stay here and die alone. Not that the truth would have been a comforting bedfellow, but nor was the contrived, failed lie.

"You can talk to me, Ma. Talk to me."

She looked at him for an eternal moment then turned her head away, "I can't talk to anyone."

"You had a happy childhood, didn't you, Max?" Rita asked a few minutes later. She passed the summit of her anguished silence, and emerged on the plateau.

"Sure, Ma, I think I did," he answered. "I certainly had everything I wanted, and you were always very understanding. Strict, but understanding."

"And your father?" She searched his face for a hint of deception behind his answer.

"He was great. None of my friends had a father who would take them places, spend time with them."

"He loved you, Max, still does. Thinks everything you do is wonderful."

"Not since I told him I would not become a physician."

Rita waved her hand, dismissing the charge, "He wanted you to become what he never could because of circumstances, partly because we married so young, and partly, well, maybe he just didn't have it in him. But he's a good man, Max. Try to understand him."

"I was afraid," Max said. "For so many years I was afraid to even think that what I found in music was something I couldn't ignore. I couldn't tell you that it was touching a part in me that would never be happy if I studied medicine, or law, as you suggested."

"Only because you could think on your feet so well, and have that kind of mind."

"But you never stood up to him and said, 'your dream is yours,' Max has to live his own life."

Rita smiled with a trace of sadness: "How many times you'll never know!"

"When I began to become a good piano player, and was playing at dances as a teenager, and then with the band in the Catskills in the summers, he liked it. Even when my friends used to come over for jam sessions it was okay with him, but as soon as I decided to be a composer the roof fell in."

"You were destroying his dream, Max. Can't you see that? He struggled for a living all of his early days and finally began to achieve respect for himself and a good income with all of its benefits, and he wanted the same for you. He didn't want you to struggle."

"I think it was more than that, Ma . . ."

She waved his objections aside: "Don't complicate simple issues, Max. You always had a way of doing that, which is why I thought you would be a good lawyer."

He didn't answer because he could feel himself getting annoyed, and how could he, with her, especially now?

"My father wouldn't even let me play the piano," Rita said. "So what have you got to really complain about? We had a piano in the living room, a Steinway grand that was my mother's — my real mother's — and it just stood there. When I was already working I began to take lessons without telling him, but when he heard me practicing, he wouldn't let me play. He said I would break the piano. Can you believe that?"

"Break the piano?"

"Yes. I was learning to play ragtime. I loved it, and he said it was trash. 'The work of the devil' were his words, and he wouldn't let me play. So the piano just sat there, closed, and I stopped my lessons."

"Why did you let him do that to you, Ma?" Max asked.

She smiled indulgently: "Max, you're naive. In the old days if your father said something, wrong or right, that was it. You and your sister were given so much freedom that you don't know what the opposite is! So when Daddy disapproves of something you do and lets you know it, you think you're suffering." She laughed bitterly and continued: "But he doesn't threaten you, beat you, throw you out in the street, make you leave school and go to work. You don't know!"

"I guess I don't," he admitted.

"Why do you think I got married to your father so young? I was only seventeen. I went from an evil man to a good one, and whatever he says, however cranky he can act, don't forget that your father is a good man."

42

Rita seemed to perk up as she told him some of her history, parts of which Max had heard before, but in the circumstances, the stories took on a new aspect.

◆

Rita's father, Nachman Peretz, groomed her younger brother, Phil, to follow his father's path into the undertaking business, and made sure that Philly — that's what they called him — received everything: schooling, clothes, pocket money, his own bedroom with a desk on which to do his homework.

She didn't get the royal treatment her brother received. She slept in the living room on a folding cot that was kept in the hall closet, and she couldn't go to sleep until her father and stepmother, Yetta, went to their bedroom.

"Can't I sleep in the dining room?" Rita asked.

"Dining rooms are not for sleeping!" Nachman said.

"You'll get up in the dark and break something or scratch something!" Yetta said.

And Rita needed to have her sleep because she had to get up early to go to work.

"Public school is enough for girls," Nachman told her. "Why do you need to know more to wash floors and have babies?" He made her leave school at thirteen, after she received her elementary school diploma, and sent her to work, "to help pay your keep."

The only job Rita could find was in a bakery, where she put in a twelve-hour day from Monday to Friday. Evenings she cleaned up the dishes after dinner. She gave all of her salary to Nachman, who gave her a few cents for pocket money. In return, she was allowed to sleep in the living room. On Saturday she washed and waxed the floors while their father went to *shul* (years later Rita learned that he visited his mistress on Saturday mornings), and Yetta slept late. At noon she prepared a lunch for him when he returned from a morning at diligent prayer. Rita worked in that bakery again on Sunday morning, but if there was no "company" on Sunday afternoon requiring that she help to cook, serve and wash up afterward, she had only those few hours free.

For a while she tried going to night school because she wanted a high school education, but after twelve hours at the bakery and then the clean up after the evening meal, she was too tired to do anything but fall asleep in class. The choice between sleep in class and sleep at home — on Phil's bed, until Nachman and Yetta went to bed and she could open the cot and make it up in the living room — the choice was made by her body, not her will.

From the time she was fourteen, as Rita developed the features of a woman, indeed blossomed, with a bosom and hips that made Yetta look plain, the stepmother encouraged her every day, "Why don't you get married? Then you could have your own place."

More than that, Yetta didn't have enough room. Gertrude, the baby who cemented her marriage to Nachman — or caused it perhaps, — was getting too old to share her parents' room and was moved in with Phil. But in a short time Yetta looked forward to giving her only child a bedroom of her own by putting Phil in the living room. Rita's days in the house were numbered. Moreover, the girl looked too much like her mother, and Yetta didn't think her own marriage profited from the constant reminder to Nachman of his past.

◆

"In any case," Rita broke off her story, "it's all over now, history."

She looked away from Max, stared at the ceiling, and said no more. The red leather diary was still clutched in her bony hand. She handed it to him.

"This is also history, a different kind. Take it with you, Max, and read it. Maybe it'll make some sense for you," Rita said, after an awkward silence dragged its own weight across the space between them. "When I was young I was told that my mother died, and only years later — I was about sixteen — I found out that she was in an institution all the while, and had just died. I never knew her. But she kept this diary, and I inherited it. You were always curious about

44

the family, so I thought you might find something here. Nobody else would."

When Max left for the airport later that day, he felt guilty for being alive, terrified at the realization that he wished his mother would die soon, and spare herself the agony of the ambiguous living purgatory decreed for her. He'd be back around Thanksgiving, he said, and he knew she'd be better by then, hating himself for furthering the charade. From the way she looked at him when he said the words, he knew that she knew the truth, but there was unspoken conspiracy of silence between them, sealed by the trust she exhibited when she gave him the red leather diary.

His mother never spoke of the diary again, and within the year she was dead.

◆

"Saying the Kaddish for your father is not something you should take any liberties with, Maxie," Uncle Phil was saying. "A man has certain responsibilities he should accept without questioning."

"Like saying prayers that have no meaning for dead people for whom prayers do no good?"

"Be a *mensch*, Maxelleh," Uncle Phil cajoled. "You don't have to examine everything, ask questions all the time. Some things you just do, because you're a Jew, and that's what we do."

Phil sat down next to him and put an avuncular arm on Max's shoulder. "C'mon, everything looks lousy at a time like this. Nothing makes sense."

A disbelieving look spread across Max's face, a grimace he couldn't control.

Uncle Phil gripped Max's shoulder and said: "I'd better shut up, huh? I just open my mouth to change feet."

The tension broke into laughter.

Max couldn't ever fault Philly for long. He always liked his mother's brother, who was warm, affable, and jocular with Max when they saw each other, which was only at family dinners or special occasions. He never really sat down and talked to Phil alone to find out how he felt, what he thought, what kind of person he was. It was as though his uncle, and all the family, were born into the world complete with all their attributes, shortcomings, the works. They acted roles in a play written and cast by Max and couldn't change parts; any change meant that something in the drama was being revised, and that couldn't be done except by him.

"I'll think about it, Uncle Phil," Max said, moving a little and turning toward his uncle so that the hand on his shoulder slid off.

"Well, that's better than nothing," Phil said. "At least you'll keep an open mind."

"I don't feel it," Max said. "I don't feel the need to say Kaddish, and I like to know why I do things before I do them."

As he said this he realized that he was not being truthful. Did he know why he stayed at the grave earlier today, or why he walked through the streets for an hour, or why he sketched the music that echoed through his head? Did he understand what made him not want to do whatever anyone else wanted him to do? Why anyone's demand on his time or attention would be rejected out of hand, even though it might be justified? Max didn't know any of this, so why did he try to wear the appearance of a rational philosophical temperament to his uncle, as though Max Bergman were merely a phlegmatic man who acted according to reason. It was an illusion he liked to foster.

"Sometimes you do things first," Uncle Phil said, "and then you learn the reasons why. Who understands these things? Why argue?"

"Oh, here's your sister with some food. *Ess und gedenk!*" he added.

Arlene placed the bagel, stuffed high with cream cheese and tomato, in front of him. Another dish held small mountains of chopped herring, potato salad, cole slaw and lots of olives. A steaming cup of black coffee accompanied the platters. Max leaned forward over the glass and steel cocktail table and dove into the food, each taste filled with history. Arlene might be irritated with him, but not with his stomach. What would she do if she liked him?

Phil talked to Eddy about cars, Ursula discussed college with Ellen, and Arlene listened as Aunt Charlotte from Cincinnati, their father's widowed sister, described in minute detail the lives of her children, their wives and husbands, her grandchildren, especially Mark, who recently began medical school in Chicago. Max watched his sister being attentive to their aunt, asking an occasional question and seeming interested in everything Charlotte's non-stop mouth continued to babble. Where did she get the patience and stamina? He couldn't do it. The world out there was full of cousins Max didn't know, or want to. Was he wrong?

Leaving her conversation with Ellen, Ursula sat down next to him and asked, "What were you doing, Max, when you didn't come back with us?"

He pointed to his mouth, so filled with the first bite of his stuffed bagel that he couldn't even reply properly: "Blrwyng vrm mszchk indrhthing . . .."

"Okay, don't talk," she said, laughing. "But let me tell you that I don't like having to run defense for your moods, especially with your sister. You put me in a very awkward place; she's always looking for me to confirm what a flakey character you are, and is miffed with me because I won't, at least not in front of everyone."

Max succeeded in getting the food past his mouth on its downward trek to nourishment, and before taking another — and smaller — bite, he answered, "But in private, you agree with her."

"In the style of life you — we've — chosen, lover, no. But you're among your family now, so at least do what they expect of you and stop trying to have your own way. It's childish."

"Whose side are you on?"

"Yours, you lummox, but when in Rome . . .."

"Spare me platitudes, Ursula. Today's been too full of them," Max said and bit deeply into the bagel again as he gained some armor by doing this. No questions, no answers.

He saw his niece Ellen watching him from across the room. She looked at him, he thought, with a mixture of suspicion and admiration. No doubt she heard many a family lament about Max disrespecting the idols of the tribe. Curiosity showed through her passive mask.

"For this week, at least, Max, do what they expect of you," Ursula continued in a lower tone, "and then you can be done with it. Why do you have to try to convince them that you have a better way, or that you don't give a damn for their rituals. Pay your respects, and then be quits, if you want to."

"Sit and listen to Aunt Charlotte's inane stories about her grandson's oatmeal and her son's paint job, and . . .?" he spluttered, forcing the food down quickly.

"Yes," Ursula interrupted him.

"It won't cost you so much! And maybe you'll learn something about how other people, who you think are less exalted than you are, live and think."

"You sound like my father, another reality instructor."

"You need one; it wouldn't hurt!" she laughed. "You see, after years with you, even a *shiksa* look-alike can sound like a Jewish joke. Besides, a lot of what Ben used to tell you made sense, you've admitted that to me yourself."

"But never to him," Max said. "and now I can't anymore." He felt a surge of tears coming.

"And if he were still alive you still wouldn't," Ursula said, "so stop bathing in self pity and learn something."

He couldn't answer this time. No words came. Instead he changed the subject, told her about the chorale melody he earlier charted. "I'm going to go downstairs and use the piano in a few minutes while it's still fresh."

"Must you? They'll see it as an affront," she said, motioning her head toward the family.

"It's not; it's my way of memorializing my father."

"Not for them. You're starting something when you needn't."

"In a minute, you'll tell me that it's 'not nice' and all of that kind of crap."

She smiled sadly: "It's not nice, Max. I'm sorry to have to tell you, but today's not about you."

"Shut up, Ursula!" he growled, bits of bagel tumbling from his mouth. "You think sitting here talking about cars and grandchildren is 'nice,' but creating something that moves *me* because of my father's death isn't?"

"For the time being you ought to be fulfilling their expectations, Max. But no — you have to wave the flags of rebellion in everything you do. You think you're going to get these people to see it your way, to educate them? Never. Please wait until you get home to work out your ideas on the piano. Don't make trouble here. I beg you, for your own good. I hate to say it, love, but grow up a little, if not for them, for me."

Ursula stood up without waiting for his response and walked back across the room to Max's niece, and they seemed to pick up where they left off.

The girl kept glancing at him. He hadn't been much of an uncle to her, and had shown little interest in her when she was a child — too busy with himself. But Ellen had formed a strong alliance with his father, Max knew, because Ben often spoke of her, of how smart she was. In Ben's praise there was an echo of his earlier affection for Max and a distinct difference from Ben's endless petty bickering with both Max and Arlene. *What did the kid have going for her?* Max made a mental note to find out. Whatever good it would do, he didn't know.

Ellen continued to look over at him while she and Ursula talked on. *What was it? Horns growing on his head? What had she heard about her uncle, the strange man who was her mother's brother, from Arlene, from Eddy, from Ben? Enough to think him weird, an object of derision, thus someone to hate?*

Ursula noticed the stare and shifted in her seat so that Ellen needed to turn away.

# 4

MAX MET URSULA during his first year of college. She was an art student at Cooper Union, and a classmate of Jules, Max's best friend, who introduced them. Max was smitten by her attitude, an aesthetic shield she carefully constructed around her daily life. Though she commuted daily to Greenwich Village from Scarsdale, where she lived with her parents, Ursula looked as if she had just rolled into class from a loft studio nearby. She lived in Paris while still a child, summered in Rome, visited Florence with her mother on a chaperoned Grand Tour, and had an easy familiarity with Jacob Burckhardt, Miguel de Unamuno, Benedetto Croce, Bernard Berenson, George Santayana and other philosophers of art. They were household gods in Scarsdale, where Mrs. Miller, Ursula's mother, set up as a sculptress, and her father, a physician, collected master drawings and encouraged all the artistic talent in his family.

Max first saw her in Washington Square Park sitting on a bench with Jules. She was reading aloud from a small book with a green leather binding, and Jules was studying half of a salmon sandwich. Pale sunshine filtered through the browning leaves and was caught in her long, blonde hair. And so was Max. His clothes still smelled from the hydrogen sulfide of the morning's chem lab, and the image of this beautiful, long-haired girl reading aloud to Jules made him want to leave the chemicals to their own reactions forever. If only he could sit like that and be read to by such a creature for the duration.

"The body bent forward toward the earth . . ." she read to Jules, whose eyes swept from the diminishing sandwich to the intruder, Max, and signaled "no!"

". . . the arms clasped full of hay . . . that pricks heat into the arms and the skin of the breast, and fills the lungs with the sleepy scent of dried herbs; the rain that falls heavily and wets the shoulder. . . running in a trickle towards the loins, secretly. . . "

Max, standing behind her at a small distance, wondered why he never felt that way about rain and labor and hay.

". . . this endless heat and rousedness of physical sensation that keeps the body full and potent, and flushes the mind with a blood heat . . . .. It is the life and the fulfillment of the peasant . . . "

"Ursula . . . this is my friend Max, the musical doctor," Jules said, interrupting before she read on, and then taking a huge bite of his salmon sandwich, poised as expectantly as Max.

"Nice stuff," Max said. "Who is it?"

"D. H. Lawrence," Ursula said, looking up at his face and then down to his shoes in a classic woman's size-up. "From *Twilight in Italy*."

"We're reading *Sons and Lovers* in my English class," Max said.

"I'm living it!" Jules said.

"You should try *Women in Love*," Ursula said.

"He does, without much success," Jules said, his mouth full of salmon.

"Who is your friend?" Ursula asked Max, feigning annoyance with Jules.

"Just a kid from the old neighborhood," Max answered, "and my best friend in the world."

"Ah, it's enough with that rhapsodic bullshit, the dignity of labor, the currents from the soil, the prison of the body," Jules said. "By the way, Max, she plays the cello too."

Ursula was piqued: "Lawrence found beauty in simple things;

52

you insist on squalor. That's the difference, and I'm not a good cellist. You're romanticizing."

"So what?" Jules answered. "I thought you were okay."

"Back to Lawrence, please," she ordered.

"Why didn't he write about that same wonderful peasant picking his nose and farting, stinking with the unwashed sweat of all those bathless years of 'spiritualizing' labor and dying at the age of forty without a tooth in his head?" Jules asked, asserting his anti-romantic nature.

"You are really intentionally crude," Ursula said.

"*Me?*" Jules looked surprised at her accusation. "Not me! It's more of a crudity on your part to accept that kind of glamorizing of plain dumb hard work on the part of someone who never held a shovel or a pitchfork in his hand all through his life, except maybe to admire their design, so that he could write reams of paper about the 'inherent relationship of form to function in primitive implements of the agrarian cultures'. The only implement he ever used was a fountain pen."

"And the only one you ever use is a paint brush or a palette knife!"

"Yeah, but you won't catch me praising the organic unity between the cab driver and his cab, or the street cleaner and his broom," retorted Jules.

"You're impossible!" Ursula said irritably. She shook her hair as though to rid it of the unpleasant atmosphere of proletarian "reality" Jules invoked.

Max leaped in: "You don't have to accept the writer's vision for your own in order to see that it's beautiful, Jules, just as you can look at a religious painting, a Christian one, for instance. You don't have to accept the entire belief system of Christianity in order to see that Michelangelo was a great artist. You know that."

"My hero," Ursula said.

Feigning great sadness, Jules said, "*I'm* not? No laurel crown?"

"You don't deserve rewards for your garbage-focused mind, either," Ursula said.

"What you call 'garbage,' and thank you for not saying 'shit,' is actually my original contribution to aesthetics. You just don't appreciate the finer things," Jules said. He assumed a hortatory tone, and gesturing with self-important mockery continued, "We can add to the aesthetic of my illustrious teacher, Aristotle, by swelling the number of prescribed or described artistic unities to four. In addition to the unities of time, place and action, I should like to add the unity of excrement. That is, within a given context — an age, a family, a society, an institution of any sort the writer may care to discuss — there is a similarity in the kinds of mental shit, including horseshit, bullshit, etcetera, that the characters are evacuating. Such excretia are, of course, self perpetuating and renewing. As long as the biological process we call life continues, there is an unending supply of excrement, varying directly with the amount of mental and literal food that the organism ingests. The best writers, to my observation, maintain a consistency in this: all the members of any given group, from a family to an entire culture, give out the same shit. Failure to observe this will result in a failure of communication among the characters, thus lessening the possibilities of conflict."

Ursula applauded. Jules stood and bowed and she caught his head and kissed his cheek.

"How can I be angry with such a clever clown?"

Jules beamed pleasure, and then screwed his eyes up at Max, expecting some reaction, but Max unwrapped a sandwich he'd bought before walking over to the park, made the obligatory offer of half to Ursula, who refused, and began to eat. He lost Jules for the moment and could only focus on Ursula. She had very delicate wrists, Max noticed, and he liked the way she held her head, slightly to the side when she talked. What was the rest of the conversation? He tried to remember, but he couldn't bring the words back. He knew it was about his goal to become a doctor, hers of being a painter, and how she wanted only to spend her life making beautiful things; nothing else mattered very much.

"I want to be a doctor," he said.

"Why?"

He couldn't answer.

For the first time in his life, sitting there in Washington Square, with his old friend Jules, and this new girl, Ursula, he couldn't answer. The sun came through the leaves in the same way and the air still vibrated with dusty beams of light. Ursula sat with her head cocked to the side, and Jules studied his salmon sandwich with great concentration. Nothing had changed. But everything had.

"From imperious courtship in the mighty and majestic undulations of the Pacific, the noble salmon, royalty of fish, wend lovingly towards the shore, driven by impulses whose magnitude is immeasurable," said Jules aloud, addressing his half-devoured sandwich in the breach of silence Ursula's question produced, "and cavorting with the earnestness coded by millions of years of genetic compulsions, thresh their way up the mighty Columbia River. Silver clad, flashing in the sunlight like crusading knights of old, they battle their way towards the grail of their destiny, and culminate, ah, yes, saluting the glory coursing through them, reach their goal finally when mashed together with mayonnaise and spread on soggy white bread by my mother, who nurtures her only begotten son for the glory of ART! That's in capitals."

It was a Friday night several weeks later, and when the candles were lit and the blessings said, Max announced that after dinner he was going back to the city for a date. He wouldn't be staying in Queens overnight, a newly established ritual for the Bergmans.

"You're too young to be serious with a girl," Rita said.

Ben defended his son, "What serious? What are you talking about?" "The boy needs some healthy recreation, some company of girls. What kind of doctor doesn't need biological experience?" he asked, winking at Max.

Arlene look at her brother stonily.

"Since you were a young man, that's all you think about," Rita snapped at Ben. "Your own animal satisfactions."

Ben winked again at Max: "Her father's a doctor, Rita. That's a good thing, a good influence . . .."

"What are you both doing?" Max protested, easing some chopped liver off the hated bed of lettuce. "I have a date with a nice Jewish girl I met a few weeks ago. End of story!"

"And you let that interfere with your family obligations!" his mother asked.

"I'm here for dinner, no? Isn't that enough? What more do you want from me?'"

"But you usually stay over."

"He fulfills something by sleeping here?" Ben asked.

"Better than sleeping with some girl!" Rita snapped.

"Ma!" Max said.

She cast her eyes downward toward the table and wouldn't look up at her husband and son.

He continued, "I go out with her two or three times and you've gotten me married off already. What is this?"

"You're jumping the gun, Rita." Ben said.

"He's too young to be serious with a girl!"

"Who's serious?"

"You are," she said. "I can tell. A mother can tell!"

Max pushed the lettuce aside and scraped the remainder of the chopped liver off the plate.

"What's wrong with the lettuce?" Rita asked.

"I don't like it," Max said.

"What's not to like about lettuce; it hardly has any taste," Arlene butted into the lettuce debate as though to support Rita.

"Dry up!" Max said to her.

"Don't talk to your sister like that," Ben said.

"Do you come down on *her* because *she* has a boyfriend?" Max asked his mother.

"And his father's not a doctor either," Ben chimed in helpfully.

"I want to see my children firmly established in careers," Rita said, "before they get seriously involved with anybody."

"I like her company. Period," Max said, "and already you have me married. Jesus Christ!"

"Don't swear," Ben said. "And to say *that* name on the Sabbath in a Jewish home . . .?"

"Her boyfriend can practically live with her," Max said, nodding in Arlene's direction, "I go out with a girl more than once, I'm chopped liver."

"If by 'her,' you mean your sister Arlene," Rita said angrily, "then the answer is that she already finished college with honors and is in her second year of medical school. I don't think that Arlene will let anything get in her way now, including Eddy!"

"Maxie won't let anything stop him either," Ben said. "Will you, sonny boy?"

Max shook his head.

"You see?" Ben asked Rita, triumphantly.

Rita looked up with tears in her eyes.

"Why do you always have to compare me with Arlene, Ma?"

"Who else should I compare you to, the man in the moon?"

"And will you compare Ursula to Eddy when you meet her?"

"I don't want to meet her," Rita said, sobbing. "The girl who distracts my son away from his family."

"Compared to Eddy, she's a genius, and good-looking too!"

"See, I told you," Rita raised her voice. "He's serious."

"What's wrong with Eddy?" Arlene asked, ready to fight.

"He's a jerk!" Max said.

"He's always so nice to you, you little twerp."

"He's as phony as a three dollar bill," Max said.

"Will you two stop it?" Ben demanded.

"All he's got is his old man's business and a fancy sports car," Max went on, unheeding. "This qualifies him for Arlene. But I get a different rating system!"

"How dare you!" Arlene said.

"You wouldn't defend yourself so much if you weren't serious with this girl," Rita said.

"I'm defending my rights, that's all," Max replied.

"The boy told you that he wasn't seriously involved. Now will you let him alone?" Ben said firmly to his wife. "Let's have a peaceful supper. Come on, Rita," he changed to a cajoling tone.

"I don't like to be lied to by my children," Rita said, standing up, her eyes narrowed and full of angry tears. She gathered their dirty salad plates.

"He told you the truth, Rita," Ben said. "Didn't you, Max?"

Max didn't answer as Rita's eyes bored into his skull. Arlene glared at him and reached for her mother's hand. Ben sat expectantly, smiling, waiting for an answer from his son that would calm Rita and allow them to continue supper in peace.

But Rita pulled away from Arlene, put the dishes in the sink and said, "Eat by yourselves. I lost my appetite." She stalked out of the room and slammed the bedroom door. Ben got up and followed her, while Arlene and Max sat where they were, not seeing each other, and listened to the raised voices but unintelligible words from the other end of the apartment.

"You're a little bastard," Arlene said, when the voices stopped and they heard the bedroom door open.

Max didn't answer her.

Ben came back and took his seat, with a sheepish grin on his face and a shrug of futility in his shoulders.

"Arlene, would you dish out the rest?" he asked.

The men sat in silence while Arlene portioned out the chicken, potatoes and carrot pudding.

"So tell me," Ben said when the food was before them and Arlene seated once more: "What kind of doctor is this girl's father?"

"I don't know, but they live in Scarsdale and they're Jewish. Okay? That's all I know."

Max was serious about Ursula, he realized the next day, when he woke up next to her in the bedroom of a loft she "borrowed" from one of her mother's friends. It was something about her, so different

58

from the people who lived in the world Max knew. A softness, an openness to experience, a birdlike fascination with little things: the way a leaf hanging on a tree shivered in the late autumn wind, the way sunlight appeared on the side of a building. She saw everything with the eye of a painter and her usual words were: "Isn't that wonderful?" whether she was talking about a bird in flight or the grizzled old man who sold hot dogs and soft drinks from a rolling cart with a large blue and orange umbrella in Washington Square Park.

Max, conditioned by a more practical cause-and-effect world combining the pragmatic dreaming of Ben and the refusals of imagination that were Rita's, felt that he was being inducted into the service of a force he never knew. His goals seemed less important than before. Only Ursula and the moment and their combined bodies were.

On Monday nights she came to see him perform at a small bar on Macdougal Street, and listened intently as he played piano with a jazz trio, who were sitting in when the regulars were off.

Max began to write songs — complex harmonic progressions with brief flashes of lyricism — dedicated to Ursula, and he wrote lyrics. "Autumn Meeting" was the best. He sent them all to her by mail, even though they now saw each other every day at lunchtime, meeting in the park if the weather was fine, or at the NYU Commons, Phebe's or the old Cedar Tavern, a hangout for the abstract impressionist painters Ursula and Jules liked to identify themselves with.

Jules was with them most of the time, choosing to be oblivious to their need to be alone together and forcing them to be evasive when they wanted to spend the time in the painter friend's loft. Ursula now had both the key and the unspoken blessing of her mother's suburban, bohemian friend, who apparently also used the place more for her own affairs than for art work. Max was in love, and Rita knew it.

"You think a girl like Ursula will make a suitable wife for a doctor?" Rita asked.

It was the Saturday after Thanksgiving and Ursula joined his family for the Thursday feast; her own parents were away for the long weekend.

"Why not?" Ben answered. "She has watched her folks long enough, a professional family, and learned from her own mother, no doubt."

"I'm not talking to you, Ben," Rita said. "I'm asking Maxie!"

"Who is getting married?" Max asked. "What are you talking about?"

"You know very well what I'm talking about," his mother replied. "The fact that I saw this coming and you denied it before gives me the right to an honest answer from you."

"I'm not getting married," Max said. "What for?"

"What for, he asks. What for? Max, thick you're not. Pretend though you may, you're human like everyone else."

"I know what Ma means," Arlene chimed in. "She's saying that your Ursula's a flake, an artsy-craftsy dilettante with her head in the clouds."

"Who asked you?" Max said angrily. "Who gave you the right to judge?"

"Oh, the little prince can judge my friends, but I can't say a blessed word about his. Is that so?"

Max tried to kick her under the table but missed.

"Ma," she shrieked as she felt his foot whisk past her shin.

"Max, answer your mother," Ben ordered.

"I'm not getting married so soon."

"What then, you'll wait a few weeks?"

"No. I'm not getting married! Why should I?"

"Oh, you have no normal drives like everyone else?" Rita asked. "Then you should pardon me, I didn't realize I was talking to a saint."

"A saint I'm not, but I don't see why people who want to have sex" — he caught the warning beacon in his father's eyes too late to stop — "can't do what they want without the ceremony and a stupid piece of paper."

Rita now blazed: "You think that makes it better? You think what you are telling me offers any assurance. No! It makes matters worse. Not only is the girl unsuitable, but she's loose. Nice girls don't do that until they're married."

"At least engaged," Arlene said, eying the ring Eddy gave her the week before.

"Even then," countered Rita. "And nice boys don't do that to nice girls," she went on, raising her voice again, her face turning apoplectically red.

"Ma, this is 1970," Max protested.

"I don't care if it's 2070!" Rita yelled, "that's the way it is now and always in my book."

"Your book is out of print!" Max yelled back at his mother.

"Don't you talk to your mother like that!" Ben said, raising his voice and his hand as though to slap Max.

It was now Max's turn to slam doors, although once out in the street, walking towards the train back to the city, he regretted the scene. He didn't start it, but he should have controlled it better.

# 5

ARLENE WAS DONE IN THE KITCHEN. She had helped Samantha put the perishables away; not that her full-time maid of many years couldn't do the job herself, but it made Arlene feel that she was on top of things if she knew what was under each Tupperware lid, or surrounded by every bit of Saran Wrap. Such details, the knowledge of the territory, gave a precision to her everyday life. She felt uneasy and uncomfortable with anything sloppy, inexact, or undefined. Her office, her hospital work had order and clarity, and she wanted her home life to echo her profession.

Office assistants didn't last long, as none of them could ever meet her expectations, but Samantha had been with Arlene for many years, and knew her ways. Moreover, Arlene came to rely on the West Indian woman and needed her regularly in the house. To avoid the kind of dissatisfaction that gnawed at her until she would be irritated to the point of letting Samantha go, Arlene performed little tasks herself. It saved explaining and ragged nerves.

Arlene could not understand Max and how two children who were so different could come from the same parents. She was pragmatic and focused on the present, like her mother, she even looked like her: short, sturdy but shapely, dark hair, green eyes. Her tall, thin brother, who looked like Ben, was a dreamer. He lived in, mulled over and was even tortured by the past. He was forgetful of his present obligations, but could remember precise details of events from twenty years ago. And while remembering what was long past, he'd forget to pay his bills, have his shoes fixed, call his family. She didn't know how Ursula put up with Max. Maybe he was what she had instead of a child. She'd probably make a good wife to him, if only she could get him to agree to marriage. Ursula said she didn't want to marry either, but Arlene was sure that it was defensive: any woman wanted some security from the man she kept house for, or "with" as her brother and putative sister-in-law stupidly insisted.

As though Max was really a sharer of housework! He couldn't even sew on a button and was the world's disorder king, never putting anything in the same place — even when he was a kid. On the other hand, he did enjoy cooking, and always helped around the kitchen when he lived at home while their mother was alive.

"There are things a man doesn't do," Ben would say to deaf ears. "Let your sister help in the kitchen, Max. What do you want . . . to grow up to be a fairy?"

Eddy was cut from the same domestic cloth as Ben. He never lifted a finger to help with anything in the house. And he was right to do so in his father-in-law's eyes, despite his failures. Eddy, however, couldn't take it that Arlene made more money than he did, and that after his business went under, and he became someone else's employee, there was no more big shot, expense accounts, fancy cars, custom suits. He also resented Arlene's six-figure income. When his couldn't compete, he became less of a man. Even in bed, he never wanted her on top, and then when the shysters took over his company, it was as though he had been shot full of saltpeter.

Thinking about her marriage made Arlene horny. She'd talk to him later, and maybe next week "get together" with Eddy. When he was on his game, she had no complaints in bed. But he married again. Well, so what! He was still her only husband, married or divorced, and she still wanted him when she needed sex.

Max brought his dirty plate and cup into the kitchen, and put them in the dishwasher just as Arlene finished securing the last shred of Saran Wrap around the leftover potato salad.

"Would you mind if I went downstairs and worked out something on the piano?"

"Now? With everybody here? What are you, crazy? Of course I'd mind. You aren't supposed to play music during this time."

"I'm not playing, Arlene. I'm working. I have an idea I must hear before it escapes me."

"Can't you write it out?"

"I did, before I got here, but I have to hear it."

"That's what kept you?" she asked, annoyance lighting up her eyes.

"It only took a couple of minutes, Arlene. I just wanted to be alone after the funeral."

"Well, maybe I did too; did you ever think of that? Did it ever occur to you that other people besides yourself have feelings that they can't always act on? That some of us just hold those feelings in abeyance and do what's expected of us. Where do you think the world would be . . . ?"

"I don't know," he interrupted, "but the people who do hold it in and wait for the right moment may be wonderful diplomats, or ulcer candidates, but they aren't artists."

"They also aren't babies!" she said loudly.

Just then the telephone rang, and Max didn't respond to the intended slur knowing that in some respects he was whimsical and capricious, suddenly motivated to tears or laughter, and often either oblivious or indifferent to convention. He saw no reason to defend himself, as that would only have convinced Arlene of the accuracy of her judgment. As for Arlene, he knew she coped with any impulse not conducive to her ideas of order by suppressing it in herself and discouraging it in others. Of all the things she feared, chaos was the most abhorrent, and showed its ugly face in deviations from the norm. She prided herself on being her mother's daughter, and conducting her everyday life along lines set down for her from the cradle.

Arlene answered the phone, then summoned Max to speak to Aunt Gertrude, his mother's younger sister, in California. She had been informed of Ben's sudden death, but after making a quick evaluation of the benefits or losses to be accrued by attending the funeral, she decided that it would do the deceased brother-in-law little good. Business — she was an agent for scriptwriters — didn't permit her coming east at the moment. "But I'll be in New York on business next week," she said, "coming in this Friday. Maybe you and Arlene and I can get together for a drink, or perhaps dinner. I'll call."

She said she was sorry for Max's "great loss," and that she liked Ben and was sorry she had been out of close contact — she sent a yearly Chanukah card and called once every three or four times she was in New York. Max asked her a few perfunctory questions to be polite. Cassy, the woman she lived with, was fine and sent her condolences, too. He then took the portable phone to Uncle Phil in the living room.

"What else can you expect from her?" Arlene said.

Peeved when he didn't answer her, she quickly returned to the living room, where the rest of the gathering was now seated in one of those deadly family circles talking about Gertrude, Rita's and Phil's half-sister.

Max usually enjoyed sitting and talking to one, two or even three others. This circle, however, in addition to being family and having a common thread running through their lives, was exactly the number he thought to be deadly. Seven. Too few to break up into small groups of two or three, especially because there was little for them to discuss besides the family's new gossip since the last wedding or funeral took place. After "Hello, how are you? What have you been doing lately?" there was nothing left to say. They were like seven different radio broadcasts on seven different frequencies with occasional static when they all mingled in a buzzy blur. Not that he didn't like cacophony, but only when musically useful.

He began to imagine what he could do if he were a playwright, how he could take these many voices and orchestrate them as they all talked at once or separately; they interrupted, picked up a phrase, a tone, a melodic leap, formed a chord, passed over a theme from one to the other. How the printed page became no more than an approximation of what the author intended, just as the printed music was also an abstraction, a way of organizing and transferring the idea of sound so that others could approximate what he had in mind, what he actually heard. But he couldn't control these conversations with musical notation, couldn't get them on paper quickly, and it bothered him.

Max tuned out the general blur of conversations and began to listen to individual voices as he sat down on the couch again, next to his niece Ellen this time, who was seated between himself and Aunt Charlotte from Cincinnati.

"What makes you say Aunt Gertrude is a lesbian?" Ellen asked Charlotte.

"You know when you see her," Charlotte answered.

Ursula injected, "Last time I saw her she looked perfectly normal to me. What does a lesbian look like?"

Max wondered why she was doing this, after she cautioned *him* not to make waves.

"What do you think?" Charlotte retorted hotly, "just because I live in Ohio I don't know anything, see anything? Besides, don't forget I grew up in New York, and we got plenty in Ohio, too!"

"Tell us then, Aunt Charlotte," Ellen piped up from next to Max.

Arlene wished that her daughter hadn't asked, but youth had already asserted its impetuous way.

Now Charlotte seemed impatient that she must explain the obvious. "Ya' know . . . dykes!" she said, pronouncing the word as "die . . . keys," which forced Max to put his hand over his mouth to prevent a chortle, "with the short haircuts and the men's clothes. They wear the motorcycle jackets with silver studs, and they smoke Camels without filters and God knows what else!"

Chins around the room were pressed down to chests to conceal smiles of dismay.

"Gertrude doesn't play that role, Aunt Charlotte," Ursula, now the peacemaker, said, "but she has lived with Cassy for fifteen or eighteen years, as though married. They share a bed and they love each other, like any married couple. Max and I stayed with them when we were out there. They were great!"

Charlotte's jaw hung open: "You could have fooled me, but is her friend like a man?"

"No, she's very womanly," Uncle Phil said. "I met her a number of times. She's a regular, good looking woman."

"So what do they do it for? Why don't they find guys? It's so perverted," Charlotte said. "How come you're all so blasé about it?"

"Look, what do I know?" Phil said. "Cassy's nice. Gertrude's nice, And they got a good life out there, lots of friends, they run this agency together. What the hell's the difference? They're happy, they love each other, and they don't make no one else uncomfortable with it. 'Live and let live,' I say."

"I wouldn't want anyone like that teaching my grandchildren!"

"Two of my professors are lesbians," Ellen said, and then as an afterthought, "Well, one I'm sure about, the other only half."

"And they don't try to talk the students into it?" Charlotte asked. "I'd be afraid to let my kids go there," she said, looking at Arlene.

"I don't like the place," Eddy said. "There's too many snotty rich girls, and with only a few weird guys and artsy-fartsy professors. Look, who can tell what might happen?"

"Oh, shut up, you asshole," Arlene said to him. "You don't know what you're talking about. You visited the campus only once, and, besides, you don't pay the bills, so butt out. Anyway, I have enough faith in Ellen's good sense."

"My roommate is gay," Ellen volunteered.

"Trisha?" Arlene asked incredulously. "Did she ever do anything, proposition you, try to talk you into it?"

"She asked me if I was straight or gay," Ellen said quietly. "She really believes in any woman's right to choose what she wants to do with her own body."

"What did you tell her?" Arlene interrupted.

"I told her I wasn't sure. That I liked boys, but that since I never had anything in the way of an experience with a woman, I couldn't know."

"You see," shouted Eddy, "the kind of place you send her, and look what happens."

"Nothing happened," Ellen said, eyes on the floor.

"But it might?" Arlene asked, her lips trembling.

"I doubt it," Ellen answered, "but it might!"

"I forbid it!" Eddy said. "I absolutely forbid it!"

"What could you do about it, you yo-yo?" Arlene snarled.

"I'll call the cops, the governor. I'll disown her. Over my dead body. You better not!" He waved an angry finger at Ellen.

"I happen to agree with you, Charlotte," Arlene said. "I don't like it any more than you do, but there's nothing I can do about what people do in private, except to make it clear it's nobody else's business. Toleration doesn't equal approval."

"Did you make it clear to Vassar?" Eddy asked.

"You oughta!" said Aunt Charlotte.

"I never knew about it until now," Arlene answered, "but I think of women's rights and equal rights. I am in favor of that, including sexual orientation and so on."

"You are?" It was Charlotte's turn to be incredulous. "You believe in shared bathrooms, and women drafted into the army?" She was twisting her handkerchief, looking pained, as though she didn't understand what the world was coming to.

"That's for the lunatic fringe," Arlene said. "I mean jobs, the right to say whether or not you want an abortion and not have old men decide what's good for your body, or young men either. That's what I'm for." Max was surprised to hear his sister speak so calmly and reasonably. He gave her a point in the credit column.

Aunt Charlotte's dismay deepened, and she rolled her hanky into a tiny ball, pressing it until her fingers turned white. "I never thought I'd hear such radical ideas from you, of all people. Your mother would turn over in her grave," she said. "You sound just like your father when he was young, except about the sex stuff."

"Ben was practically a Communist!" said Uncle Phil.

Max couldn't tell whether Phil was teasing or not. Arlene looked more shocked to be compared to her father than to hear him accused of being "practically a Communist." She modeled herself in the measure of her mother and never let anyone else forget it.

"Yeah," Charlotte said, nodding her head to affirm the truth. "He was once gonna save the world from the rich, remember that, Phil?"

"Until he became rich himself," Phil answered, running his hand over his shining dome, as he had probably once run it through his hair.

"How can you say he was rich?" Arlene asked. "He was always a working man."

"But he was a professional!" Aunt Charlotte said with pride, "and a self-made man, and, believe you me, it wasn't easy for him."

"When was he a Communist?" Max asked. He knew Ben had been interested in politics, but he didn't know whether his aunt and uncle were talking about some radical ideas, or if Ben Bergman was a card-carrying member. His father the revolutionary? Maybe they were talking about someone else.

"It probably started with the cousin you're named after," Charlotte said. "Cousin Meyer."

"I never knew him," Uncle Phil said.

"Of course not," Charlotte answered, "because by the time Ben met Rita, Meyer had gone back to Russia. You got to know the Bergman family at a later date."

"I never even heard about him," Phil said.

"Sure you did," Arlene said. "You just don't want to remember that he was a Communist."

"What a stupid thing to say," Uncle Phil said to her."Why shouldn't I want to remember something like that?"

"Because Meyer was a big *macher* with the Communists and maybe you were afraid the House Committee on Un-American Activities would subpoena you."

"Hey, what kind of bullshit is that?" Phil asked angrily. "What the hell does my business have to do with what Ben did fifty years ago?"

"More," Charlotte said. "Meyer went back in 1935."

"So, I was almost right, fifty-five years ago," Phil said, "and why should I forget purposely? Some big Communist Ben must have been as a fifteen-year-old!"

"I remember Papa talking about this once, years ago, at a Thanksgiving dinner," Arlene said, "and you and your whole family were there."

"*I* don't remember," Max said, "and I must have been there."

"Sure you were," Arlene said, "but you were nine or ten. Why should you remember?"

Max shrugged. Specific events had a place in his conscious memory, but those family dinners were all a blur. The facts intermingled. Cousins, food, giggling, fighting, tears, boredom with the adults, playing hide and seek in the bedrooms. It was all a large stew simmering with vague ingredients. Servings of his individual experiences were on single platters without sauce.

"Anyway, so what happened?" Uncle Phil asked impatiently.

"Meyer was my father's favorite cousin, and a big influence on him," Arlene answered. "He returned to Russia in the 1930s and never came back. It was a big disappointment for our father."

"That's no story!" Phil said.

"If you'll let me continue, maybe I can tell you something," Arlene retorted.

"Let me tell it because I was there," Charlotte said. "At least I got the facts."

Arlene shrugged her shoulders and yielded reluctantly to Aunt Charlotte, who was there and probably did know more details, though the story would get longer.

"My father, Isaac," Aunt Charlotte began, "Your grandfather," she informed Max and Arlene, "and your great grandfather," she said to Ellen, to be sure that everyone had the relationship straight . . ..

"And the father-in-law of my sister Rita," Phil interrupted.

"Yeah," Charlotte said, at first looking pleased that someone was grasping the complexity, but then she became annoyed when she realized that he was putting her on.

"Why can't you be serious, Phil? Since I know you, always the same joker and it's not so funny anymore. Not now at least," she scolded him. He looked sheepish and stroked his head, saying nothing.

"Anyway, Isaac came to this country in 1910."

"I already heard this story many times," Eddy piped up.

"Nobody's keeping you," Arlene snapped at him.

"I'll take a walk," he said. "I need some air," and he left the room.

"He should choke on it," Arlene muttered.

Ellen looked at her sullenly.

"Keep walking 'til you *plotz*," Arlene said as she heard the front door close.

"Ma!" Ellen said.

"He's a phony," Arlene answered her daughter. "He comes here with his hearts-and-flowers sympathy, pretends that he's a member of the family. When he really doesn't give a damn. He probably thought he'd get in my good graces. Well, he's got the chance of a snowball in hell."

"That's your father speaking in you," Phil said. "He never forgave an injury."

"Can I continue with the story?" Aunt Charlotte asked, and without waiting for an answer went on.

Later, Max recorded and edited Charlotte's telling for his notes because, though she rambled and digressed, he liked the story and wanted to make it coherent.

◆

Isaac Bergman emigrated to America from a small *shtetl* near Minsk in 1920, and settled into a tenement apartment on New York's Lower East Side with his wife Sarah Leah. Max's father, Ben, was born that year; Charlotte, two years after that. Later they moved to Brooklyn.

Because Isaac was the youngest son of a well-to-do merchant in Minsk, he was a pampered ladies man and a layabout. Pogroms and the threat of conscription into the army drove him from Russia, where he otherwise would have been quite content to remain. A gentle man given to random study and much speculation, in America Isaac was content to earn a scanty living in a garment factory, and was willing to barter his poorly paid long hours in the sweatshop for the privilege of enjoying his evening meal in peace, secure that the Cossacks would not destroy his little island of domestic pleasure.

Saturday afternoons when he returned from the synagogue were his great joy of the week. Then he could sit by the white porcelain enamel-topped kitchen table, drinking endless glasses of tea from the samovar, smoking Turkish cigarettes (while Sarah Leah fussed about and complained that he shouldn't smoke on the Sabbath), and entering into long philosophical conversations with relatives, friends, and comrades who dropped by.

Sarah Leah, a short, square woman with braided hair, said that they were talking nonsense about things she didn't understand, and sat reading the Yiddish newspaper, clucking her tongue. Her greatest pleasure was her sympathy for disaster stories and the wailings of the agony columns, especially the letters to the editor about the misdeeds of errant relatives, thankless children, and runaway husbands.

Most welcome to Isaac's Saturday afternoon conversations was his "nephew" Meyer, son of Isaac's cousin, Samuel, who also lived in Brooklyn.

An invalid, and older than Isaac, Samuel had a somewhat superior attitude toward Isaac, and Samuel's wife, Minna, actively disliked Sarah Leah. The relatives did not see each other frequently even though Isaac's father Noah and Samuel's father Jacob were brothers.

But the cousins' differences were the work of history: Jacob, a lowly conscript during the Crimean War was promoted on the field to non-commissioned officer for a daring act of bravery. Highly unusual as it was for a Jew to be so honored, the status entitled him to send his children to the official *gymnasium* and to the University.

Hence Samuel's branch of the family was educated; after coming to America they had the background and confidence to become prominent in public life as well as business in the United States. Some of them, who by dint of their education and the subsequent sense of being Russian (rather than merely Jewish outsiders existing beyond the Czar's "Pale on the Settlement") obtained permission to move to the cities of St. Petersburg and Moscow, where they managed to find employment in the civil service. The pogroms were mostly rural phenomena, and did not touch their lives directly other than with sympathy, and they did not feel the pressure to escape from Russia as did their country shtetl kin.

When the waves of social upheaval struck Russia in the early years of the century, the urban branch of the family supported the political spirit, if not the bloody action, and stayed around to become party members when the struggle for power was resolved. Those who emigrated to America, not having quite the faith in the promise of the Russian Revolution as did their relatives, took as their ideal the motto *"Novus Ordo Seclorum"* — A new order of the ages — on American currency. In the New World you could go as far as your talent and ambition took you. They became, for example, editors of newspapers and magazines, founders of banks and brokerage houses, real estate developers, university professors, lawyers, surgeons, politicians, movie producers, actors, entertainers, among other success stories.

But the grandchildren of Jacob tended to look upon the grandchildren of Noah as ordinary, poor and ignorant, and kept them at a discreet distance. Isaac was forgiving, and gentle in forgetting the slight, but Sarah Leah never gave up a grudge. Cousin Meyer bridged the gaps with regular visits to his "uncle," whose company he seemed to enjoy.

It was an odd pairing too, this strong bond between gently stoical, somewhat dreamy Isaac and the younger ardent Meyer, a dedicated Communist who repudiated religion, but stayed culturally Jewish. Meyer did not want to sit around waiting until the millennium for social progress in America beyond making money. He believed it was happening right then in the new world of the Soviet Union and didn't want to miss it. Although born in the USA, he grew unhappy here; he longed to return to the land of his forefathers and work for earthly paradise.

The revolutions of 1917 were long past and he didn't want to fight in the streets, but by the early 1930s he had begun to fear the rise of Hitler and knew in his heart that the long simmering hatred between Russia and Germany would erupt in armed conflict, especially since Hitler loathed both Jews and Communists, and Russia had plenty of both. Meyer wanted to make history rather than to be made by it, to stand in the middle of time rather than outside. Watching the hours pass with the mild acquiescence of his "Uncle" Isaac was not for Meyer.

A man of broad and deep culture, well acquainted with classical and modern European writers, no stranger to either Dostoyevsky or Georges Sorel, Meyer read in his ancestors' Russian as well as French, German, English, and, of course, Yiddish. He had a passion for the opera and would often go to the old Metropolitan Opera House on Broadway and 39th Street. Not able to afford seats, he paid for standing room and became practiced in spotting an empty place into which he could zoom at the end of the first act. The rest of his modest discretionary funds were all spent on phonograph records and books.

His trade? Shoemaker.

Not a repairman or a cobbler though, but rather a craftsman who made and built fine, custom shoes for men and women, he was employed by a small factory that prospered in the trade from Brooklyn's well-to-do.

In those days it was standard in shops where there was an the absence of noisy, heavy machinery, that employees in the skilled trades would chip in a small amount each to hire a "reader" to read to them as they worked. It was in this way that Meyer first heard the early works of Marx.

The shoemakers of Bendelsky's Custom Made Shoes for Ladies and Gents chose to listen to a variety of books. Marx's *The Eighteenth Brumaire of Louis Bonaparte* was popular, as were the writings of Rousseau, Voltaire, Freud and Dewey. Dostoyevsky, Tolstoy, Dickens and Trollope were among their favorite novelists, and American social realists like Dreiser and Lewis were also of interest. Only rarely did they listen to the newspapers being read aloud, because each of the five craftsmen in the shop differed in his journalistic preference and found the editorial position of the other papers intolerable.

The men spoke only Yiddish with each other, even Malik, a non-Jewish Latvian, who learned the language from his co-workers. By agreement, however, everything was read in English as this was the language they all wanted to improve. The reader was always a native speaker, and the men acquired vocabulary painlessly.

Occasionally they spoke Russian, but only when a passage translated from Tolstoy or Dostoyevsky seemed incorrect. Invariably one of the them would bring in the original text on the following day, and during their lunch break, the arguers would lend authority to their positions by speaking the language whose distortions were in question. Work, instruction, and entertainment combined.

Cousin Meyer especially liked his "Uncle" Isaac, and his young cousin, Ben. Perhaps this was because Meyer's own younger brother, Joe, was interested in neither music nor literature, nor political thought. Oh, to be sure, Joe was a socialist, but that was simply his inclination. He had little concern for the fine points of anything except baseball.

Meyer became a surrogate older brother for Ben, and a mentor who tried to shape the boy's thinking by bringing him books to read and taking him to concerts, thus acquainting him with the cultural richness of New York, which if they could neither own it nor be first class citizens, then at least they could explore. Under Meyer's tutelage, Ben heard *La Boheme*, *Tosca*, and *Madama Butterfly*, saw John Barrymore do *Hamlet* on Broadway, heard Rachmaninoff perform at Carnegie Hall, and saw Toscanini conduct Beethoven.

Through Meyer, the reading room at the New York Public Library lost its mystery, and Ben began a nodding acquaintance with great thinkers who shaped Meyer's world. But Ben was restless, and he wanted the future Meyer believed in to happen right away. He didn't have Meyer's patience, a patience based upon his unswerving religious faith — and Marxism was for Meyer nothing if not a religion — that things must change, would change, as decreed by the iron laws of history; these were Meyer's gods.

Then, in 1935 two events had great impact on Ben: he dropped out of high school, and Meyer returned to Russia.

Ben became impatient with the "lies" he was being taught in his history class, and irritated by his teachers, who were simplistic and reductive in order to bring culture to the "peasants." Ben suspected that his teachers were basically ignorant people in positions of authority. The English teachers, especially, reinforced their own status by regarding their rights over the novels, poems and plays they taught as proprietary. Born to the language, they thought they owned exclusive claims to the great works of Shakespeare and Dickens. Tolstoy and Dostoyevsky they regarded as "foreign," like their garlic-breathed students, and not to be studied in class. They never heard of Freud, whom Meyer extolled as the greatest philosopher of the mind. Ben's probably justified dislike for the instructors in the liberal arts paired with his unjustified dislike for the teachers of mathematics and science, who became gross malefactors in his eyes because they insisted that he study, do his homework, and pay attention in class.

There was nothing Meyer could do to prevent his young cousin from leaving school. He told Ben that he was disappointed in him for making the wrong decision. It was cowardly, he said, not to face up to responsibilities, even though they were not the most pleasant. Ben protested with the rationale for his complaints, but Meyer told him that all societies, advanced, transitional and progressive, were run by people who possessed the credentials. Ben was choosing not to be a leader but a follower.

"The future needs trained minds more than strong backs," Meyer insisted."

They were standing in front of the Public Library on 42nd Street at the time.

"The lions," Meyer continued, "guard you in the morning. In the afternoon and evening you have to protect yourself."

Then he walked to the subway, leaving Ben standing there, his expression blank, his frozen by his inability to understand what Meyer just said to him.

Meyer did not appear at Isaac's house for three weeks, and when he did, one Saturday afternoon, he announced that he was leaving for the Soviet Union in a few days. He felt that his future was there. "All hopes disintegrate in America," he said, glancing at Ben, who sat by the kitchen table sucking on a sugar cube. "In Russia, at least, they're trying to make a new world happen, integrating human beings into a national community, with a respect for ethnic differences."

"It sounds like heaven," Isaac said, "But that's for you young people to believe in."

"Better I should sit here waiting for the Messiah?" Meyer asked.

"You're a Jew, aren't you?" Isaac responded. "That's what we're supposed to do."

"I'm a different kind of Jew," Meyer said. "I'll decide what my heaven is."

Sarah Leah looked up over the top of the newspaper she had been reading, frowning and clucking her disapproval of Meyer's declaration.

Anya Dorfsman, Meyer's fiancee, fidgeted uncomfortably on a kitchen chair. She had come with Meyer to say goodbye to his family, and had experienced similar discomfort all week as they went from relative to relative to announce their — really Meyer's — decision. Behind her dark, almond-shaped eyes that were the glory of her round, swarthy face, there was a look of apprehension.

Meyer insisted that they would marry in Russia, under laws of a state that he could respect, and he promised they would have a rabbi perform the traditional ceremony, too. But it would have to wait until after they arrived, and found a Russian rabbi they liked.

Anya's family didn't want her to go, but she "needed to do what was right and just."

"Okay, then, if that's the way things are," Isaac said, shifting his weight on the hard chair and reaching for another glass of steaming amber tea. "It's not a bad country, America," he continued. "In fact, I think it's wonderful here. A man can earn a good living if he works hard, and at least the Cossacks don't come and kill you every time they get drunk and tired of fighting with each other."

"Oh, yeah, wonderful," Meyer said, lighting a Fatima cigarette. "Isaac, you were always a dreamer, and you see the world through rosy glasses! America's only about making people want to be rich, because the rich control all."

"So substitute the Communist Party elite for the rich and it's the same play on a different stage, different costumes."

"Meyer! It's *shabbos. Rauch nicht!*" Sarah Leah interrupted the by-now classic face-off between her husband and his brother's son, waving the smoke away from her face with an impatient flick of her hand, as though even to smell the fumes was a sin in the eyes of God.

"Anyway, there are no more Cossacks!" Meyer said.

"Who's the dreamer now?" Isaac snorted. "They just changed their pants!"

Meyer reconsidered a little, " Well, at least they're our Cossacks."

◆

"And that was the last we ever saw of him," Aunt Charlotte said with a sigh.

"What happened to him?" Max asked. The story had promise. Maybe he'd use it someday.

"He became a great macher . . . a general or a commissar in the army and was a hero in the war, the siege of Leningrad, I think," Charlotte said. "He only died about ten years ago."

"He's dead?" Max asked.

"You're named after him, dummy," Arlene said to Max with a snort of disbelief at his ignorance, "so he has to be dead. Some Jew you are!"

"So then how could I be named after him if I was born before he died?" Max asked.

" I don't know, but you are," Arlene answered.

"You are," said Charlotte, "because that was the way your father wanted to honor Meyer, who had such an influence on him. And he didn't care about what he used to call 'Rabbi Rules.' He made his own."

"Apple doesn't fall far . . .," Arlene said.

Charlotte went on, around the interruption, "Oh, Meyer wrote to Grandpa Isaac for years, and then, after Meyer died, Anya wrote. I still get a letter from her about twice a year. They had three children. All of them became very important people over there. The first son, Mikhail, is in the government, in the agriculture department, and the daughter is a journalist, her name is Nadya, and the youngest, Boris, is a professor of physics at the University of Leningrad and he also writes novels. Here — I have some pictures." She reached into her handbag and pulled out a large black picture case.

A family group with three young children looked out of an old sepia -tone snapshot Max held in his hand. Foreign lives he never knew leaped across time at him. Strangers staking their claims on his territory. Meyer was thin and wiry with a Stalin moustache and stood like a soldier. Anya was short and full-figured, and wore a suit with a long skirt. The kids were all wearing white shirts and dark neckties and smiling studiously as though for a school photograph. A family day in the park?

Then there were some individual snapshots of the kids grown up. The professorial looking man in a suit looked cannily at the camera through wire-rimmed glasses. Mikhail. A beautiful, strong–jawed woman of about forty smiled as though greeting a friend. Nadya. And a younger son with a shock of hair atop his head looked out at Max as though confused by the camera. Boris.

"The family resemblance is amazing!" Max said.

Charlotte nodded her head. "Mikhail looks just like his father and Nadya is the spitting image of her mother."

"And Boris looks just like Uncle Max!" Ellen said, leaning over to scrutinize the picture Max held. "Take away that silly hair and they could be twins!"

"I don't see it," Max said, embarrassed to admit that he was thinking the same thing.

"Let's see," Arlene said, reaching over for the snapshots.

"I never thought of that until now," Aunt Charlotte said, "but you know what? You're right!"

"How old are they?" Max asked.

"Basically about your and Arlene's ages, because Meyer and Anya didn't have kids until after the war, so now Mikhail is mid-forties, Nadya is a couple of years younger, and Boris is just about your age. Maybe you could make contact. I'll send you Anya's address."

Uncle Phil, who was dozing off and on throughout Aunt Charlotte's story, reached over for the pictures. "Let's see the Commie cousins," he said, laughing at his own jibe, but as Eddy was outside at the time, nobody joined him.

"You never told us about how Ben became a Communist," Max said. He saw a quick glance between Arlene and Phil, a mutual eye roll.

Charlotte missed the look, because she was so caught up in the family history she was remembering, and was so incapable of sticking to a single point, that she lost the thread. She sat staring down, concentrating.

It was unusual for anyone to listen to Charlotte at great length. She usually dumped on any listener all the trivia that occurred since her last visit, and no one was really interested beyond the initial few minutes. Asking her the question that led to the endless flow of details and gossip, only to be polite, was considered a family sin.

This time, however, there was something that kept them all attentive. Enjoying her role as keeper of the family chronicles, Charlotte went on and on. The family history, removed from her listeners by half a century, was unique to them, romantic even — except to Phil.

Phil was seven years old when Ben lost Meyer, and he didn't even know the Bergman family then, so he was about as interested in these distant lives as he was with anything else, which was hardly. His dreams were more important to him. But the family was used to him nodding off, even at the dinner table, so nobody else paid attention to his slumping head and closed eyes — and he probably took that as approval.

"You never told us about how my father became a Communist," Max repeated.

"Another time," Arlene said, rising out of her chair. "We've got a whole week, and the kitchen calls if you want to eat tonight," and she walked out of the room.

"About three or four years later," Charlotte answered, ignoring Arlene, "Ben went back to night school, got his diploma, and then married your mother and joined the Party at the same time."

"I heard all this before," said Uncle Phil, opening one eye.

"But I didn't," Max protested.

"He's right," Charlotte said, "I talk too much. I'll tell you more later."

"Her mouth needs some sleep," Uncle Phil said, laughing.

"That's not very funny, Philly," Charlotte said angrily, getting up and standing over him. "You've been teasing me for years and always nasty. Who gives you the right? At least I listen when people talk to me. I don't fall asleep like a hippopotamus."

"Look who is calling who insulting," he said huffily. "Do I say anything about the way you look?" He stood up and walked away, toward the kitchen, Charlotte following.

"Who said anything about the way you look?" she asked his back.

Max followed, stopped at the hall closet, removed the paper with the improvised music he'd jotted down earlier from his jacket, and slipped it into his trouser pocket. Glancing around to make sure no one was watching, he eased along the corridor to the kitchen trying to look nonchalant, as though he were going for another cup of coffee. He heard the raised voices of his aunt and uncle through the swinging kitchen door, and then quickly Max stepped through the door to the basement, closing it quietly behind him.

# 6

FOR MAX, MUSIC WAS HIS LINK with the deities of both heaven and hell, and he knew that what his mother's mother, Adelle, spoke of in her diary was hell. She was married to a husband who didn't love either her or their children, spent his money on other women, gambled, and lied; and finally, after he provoked enough tirades and broken crockery, he had her committed to an institution for what used to be called a "nervous breakdown."

After she was "cured," Adelle chose to remain there; returning to her husband was like going back to hell voluntarily. She refused, though it meant giving up her children. Her husband, Nachman, obtained a divorce decree for abandonment that included Adelle's surrender of any parental rights, and took custody of all her monies to pay for her upkeep. Then he told eight-year-old Rita and five-year-old Phil that their mother had died.

But Adelle didn't think of the upstate sanitarium as heaven either. Memory was her roommate. She wrote in her diary:

> He had promised to forsake all others, he had sworn
> himself to me in sickness and health for the bitter with the
> sweet until death. Then all of a sudden it wasn't true and I
> didn't know why. Nothing I did had changed. The women

whispered in the market when I passed, and first I didn't care. Later I thought that it was just envy. I had a man who earned a good living because undertakers have steady work. I had a nice apartment with a piano and a rug on the floor, books, a statue of Beethoven and two healthy children, my sweet Rita who was so smart she could already read, and the baby Phil, who ate like a horse and never cried. The *yentas* wanted what I had, I thought, and they were green with envy. Let them choke on it.

Later, this retreat from the world was sometimes an elysian setting, a pastoral idyll, a bucolic environment where she was freed from the turmoil of the city, away from the normal grind of living, the everyday struggle, but was this heaven for Adelle? If you had enough to eat and a roof over your head, if you earned a good living or did what you were supposed to do as far as raising a family was concerned, if you had nachis from your children, then it was heaven. But she gave up all that.

Why? Was it because the director of the institution came into her room at night and made love to her, and she didn't mind too much once she got past the sin of being unfaithful? She wrote:

Nachman left me here to rot so why should I care? Dr. Miller was gentle and loving and knew how to thrill my body . . . I felt shame the next day, and thought of my little Rita and Phil a lot, but when Morris — he wants me to call him that — came to me a few nights later, I took him with abandon, and never felt anything better in my life. Little by little, I thought of the my children less and less, of Nachman hardly at all. Only of Morris, and when he would take me away from here to live outside as man and wife. When he left without a word of goodbye, and never wrote to me, I wanted to die, but couldn't.

86

Her love for Morris, her sexual fulfillment, and her joy in imagining the future? All over.

> With a swift cut at my heart I tried to end my pain, but the knife betrayed me too. Did Morris know? Did Morris care?

Adelle's attempt at suicide was used by Nachman to get a judgment of *non compos mentis* written into the final divorce decree, and with that she could not reclaim her children unless the judgment was reversed.

Adelle was both the victim and the cause of her life.

◆

*Faust:* Where are you damn'd?
*Mephistophilis:* In hell.
*Faust:* How comes it then that thou art out of hell?
*Mephistophilis:* Why this is hell, nor am I out of it !

Christopher Marlowe, *Doctor Faustus*

And Adelle's grandson Max was Faust in the closet, dreaming through his art for liberation from death, for the ascent to the immortal, only to have others' demands on him plunge him back into the everyday. Why didn't the apparition appear for him, the demon granting magical power in exchange for Max's soul? He knew the power was within him, as was the demon.

Like Faust, Max wanted to be ravished, to be transported, to transcend the bounds of earth, and it happened when he was enrapt in the music he played, wrote, and dreamed. For him, his music permitted such ecstasy to exist in this world in the guise of art. It allowed certain freedoms, a hieratic link with the dark voids beyond understanding.

Right there was the borderline Max wished to cross and explore, convinced that he could discover the way to transform neurotic misery into ordinary unhappiness. Not a goal for those who want to be normal but a part of what every creative artist does, and is torn between the demands of his daily existence and the difficulties of art.

Max began in creative rebellion against the expected, the ordinary.

Then came overwhelming forces of music in apocalyptic visions that plagued him.

He saw colors in sound. He heard the organs of the heavens in the deep rumblings of the earth, the discordant harmonies of the city, and out of this and his personal hauntings fashioned an art.

Was that neurotic or even psychotic? Conventional definitions irritated him. Should he labor to transform these communions into the ordinary? Had he asked his sister or his father, he knew what the answer would have been. They told him without his asking. Could he risk the downside if these changes would only affect his day-to-day doings and yet leave his art intact?

Now he was suddenly invaded by his aunt's story of Meyer, who — like Rita's mother Adelle — had opted out. Max did not know all the facts yet. The consequences of this airborne assault and the subsequent occupation by the information would only become clear later. Through Aunt Charlotte's tale, however, Max began to re-invent Meyer, as he had done with his maternal grandmother. But Meyer chose another real life, not a cloister, a refuge; he engaged the world to change it, not to retreat. Max was fascinated. Perhaps another dramatic creation would emerge. He'd let the idea ripen itself.

Most people use and think of stories they hear in a self referential way. Max, and perhaps most artists, used such material differently — as battering rams to break down the structure of the mind, to knock down the walls of "shoulds" that cultures erect and live within for safety. He actually enjoyed these assaults because he was engaged in the reconstruction of himself and the world, reinventing others, or rather those whom he wanted to reinvent, by taking their stories, allowing the raw forces therein to breach his walls, and then subtly integrating the conquering army with his own population, sending the hybrids out as his own.

Were Max a writer or even a painter there might be some value to him in these analogies. But though the literary element was strong in Max (he had, after all, done the libretto for his opera himself), he was fundamentally a musician. Everything he heard or thought was translated into patterns of sound. Tones, chords, progressions, melodic lines and counterpoint, and the various concatenations meant something to him, something that ultimately could not be articulated in words without doing injustice to the abstraction.

Music was a language for Max, a language that permitted him to speak freely, but kept him from being understood by all save a few. In fact, he was not convinced that anyone understands, beyond the technical, what a musician or a painter is "saying," after program music or paintings with figures in them have been bypassed. How the paint is blended and applied, of course, that's technique, as is the structure of a certain harmony, or modulation.

But what is being "said" is only what it is, and only what the artist understands, which he or she cannot say in any other way. His own commentaries were therefore futile. Guesses, approximations — which shell conceals the pea? Does even the sleight of hand man know?

Max was using his own music language to reinvent himself too, fed by whatever meanings the stories of ancestors had for him, on an endlessly renewing, continuous basis. This is what probably made him so difficult for his family to understand, or even want to. Living with all their own more normal convention of time as a progression — past, present and future — they could not understand that for him it was a continuum, everything existed all at once. His father crossing the street with Max and responding to the child's question about a future profession, the food Arlene gave him today, the story of Meyer, and his grandmother's diary were all real and current, mixing and mingling in his mind along with the riots of sound that echoed through his imagination. Everything was all at once and together.

He didn't see Adelle's inability to cope as a weakness, nor did he condemn her abandonment of her husband and children as irresponsibility. Rather, he admired the courage she showed and was intrigued by her daring.

Meyer filled a gap too; he represented history for Max. The battle between ideals and expediency. Not history in the sense of chronicle, but "History" as the god deified by the Marxists. Meyer too ran, not away, but toward. Max was fascinated by obsession in others. It made him more comfortable with his own. But familial expectations of normalcy had to be asserted forcefully for the sake of peace. Expectations aroused by the images of his own mind must wait.

◆

Meanwhile, back in the kitchen, what Arlene wanted most was to do things as they ought to be done. The funeral arrangements, the shiva observed, the appropriateness of all the details, and the unification of the family around their common grief, as tradition prescribed. This was all very important to her, and, unlike her brother, she didn't question it or examine her motivations. She did what was right and only thought what she wanted; it was nobody's business but her own.

Men always messed everything up, raised objections that were all about them and not the situation, and that was confirmed for her again and again. Just look at them: Max had to be different and difficult about everything; he had to linger at the cemetery, had to come back to her late, had to play the piano when she specifically asked him not to. She really didn't care whether he played it or not, and if just the two of them were in the house, she wouldn't have blinked twice at the request. But how could he do that when all the family was sitting in mourning upstairs? She felt embarrassed, ashamed of him.

It always seemed like someone felt the need to protect Max, explain his bizarre behavior to others. From the moment he was born, he could do no wrong as far as their father was concerned . . . until he decided to drop out of the pre-medical program. Then he could do no right as far as Ben was concerned, and Rita took up the cudgels on Max's behalf.

But Arlene, she had to fend for herself with Ben, always. Though Rita was usually on her daughter's side, she could never deflect Ben's disapproval of almost everything Arlene did, even though Arlene always tried to please her father. Rather than relish her decision to study medicine, Ben saw Arlene's choice as competition for Max, and thought that Arlene's success would hurt the boy.

She would have been glad to help her brother with his studies when he seemed to be floundering, but it wasn't for lack of talent or intelligence that Max refused to become a doctor; it was the damned music, like a disease that ate away at him, an obsession. Nothing else interested him, and when he'd made the choice, even when he tried to make it clear to their father that he was going to be a musician because that was what he wanted, Ben said that Max merely declined to follow in his sister's footsteps for spite.

Then there was her marriage.

Ben actually liked Eddy, who was a friend of Mike Frank, the husband of Rita's cousin Viola. Eddy was bluff, hearty, a *kibitzer*, and though he wasn't well educated, he was street smart and shrewd, a comer in the rag trade. Rita wanted better for her daughter and said so, once. But after Arlene made her decision, Rita said no more. She accepted the choice and made the best of it. Ben was more devious. He would praise Eddy to his face and talk about him behind his back. What did he want? Eddy was a good provider; he supported Arlene comfortably through the last two years of med school, and her internship and residency. He even took good care of Ellen when Arlene was on night shift, or had a long, tiring day. He couldn't be faulted for that.

But no sooner did Eddy's business begin to slide downhill than Ben began an endless litany of "I told you so's." It not only annoyed Arlene, but affected her. She began to believe that her father was right, although she wouldn't admit it to him. The flash, the *savoir vivre*, all the enjoyment of everyday experiences Eddy showed began to grate on her. How could he be so cavalier when his own lack of managerial skills cost him his credit line at the bank, without which survival in the seasonal garment trades was impossible, and then how could he, without telling her, go to the loan sharks and sign over sixty percent of the business his own father spent a lifetime to build up? He wasn't even smart enough to go to the cops, or to try to manipulate his way out of the jam. Of course he never told her there was any trouble. He continued to have his suits custom made, drove a new Jag, insisted on expensive vacations, until one night he didn't come home, but went to the hospital instead, badly beaten up by Mafia musclemen because he hadn't met his payments and wouldn't do what the big shots wanted him to do with the business.

A few days later he agreed. He signed, and became an employee. It was that or the East River.

The loan sharks were nice to Eddy after that, and the business seemed to thrive, but something went out of Eddy, especially as Arlene was doing better in her practice every day. He grumbled whenever the phone rang at night, whenever she had a delivery in the wee hours, whenever they had to cancel a dinner date or an evening out for the theater because of an emergency. She began to sleep in the spare room, and had her phone installed there so calls wouldn't wake him. He retaliated by staying out later and later, and eventually not coming home at all. Finally he moved into his secretary/ girlfriend's apartment in the city and said he'd pay for the divorce.

Eddy and Arlene signed an elaborate agreement in which he took financial responsibility for Ellen right through college and graduate school, but after a few months of late payments, he stopped paying altogether, pleading poverty. Arlene really didn't need his money, and didn't want to hound him or unleash the law on him, so she just let it ride. According to her most recent calculation, Eddy owed her about $165,000, and she had about as much chance of collecting as she had of her parents coming back to life.

They were babies, these men, deluded fools who held on to crazy pipe dreams and shoved everybody and everything into or out of their plans as it suited their needs. The ordinary details they left for the women to work out: what you ate, whether your clothes were cleaned and washed, whether your sheets were changed, whether there was money to do what was necessary — there always was money to do what wasn't — that was left to the women, and the men depended on women like herself, like her mother. Even her brother depended on Ursula for the daily wherewithal in his life. He wouldn't know where his shoes were unless she was around to find where he dropped them, and she was no model of efficiency — but a paragon compared to Max.

*Oy*, men — who needed them?

Maybe there was something to all that lesbian stuff. Women were better than those nincompoops. She saw the way they handled things: in childbirth, in frustration, even death. Women had knowledge that the male dreamers — fantasists all — didn't. Women knew who they were, knew their place in history, in the order of things, and that was very important to Arlene. Even their bodies were nicer than men's. But medical awareness of the morphology of genitalia and her clinical experience notwithstanding, Arlene thought that the penis and scrotum were silly looking and held no attraction as objects of beauty. How could they compare to breasts, or the wonderful curve of a woman's hip that every painter knew was the ultimate in feminine attraction. Yet she felt nothing more than admiration for the female body, she didn't want to touch, feel or be loved by one. When she did need sex it was all for what she thought attractive in men: the childish dependency of their loving, and the powerful thrusts of their bodies was what she wanted when she wanted it, and that was infrequent now. Except for the lurking need to "get together" soon. Next week, maybe, but who had the time?

◆

The basement was the only room in Arlene's house that Max liked. It had been "done" for her by her decorators, but for once they hit the mark, according to *his* taste. Dark paneled walls with built in bookshelves lined the main room, and there was a comfortable L-shaped settee under the shelves. Recessed, indirect lighting gave a soft glow to the wood, and track lights were directed onto two places: where you could sit and read and onto the music holder of the ebony Steinway that stood opposite the bookshelves. A bar cabinet was concealed behind the paneling, and a Scandinavian rya rug covered the greater part of the white tiled floor. There was a smoothness in the transition from element to element, unlike the rest of his sister's house. Nothing in this room said "look at me, focus your attention on this and that."

He walked along the bookshelves reading the titles: mostly popular fiction and books about Israel, Zionism and the Holocaust. Many of them looked as if they were never opened. But there was one section of well worn volumes, dog-eared paperbacks, and a quick riffle of the pages showed him that they were Ellen's. This was more like it: Proust, Joyce, Mann, Camus, Woolf and Wolfe, Beckett, Artaud, Ionesco, Shakespeare, and an anthology of Elizabethan playwrights, along with Nietzsche, Plato, Kant, Aristotle, Simone Weill and Susan Sontag bringing up the rear.

He didn't know that his little niece was such a reader; actually, he hardly knew the girl, having paid very little attention to her over the years. Today she seemed sensitive, uncomfortable, out of place. A kindred spirit to his own. *Wouldn't that be the ironic if my sister's brassiness and Eddy's garment-center-macho bullshit had issued what they couldn't tolerate. A Trojan horse? Not quite the image. Helen? THAT sounded like Ellen. And what Troy would she run to, what siege would entail armies for ten years on the windy plains? Vassar in Poughkeepsie?*

Silly to reason through metaphor, he knew, but he had little choice. His mind worked that way. Why was he down on himself for that? Was it the pressure he felt from the family upstairs? "Be as ourself in Denmark!" What subtle irony in such exhortations, insidious corruption. He couldn't work it through. Ellen wasn't a beauty. Good looking, finely wrought, strong, something like that daughter of his father's cousin Meyer, but not the face that launched a thousand ships. He picked up *The Iliad* and thumbed through it.

Max promised himself that he would read it again someday.

Abandoning the bookshelves, he turned to the piano, lifted the cover on the keyboard, pushed the soft pedal down as far as he could, and pressed a chord into the keyboard. *There. More like it.* Overtones filled his head and the language he preferred to speak replaced the emptiness in the day. Another chord followed. He moved his fingers through some closed chromatic voicings around a common tone, F sharp for Faustus. The crudely drawn staves on blank paper were in front of him now, and he played through what he had written near the cemetery. It was a rough hymn of sorts, a four square chorale, but it had an ungodly quality to it, a diabolic urge running through, colored orange and dark red. He played a few bars of "Blue turning gray over you" for no known reason and then returned to the other side of the tone spectrum. But he came back from every key to F sharp minor, the epicenter of his hurricane, and it was dark, orange red. Mephistopheles was in it. After all the prayers at the chapel and grave, the exhortation to say Kaddish, this world was not God's alone.

Chaos and pain were everywhere, and the supernatural vision of splendor was a lollypop no one wanted to suck any more, anodyne to memory. And the trail of breadcrumbs through the forest led him to the witch's house. They weren't supposed to play there . . . Gretel had turned back. But he had to go on, peer through the door, make up songs about what he saw inside, hoping that a few would believe him.

Kaddish praised all creation: *Could I say it?* The goodness of God's bounty, the praise for He who was beyond all praise? That wasn't it, he knew. The prayer was an incantation, a song; the words had no meaning after a while. The efficacy was in the chant, entering into a rhythmic relationship with something outside yourself, a universe beyond your own, not filled with petty cares, but holding the vague promise of redemption. "*Salve Regina,*" but the Queen was song.

And yet the idea of all creation included sadness of loss, confusion and chaos of existence. The fear underlying everything was that it all was meaningless, that mankind struggled for centuries to codify a set of responses that would alleviate the fear of anomie. Subtle transformation of energy, despair into hope. The world was the Devil's too and the rush to extol its goodness and the beneficence of God's scheme for human history only damned it.

The basement door opened, and Ellen came down the stairs.

Curious? Brain waves? He must get to know her better, try to be a good uncle.

"Can I listen?" she asked, hesitantly.

He nodded. It was her house, after all.

His father, a man of dreams and plans, loved his son for what he could be and hated what he became. How could Max ever know now the passions that raged through his father's head? How did Ben feel when his beloved Meyer abandoned him and went off to Russia to pursue his own dream? *Was it his fault, that?* Sins of the fathers, a burden to the sons. Max needed to avenge the death of dreams. Be as ourself in Denmark, indeed.

Ellen sat in the corner as Max played the chords of his chorale in another key, using D flat as a center, but it didn't have the same feeling for him, and he pulled up in the middle and returned to F sharp. It was a magnet.

And his son had a son, and the son's son had nothing, nothing, nothing! Just some little black marks on paper. A group of children stuck in the witch's stove clamored for his attention. He would not have a son; there was no reason to add to the pain, to extend it into another life in the fantasy that you could ameliorate things, make a small bid for eternity.

He recapitulated the chorale melody, adding a pedal tone. The augmented $11^{th}$ chord he was hearing and using in a closed voicing to make the $F^{\#}$ tense and disturbing added an ominous quality to the bass — a steady thump of a large door closing.

He looked at Ellen sitting rapt in the music and wished she weren't there, not just then at least, because she prevented something: he wanted to meet the devil, talk to him. Did they show themselves when you weren't alone, make clear who they were? Maybe the religious had it all wrong, backward. Lucifer reigned; in the depth of his malevolence he invented God to give men false hope. The creation of illusions to mask the truth was the greatest evil of all.

Foot still pressing the soft pedal he touched the low G in a pattern of two sixteenth notes placed asymmetrically in each measure of the four square chorale writing above it. There was a scream in the center, and he was waiting for it, trying to hear it. When it came would he know, or feel where it should go? Seeds of destruction. World, flesh and devil. In which order? Vision dim with the pain of headache taking him suddenly with a bolt across his temples, shooting behind the eyes. Still pressing the low G, he took up the pencil and wrote across the top of his crude staves "Faust in the Closet: Notes on Schizophrenia," and voiced a terminating chord, running right up through the series of overtones haunting him, a diapason of Hell, then released the soft pedal and struck the whole chord's ten voices, hard and loud.

"I asked you not to do this, Max. I asked you please to show some respect," Arlene's voice said from nowhere, from the ceiling, the intercom, "but you have none, not even for the dead! Now stop it and come upstairs, and behave like a man." Her fury hissed at him, then clicked off.

Behave like a man. What else was he doing? Max stood, folded the paper into his pocket, shut the piano lid and walked over to where Ellen sat. She looked as though she was embarrassed.

"You can hear the piano right through the floor upstairs. I was going to tell you, but was afraid to interrupt," she said.

Max shrugged: "I didn't realize it, but if I were to tell your mother I'm sorry, she wouldn't believe me."

"You could try," Ellen said.

"Maybe."

"Why don't the two of you get along?" she asked.

"We never really did," Max answered, "even as kids. I guess I invaded her space."

"I wish I had a brother to talk to, play with," Ellen said.

Max laughed: "And if you had one, you'd probably wish you didn't!"

He reached for her hand and helped her up, then walked toward the stairs, "I see you read a lot. We ought to talk sometime, because I've read most of that too."

"I'd love to," she said, "but I hardly ever see you and Ursula, and I go back on Monday."

"Well, maybe we can do something to change all that when all this is over," he said. "There'll be time. Thanksgiving, maybe? What are you studying up there?"

He concentrated on her answer and avoided Arlene's eyes when he and his niece entered the living room. The day belonged to others now.

# 7

AT SIXTY-TWO, PHIL PERETZ was a sturdily-built, florid man, smoothly bald, who trimmed his fringe of gray hair close to the head, and carried himself like a soldier. Gold-rimmed glasses, sitting on a finely chiseled nose topped by bright blue eyes, made him look alert, crisp, Teutonic. Just like his father, Nachman.

Phil's wife Mildred, dead three years now, had borne him two sons, Howard and Mark, neither of whom showed up at Ben's funeral, even though Phil called to tell them that their uncle had died. Howard was an auto mechanic and Mark drove a taxi. Although Phil concerned himself with their well being by sending each of them a large check for their birthdays and Chanukah, he hadn't seen much of them since he became a widower. Howard, the older one, married a Puerto Rican girl. Mark was single, spent his leisure time in bars and poolrooms, and satisfied his sexual needs with a once-a-week whore. Their father had little to say to them, and after he began to date Frieda, a wealthy widow whose children were successful professionals, he preferred to let the boys alone. He did what he could for them and now had his own life to look after.

But his sister Rita's children were another story: from the times they were little until now, Phil always admired them. Arlene was tough, practical, and smart. She held her own in the world, differed from the well intentioned, but largely ignorant, women of Phil's generation, and managed as a successful doctor while keeping a nice house and earning a good living. Her divorce? Well, everyone was doing it. Maybe he should have years ago.

Max was a pussycat. Smart, sensitive, always a bit of a crybaby when he was a kid. At any family occasion when the cousins were younger, Max would inevitably get a punch in the stomach or a bloody nose from Mark, then Howard would be blamed, then Arlene would taunt or slap him. When this happened, Phil's brother-in-law, Ben, would always yell at Arlene for hitting Howard and comfort Max, whether or not he deserved the punch.

"Serves you right for playing with boys," Ben would say to his daughter, but reassure Max: "Mark does like you, he just gets a little wild and hits sometimes."

But all that was so far in the past, and Phil preferred now to forget the past. It was over. Many mistakes were made. Most of what he tried to do for his boys turned out wrong. They weren't interested in anything except sports, cars and girls, in that order, and even now, were still pretty much the same. So let them go, he thought, and God bless them. He did his duty by them and their mother. Let them live and be well. Let his loving, amiable wife Milly rest in peace. Phil would use up what years remained looking after himself — and Frieda was rich enough. Besides, he was tired of the undertaker business and wanted to retire.

The past was dead; Phil wanted to forget it, and that was what he told Max before when his nephew wanted to know more about the history Rita pained herself to suppress throughout her life. Why did Max want to know about these events? Phil wanted only good times from now on.

But then he shared that history.

◆

After Phil and Rita's mother, Adelle, died he lived in a succession of foster homes. His father visited him on alternate Sundays with Rita in tow, and each time it seemed like a shower of benevolence to him as he always received a dime "for being a good boy in the meanwhile." Yet underneath Nachman's smiling face — that so resembled Phil's these days that it annoyed him — lay the tissue of indifference. His father really didn't care about either of his children and was simply doing his job, spurred on by the Jewish Social Work Agency, which insisted on these "foster home" visits if they were to continue to pay the foster parents' allowance. Otherwise "Papa" would have to give his children up to the orphanage, and sign away his paternal rights. The way Nachman's mind worked, giving them up was like signing away his right to an insurance policy, an annuity. He expected that when he could no longer earn a living, his children would provide for him. After all, he was their father and had certain privileges.

Nachman remarried after five years of being single, and he brought Phil and Rita to live with him and his new wife, Yetta.

The thrill of living with his own family gripped Phil, who was treated like the little prince his father wanted him to be. He had his own room and went to school and there were no household duties for boys except going to the grocery, which Phil did occasionally when Rita wasn't around to fetch whatever their step-mother wanted. But his father rarely smiled at him anymore. The only attention he paid to Phil was limited to a smack in the face if Nachman wasn't pleased.

And then Nachman and Yetta had a baby, Gertrude. When the baby outgrew her crib, their parents wanted to move her out of their bedroom into Phil's room, but that meant he would have to sleep on the cot in the living room so that the baby could have a room to herself. At the same time they encouraged Rita to move out and stay with cousin Viola's family.

Phil did not want his sister to leave. He had spent five years of his childhood seeing her only once every two weeks for an hour, and now that they lived under the same roof he didn't want her to move away for any reason.

"Gerty can have my room," he told his father. "I'll sleep in the living room, with Rita."

"Boys and girls don't sleep in the same room unless they are married. And in the living room you can't go to sleep early enough, because we sit there at night," Nachman said.

"So, let Rita sleep in my room with the baby . . ." Phil said, but he was cut short by the sting of his father slapping his face, hard.

"Mind your own business," Nachman said. "You'll stay in the room with Gerty."

There was so much pain, all the wriggling under Nachman's thumb. Rita used to come into Phil's room and sing Gerty to sleep, then cry, until she fell asleep on his bed night after night while he did his homework at the desk, and his father and Yetta listened to the radio in the living room until they went to bed. Then he'd wake Rita and help her fix up the folding cot in the living room so she could finally sleep there.

Phil wanted to go back to the foster parents.

◆

Phil was wide awake now, and Aunt Charlotte had left the room and gone up stairs to nap.

"Never could take much of Charlotte, even when we were young. She never knew when to shut up, instead gave you all the details you didn't care about whenever she opened her mouth," Phil said to his nephew when Max dropped onto the sofa beside him. "Yak yak, all the time. Thank God your Aunt Mildred, may she rest in peace, wasn't like that. She talked, sure, liked to gossip like all the women, but she knew when to stop. Charlotte never did. She drove her husband to an early grave."

"What did Uncle Willy die of?" Max asked.

"Deafness!" Phil roared with laughter at his joke.

"Come on," Max said. "No kidding."

"Aaar-leeeen!" Uncle Phil shouted.

She came in from the kitchen. "What's the yelling for?"

"What did your Uncle Willie die from?"

"For that you have to scream?"

"Your brother wants to know."

"He's got a mouth!" she said to Phil, motioning toward Max.

"What already?" Phil demanded impatiently.

"Complications stemming from cirrhosis of the liver. He was an alcoholic, and they couldn't dry him out. Even when he knew it meant the end if he touched another drop. Don't mention it to Charlotte because she'll lie about it. She always does, she's so ashamed. He left her well fixed, but he was inconsiderate!"

"Thanks, honey," Uncle Phil said to Arlene's back.

"Yeah, thanks," Max said.

"Oh, it talks too!" Arlene said, turning slightly.

"Filled with talent," Max responded.

"I heard," she answered, and kept walking.

"What's with you two?" Phil asked. "Like cats and dogs!"

"Nothing changes, Uncle Phil. Any reason why it should?"

"You'd think your father's death might make a difference, Maxie. Ya' know, she's all you've got now."

"God help us . . ."

"You'll need Him if you don't wise up, both of you."

"Or Her, or It," Max said.

"Let's not start that again, Maxie. I'm in no mood ."

"Change the subject, then . . ."

"Okay! How come you're suddenly so interested in all this family history. You want to know about poor Willy — and I was right, deafness did kill him. He wouldn't listen to nobody. She trained him good, Charlotte did."

"Not funny," Max said to his uncle's mean joke.

"And Meyer the Communist, and that so-called mother of mine. Let them all rest in peace. They're dead. The past is dead. Let it be."

"I just never knew anything about Meyer. It's very interesting."

"What's interesting? He filled your father up with all kinds of crazy ideas, and then left. It made your father dizzy for years, all that bullshit about saving the world. The wonders of the working class . . . .. Hey, you're not a Commie too, are ya'?"

Max assured his uncle that he was not enamored of Marxism, that he wasn't even political.

"So why do you want to know all this stuff? I lived through it, Maxie, and, believe you me, it wasn't worth the trouble it made for a lot of people. They're all a bunch of whores whether they call themselves Communists or Capitalists. They want power and money like everyone else, and get all the poor suckers like you and me to work and fight, even die for the big idea, but it's never for us, really. It's for them. The guys with the silk shirts and chauffeurs."

"Forget the politics, Uncle Phil, I just want to know more about the family."

"What you have to know about the family is that you better start getting along with your sister. That's all you have to know about family. That's all there is. The rest is bullshit. You remember to pick up the phone once in a while and say hello to me, Gertrude, or even big mouth Charlotte. That's enough. But you gotta work it out with Arlene. Otherwise there's nothing!"

"Why did you say 'that so-called mother' before about Adelle?" Max asked, knowing he was risking another lecture, but he wanted to know anyway.

"You can't drop anything, can you?" Phil said. "I understand your opera is about her."

"She's the basis of the character, that's all," Max said, "because she seemed like an interesting person from what I read in that diary my mother gave me."

"Max!" Phil interrupted, exasperated, but continuing nevertheless. "How should I know anything about her? When I was about five they told me that she died, and then, a few years later, I went to live with my father and Yetta. In between there were those foster homes, two of them for me, maybe five or six for Rita. From then until I got married I lived in Yetta's house, so if I had any mother at all, it was her, and she was okay, but no prize either. I wasn't her kid, and Nachman was a cheapskate. He never gave her enough for house money, kept a lot for himself to spend on his whores and for playing the horses, and she had to make what he doled out to her go a long way. So Rita and me got shit. She had it worse because Yetta didn't like having another almost-full-grown woman in the house and, besides, Rita reminded Nachman of Adelle. She looked something like her. So whenever he got a chance, he'd smack her around too. They pushed her out."

"Is that why you don't like Aunt Gertrude? Because she was the favored kid?"

"You got that wrong, Maxie. I'm crazy about Gerty. It wasn't her fault that her father was such a bastard and that her mother was protecting her at our expense."

"How else was he a bastard?"

Phil looked at his nephew sadly. There was disgust written on his face, and Max thought he could see tears in his uncle's eyes."I'll tell you a story, Maxie, and you'll know."

◆

A bright Saturday morning in early October of the year 1942, Phil is awakened by the ringing of the telephone. Snuggled beneath an eiderdown, he hears the sound faintly, then louder as he comes out of his deep sleep, and hopes that Rita, who sleeps in the living room closer to the phone, will answer it and save him the trouble of getting up from his warm bed. He has been deep in a fourteen-year-old's dream about Betty Grable, whose picture he cut from the newspaper. She joins him at first light. The phone doesn't stop, however, and he finally stumbles out of his room, across the darkened, empty living room. Rita is apparently out of the house already, her folding bed stowed away in the alcove. The bust of Beethoven on the grand piano broods over the couch, the oriental rug, the curio cabinet and the rubber plant. He grabs the phone, which actually shakes back and forth on each ring, as if impatient for an answer.

"Mr. Nachman Peretz?" a man's voice very far away inquires.

Phil asks the voice to hold on a minute and goes and rouses his father. Yetta, cradling Gerty, is still asleep.

His duty done, he returns to his room and, with luck, Betty Grable.

"Philip, put your clothes on," says his father, poking his striped-pajamed torso into the room. "I want you to come for a ride with me," and leaves without waiting for an answer.

This is an unusual request coming from Nachman, who rarely takes his children any place, or does anything with them in the way some of Phil's friends' fathers do. There is the once each summer outing to visit relatives in Spring Valley, and a very rare visit to a restaurant, usually on Nachman's birthday. He never remembers Rita's or Phil's, only Gerty's, and that's because Yetta concerns herself with the little girl exclusively, jealously preserving her husband's affection for their child, not for the remnants of his earlier union. Nachman humors his wife, but has no real interest in any of them.

So the surprise on Phil's face, does not have a chance to register on his father. No sooner than the orders are given the door closes. No reply needed. Only one response is possible. Do it!

Phil quickly drags on the clothing he has dropped on the chair the night before and goes to the kitchen where he washes his face at the sink and wipes it with a dish towel. He puts the kettle on to make tea, but before the water boils, Nachman, his dark gray undertaker's suit carefully buttoned around his robust body, appears in the kitchen saying, "Come. There's no time for that. We'll get something outside," and hastens Phil out the door, first conferring briefly on the telephone with someone at his office.

The autumn sun is bright and warm: an Indian summer day, and for all the world to see, Nachman Peretz and his son Philip are any of many such pairs walking abroad on such a beautiful day, or on their way to the synagogue. Nachman is more than usually friendly as they walk from Rodney Street toward Bridge Plaza and the trolley depot. They could take the clanging streetcar from the corner of Rodney Street and Lee Avenue, half a block away, but Nachman knows that people in the neighborhood will see him, and it isn't fitting for a man of his standing, a prosperous orthodox Jewish undertaker, to

106

be seen deliberately riding on the Sabbath. If he doesn't observe the Sabbath, at least he will not flaunt it. Phil knows this, not having arrived at the age of fourteen for nothing, and asks no questions until they have crossed the Williamsburg Bridge on the trolley they take far enough away from where they live so that no one will notice.

Soon they are sitting at the counter in Lefkowitz' Dairy Restaurant drinking coffee and eating yeast cake for breakfast. The milky coffee is fresh and rich tasting without the chicory Yetta always insists on using to make the coffee go further, and Phil is enjoying the rare treat of being with his father, who is showing an interest in how he's doing at school.

Then Phil hears Nachman say to the counterman, "Hymie, say hello to my son Feivel — Philip — who just got a 96 in his algebra test!"

Hymie shakes Phil's hand and says that he can see how proud Nachman is and wishes that his own son was so smart. Then he puts another huge slab of rich Russian *babka* on Phil's plate, saying that growing boys need nourishment.

"Where are we going, Papa?" Phil asks just before they leave Lefkowitz's.

"I have to pick up a stiff in the country, near White Plains. I thought you should come along for the ride. It's a nice day and I don't want to make the drive alone. Besides that, you've got to begin to learn this business sooner or later."

It is tacitly understood that Phil will become an undertaker like his father, and will inherit the position his father has built for himself as partner in the firm, Goodman and Peretz. Phil has never openly questioned the assumption and knows that now is not the time to start.

After getting a van from the company garage around the corner from the restaurant, they drive all the way up First Avenue through Harlem, cross a bridge into the Bronx and soon they see open fields and farms that replace the apartment houses on the Grand Concourse. There is less traffic now.

The Chevrolet van is painted black and unless you read the legend on the door "Goodman and Peretz, Licensed Morticians" in small neat gold letters, the vehicle is no different from any other used for pick-up or delivery of parcels.

Philip glances back at the oblong pine coffin behind them. He feels queasy.

"Is that what they bury people in, Papa?" he asks.

Nachman, who has been more talkative than usual, looks surprised when his son asks the question, especially as he has just gotten through expatiating on the beauties of the countryside compared with his native area of Ödenburg in Austria.

Actually the city is Sopron, Hungary, currently, but it has changed hands so many times over the centuries that the name of the town simply reflects who collects the taxes and what uniform the local constabulary wears. Nachman does not like to be thought of as Hungarian, however. When asked — and sometimes without being asked — he tells people that he is Austrian. He does, in fact, speak both fluent German as well as Hungarian.

They ride along, Nachman talking about how scenic and beautiful Ödenburg was, and how this part of Route 9 looks just like it, when Phil asks about the coffin behind them.

Nachman laughs, "That's no coffin. It's only a box for transporting someone from where they die to the funeral parlor. A regular coffin is more like a piece of furniture. Polished, good wood, except for the real orthodox. They use a plain pine one."

Phil loses interest in the box behind them and watches the trees with leaves beginning to turn orange and red and shades of gold, and the herds of cows, and an occasional horse grazing or harnessed to a plow, trudging along a row of rich black earth. Now they are riding through apple orchards on each side of the road and Nachman stops in front of a house where a fat, gray-haired woman in a cotton dress sits with some bushels of apples for sale. Nachman bargains with the woman and then buys a bushel of apples and puts it in the back of the van.

They each take one and crunch into the thin juicy skins, his father holding the McIntosh with his left hand, elbow leaning out on the open window frame, enjoying himself, his right hand on the steering wheel. The stern face he wears habitually is gone, and Phil thinks that maybe he has misjudged the man all along, and likes him better than he ever did before. So this is what it's like to have a real father, who takes you places and talks to you.

"Mountainview Rest Home," the sign says at the big gate.

A guard waves the van through, and there are acres of property inside the high walls. Everything is clipped and clean like a park. They ride up a long, straight road between two rows of ancient elm trees for a minute and then slow down in front of a huge, white mansion with pillars in front, and several smaller buildings of red brick flanking the main house at the back.

Nachman drives around behind the house, opens the van, slides the not-a-coffin out onto a flat dolly with big wheels that fold underneath and tells Phil to stay there while he takes care of his business inside. There are some people sitting on a bench across the lawn, ordinary-looking older people except that two women are wearing long bathrobes instead of dresses. A few men sit apart, talking. One gestures toward the truck with his cane. Another, a younger man wearing a white coat like a doctor, sits apart, glances up from the newspaper he's reading to look at the men with canes and the women in robes and resumes his reading. Phil, tired of watching the people and bored with sitting in the truck, decides that he'll walk around to the front of the house for a change of scene.

But it is not the change of scene he expects. The rolling lawns, tree lined drive and pillared portico are there to be sure, yet the pleasure of the vista is clouded by a trio of people on the front steps.

His father, then livid with rage, hands raised in the air, begins screaming in Yiddish at Phil's sister, Rita, who is one of the trio!

Phil is surprised to see her and thinks that perhaps he is dreaming. He rubs his eyes with his knuckles, and nothing changes. Cousin Viola, close to Rita's age, is standing nearby, not saying anything, but looking very agitated. Suddenly Nachman lunges for Rita, and Viola gets between them. Rita jumps away, clutching a brown paper parcel, and begins to run down the long elm-lined driveway. Nachman shoves Viola aside and gives chase, but Rita has already put a lot of distance between them, and after a dozen paces, Nachman gives up, breathing heavily. He is now aware of his son observing the scene, and, ignoring Viola, strides back to where Phil stands baffled and upset.

"What are you doing here?" Nachman demands. "I told you to wait in the back!"

"I got bored and decided just to walk around . . ."

But he doesn't get a chance to finish the sentence because his father's hand swings up and catches him with a hard slap on the cheek that brings tears to Phil's eyes.

"Next time you'll listen, and do as you're told," Nachman shouts in Phil's face. "Now stop your blubbering and go back to the truck!" He then turns on his heel and walks away into the house, ignoring Viola, who has been standing alongside a fluted column, observing.

As Phil turns his back and trudges toward the rear, she comes running over and touches his arm.

"Hi," she says. "You remember me, cousin Viola?"

"Yeah, hello," Phil says, wiping his wet eyes on the sleeve of his jacket.

"I don't want to make no more trouble for you," she says, smiling. She has a broad face, curly blonde hair and green eyes. He smells her perfume and thinks she is even more beautiful than Betty Grable. Viola touches his face with her gloved fingers."Go now," she says, "we'll see each other sometime. I have to catch up to Rita."

"But . . . " Phil starts to say.

"She'll explain," Viola says. "Take care of yourself." And she moves away down the drive where he can see Rita walking slowly between the trees a long way away. He wants to rush after her, but remembering too readily the pain on his cheek, he reluctantly continues around the side of the house to the truck. None too soon, in fact, because Nachman has just emerged from the rear door with another man who helps him wheel the transport box over the gravel and lift it into the truck.

"Get in," Nachman orders Phil, and they begin the return drive.

Nachman stares ahead stonily, the side of his jaw twitching in anger, and makes a point of ignoring Rita and Viola who are walking arm in arm toward the gate. They both raise their hands to wave at the truck, and Phil, who is afraid of being hit again, hangs his arm out of the open window and wiggles his hand outside so his father cannot see. They ride in silence for about a half-an-hour, Nachman focused straight ahead at the road, no longer ready to compare what they pass to his homeland.

Phil tries to just watch the scenery and avoid looking at his father, but the weight of silence is too much. So he finally breaks in: "What was that about back there, Papa?"

Nachman glances furiously at his son and, suddenly, with a sneering smile on his thin lips, his bald head gleaming with perspiration, his eyes steely gray and cold with anger, he swerves the truck to the side of the road with a screech of brakes. The movement is abrupt and the transport box slides across the cargo space with a thump and bangs on the inside rail, spilling the bushel of apples. Phil cowers, fearing that his father will lash out again, but Nachman doesn't raise his hand. Instead, he opens the door and steps down from the running board.

"Get out!" he orders.

Phil obeys wordlessly.

"Back there," Nachman motions, and then opens the rear cargo doors to the small van. He steps into the space and, half-bent, unsnaps the lid of the large box and lifts it. A strong medicinal odor fills the air in the confined space.

"Come in here and look," Nachman shouts at his son. Phil climbs up behind his father and peers over Nachman's broad back. A dark-haired, middle-aged woman, with the same kind of broad, rectangular face as cousin Viola, lies with her eyes closed. Phil is not scared. He has seen corpses before; they look like sleeping people. This one has a faint smile and her skin is fair, almost translucent, the color of a small alabaster statue on the bookcase at home. Then Phil realizes that the face is an older version of his sister Rita's. He gasps for breath; the smell begins to overpower him.

Without turning to face Phil, Nachman says in an angry voice: "That's your mother in there!"

The space is filled with yellow flashes and suddenly Phil feels air rushing from his lungs and a tidal wave is flooding up from his insides. He lurches backward out of the truck, runs fast into the bushes at the side of the road where spasms empty his stomach, and he vomits bits of apple, babka and cheesy brown liquid into the weeds.

Nachman, meanwhile, has closed the rear doors of the van and returned to the driver's seat. He honks the horn for Phil, who gets into the mortuary wagon and stares straight ahead as his father slams the vehicle into gear and accelerates onto the road. The farms, fields, cows and horses pass by in a blur, followed by the lots of the Bronx and the bustling Saturday streets of Manhattan. Nachman says nothing, as though driving alone. When they reach the funeral parlor, he gives Phil carfare to go home by streetcar himself.

◆

Max's record of the incident that he wrote down later was more dramatic than Uncle Phil's telling. This is what Phil *really* said that evening.

> One day, it must have been a Saturday or Sunday, Nachman woke me up very early and said he wanted me to go for a ride with him in the country. He was in a good mood, even bought me breakfast out. Then we went and got his van and we drove upstate. Back then White Plains was a big trip, with the old highways and all that. So we get to this 'rest home,' which he tells me is really a nut hatch, and as we go in the front gate, I see Rita and Cousin Viola

112

coming out of the big house. Nachman stops the truck and curses Rita out. But he always does that for anything so I don't pay too much attention. But from that moment he's pissed off at everything and everybody.

Then we pick up a body in the back of the big house; it's an old mansion turned into a looney bin. Two guys come out and lift the body bag into a big box undertakers used to use for transporting corpses, and he gives them a body bag in exchange. Then we start back. But Nachman's in a foul mood, and when we pass Rita and Viola on the road he ignores them, like they don't exist. So I ask him what's the matter and he tells me to mind my own business.

Later on we're driving along, and he turns to me. This is the first thing he's said to me in maybe a half hour. And he says: "You know who that is in the box back there? It's your mother!"And then, like he's been talking about some lumber or the weather, he clams up and just drives.

I don't know what to say because I thought she was dead since I was five — nine, ten years before, and I say: "But I thought she was dead a long time ago!" And he says, "Well, she was as good as dead, locked up in the crazy house, and she's dead now. So what's the difference?"

And then he doesn't say another word, except when I try to ask him some more questions and he tells me to shut up and mind my business, not to be a snoop like my sister.

Then, not another word from him about it, ever. Nice, huh? All heart! Your father was solid gold by comparison.

◆

Phil paused and looked down at his tasseled loafers.

"I guess it's the funeral that brings out all this shit," he said after a short silence."I usually don't want to remember. You'd think I'd be used to burials already, but with your own family it's always different."

"What was my mother doing there?" Max asked.

113

Phil looked puzzled: "I don't really know how she found out that our mother was living at the home, maybe through Viola, but it was only shortly before that day we saw them there. Once Rita knew, she made some kind of arrangement to visit with her, but then Adelle died the night before the planned visit, and no one let Rita know."

He laid his head back on the overstuffed velvet couch. "I'm gonna catch up on my beauty sleep before the crowds start showing. Suggest you do the same," he said.

And then Phil's eyes closed and his mouth opened, and he was snoring.

# 8

AFTER DINNER a classic family drama unfolds.

## Scene 1

SETTING:    ARLENE'S dining room, furnished in the
            Jewish Baroque style with ornate table,
            chairs and a large glass-door breakfront that
            houses various articles of value. Decanters,
            silver, hand painted china, and antique
            candlesticks carefully arranged in the
            cabinet for display, probably never used. An
            elaborate imitation-Renaissance chandelier
            hangs above the table. Silk curtains are
            drawn across the windows. Mirrors cover
            the walls. There are no pictures.

AT RISE:    Seated around the table: URSULA, MAX,
            ARLENE, CHARLOTTE, EDDY, PHIL and
            ELLEN. SAMANTHA clears away the dinner
            plates, places coffee on the table and exits.

URSULA

I still don't see why you should wash potatoes.

EDDY

So you can eat them without worrying!


ARLENE

When did you ever worry? About the cleanliness of potatoes,
no less?


EDDY

I'm concerned about my health. What do you think, I put
anything into my mouth, indiscriminate?


ARLENE
*(growing huffy)*
. . . LY . . . LY . . . indiscriminateLY, Eddy!


EDDY
*(annoyed that she should correct him)*
Big deal!


PHIL

What d'ya want, good grammar or "good taste"?
*(Thinking this is a clever thing to say,*
*PHIL repeats the ad line.)*
"Winston tastes good like a cigarette should"?


CHARLOTTE
*(pulling herself up straight in her chair*
*and cutting Phil off)*
I think that people should speak correctly and not try to
sound deliberately ignorant.


PHIL

Who said anything about ignorant? We're just talkin' about
potatoes. Do you need a Ph.D. to talk about a baked potato?


URSULA

Most people don't even eat the skin.

ELLEN

The girls at school won't eat potatoes in any form.


EDDY

I thought all lesbians were fat.


CHARLOTTE

But men like potatoes.


EDDY

I like the skins. That's where all the vitamins are.


MAX

I can't stand the skins.


URSULA

That's why I don't bother to wash them.


ARLENE

The heat kills the bacteria anyway; you don't have to wash them.


CHARLOTTE

I always wash them.


PHIL
*(motioning toward ARLENE)*

But the scientist here says you don't have to.


ELLEN

Then they taste of earth, y'know, like dirt.


MAX

Eventually we all have to eat dirt, so why not start early?
*(gets up and leaves the table)*


URSULA

Don't you want dessert and coffee?

MAX
*(standing near the door to the living room)*
Lost my appetite.
*(goes into living room)*


PHIL
*(mimicking a Yiddish accent)*
It's a funny 'ting, doctor, but after I eat, I ain't hungry no longer.


ARLENE
Leave it to my brother to be morbid.


ELLEN
When else should one be morbid if not when there's a death?


ARLENE
As if we all didn't know that Grandpa had died. Who does Max think he is, everybody's conscience?


CHARLOTTE
This is a time for peace and quiet and forgiveness. Why does there have to be bickering at a time like this? I think that we should all make up our minds . . .


PHIL
*(interrupting her)*
Especially there should be quiet!

*(CHARLOTTE shakes her finger at PHIL as Arlene begins to slice a huge babka.)*


PHIL
*(muttering)*
Forgiveness is a *goyish* idea. I don't forgive or forget things so easily.

EDDY
*(brightly, as if he has discovered a new concept)*
How about a truce then?

URSULA
*(putting her hand on Eddy's arm, a generous gesture linking the two outsiders at the table)*
That's a very good idea, Eddy. Just a sort of suspension of hostilities when we can't solve the underlying problems.

ELLEN
That's all we ever do in this family, and the battles go on and on, year after year.

ARLENE
You'd think that you were hard done by, my child, to live in and survive such an environment.

ELLEN
*(ignoring the barb)*
May I have a piece of babka? Please?

ARLENE
*(cutting large pieces of the cake)*
You want some, Uncle Philly?

PHIL
*(looking slightly nauseated)*
No, just some coffee. I had enough of babka for a lifetime.

CHARLOTTE
But there wasn't any babka out there before. Eddy brought it back with him from his walk.

EDDY
It looked so good in the bakery window, so I figured I'd get the jump on everybody who'll come here later and bring one.

ARLENE
*(half grudgingly)*
Very nice of you!


CHARLOTTE
I think it was.


PHIL
Very thoughtful. Please pass the milk and sugar.


CHARLOTTE
You should use saccharine.


URSULA
I thought there was a truce?


CHARLOTTE
What did I do?


PHIL
Too much, as usual.


EDDY
*(biting into a large piece of cake that he
lifts to his mouth with his fingers despite
ARLENE'S disapproving stare)*
It's very good, I approve.


ARLENE
*(speaking sarcastically)*
Generosity begins at home.


ELLEN
*(exasperated)*
Ma!


URSULA
The coffee is delicious. What brand is it?

*(The doorbell rings in the next room.)*

PHIL

People aren't supposed to do that. The door is unlocked.

ELLEN

How would they know it's not locked?

PHIL

They're Jews, ain't they? They're supposed to know!

ARLENE

I have some gentile friends who'll probably come over, too.

PHIL

They're forgiven!

CHARLOTTE

Very generous, coming from you!

EDDY

I'll go get the door.

ARLENE

Stay and finish your meal. Max is out there. He can do it.

PHIL

Still, it should be unlocked.

ARLENE

So any bum on the street could walk in?

PHIL

It's a tradition!

URSULA

You couldn't do that in the city!

ELLEN

It's ridiculous. You have to go through a security check to pay a shiva call?

CHARLOTTE

I'm glad I live in Cincinnati.

PHIL

Me too!

ARLENE

Some traditions no longer apply.

ELLEN
*(sounding like a want ad)*
Those with traditions need not apply.

EDDY

What do you think, every Puerto Rican on the street wants to come in here and have some babka with coffee?

CHARLOTTE
*(incredulous)*
You have Puerto Ricans in this neighborhood?

PHIL

You know their theme song?
*(Without waiting for an answer, he begins to sing)*
"We'll take Manhattan, the Bronx and Staten Island too . . .
It's lovely . . . dah dah doo . . . in the Zoo . . .."

EDDY

That's where they belong.

CHARLOTTE

But this is Queens!

EDDY

In the Zoo!

ELLEN

You're a bigot!

EDDY

You're too innocent. If they act like animals . . .


URSULA

The city is becoming less and less safe each year . . .


PHIL

Month, week, day!


URSULA

Even in the few years I've been living in Manhattan.


CHARLOTTE
*(glaring at Phil so that he doesn't retort
"Me too" once again)*
I'm glad I don't live here anymore. In the old days it was very
safe to walk on the street or take the subway.


URSULA

I don't take the subway any more.


ELLEN

That's a shame, isn't it? That people are so frightened of
everything.


EDDY

It's not a shame, just realistic.


ARLENE

Look who's defining what is realistic.


PHIL

Shouldn't you see who came in?


ARLENE

When I'm finished with my coffee.


CHARLOTTE

Why don't you mind your own affairs, Phil!

PHIL

I didn't have any affairs when I was married, and now it's kinda' late. You got a boyfriend, Charlotte?

ARLENE
*(looking at Eddy)*

I'm glad there's some morality in this family. It's refreshing to hear that there are some standards.

CHARLOTTE

What makes you think that a woman my age . . .?

PHIL

What age? I'm older than you are, and I got a girl friend.

CHARLOTTE

Shame on you. Mildred's hardly cold in the ground.

PHIL

That's where I'll be soon too, so who's got time to wait?

*(The family continues to talk and argue)*


## Scene 2

SETTING: ARLENE'S living room — similarly Jewish Baroque in style. Furnished with small occasional tables, a sofa, several over-stuffed chairs, and some boxes loaned by the funeral home to seat extra guests.

AT RISE MAX is ushering in several guests. SAMANTHA hangs their coats in the hall closet and exits.

Cousin VIOLA, a well-preserved woman in her sixties, is fashionably dressed in a fawn-

color, silk bouclé suit with a heavy gold
chain around her neck that hangs down
to her waist and directs the eye to the well
defined cleavage of her very large breasts.
Slim-hipped with a mincing walk, she has
streaky-blond hair, worn long and pulled
back in a French braid.

VIOLA'S husband MIKE is a short, tough-
looking man, also in his sixties, with a
balding dome, broad shoulders and meaty
hands that he carries half-clenched at his
sides. He steps lightly on the balls of his
feet, like a retired prize-fighter, and he has a
broken nose that reinforces the impression.

Following closely behind, MAX'S friends
JULES and THEO. Entering the living room
and seeing that the family is not there, they
hang back a trifle nervously at the entryway,
as if they are intruding.

VIOLA
(handing a large bakery box to MAX.)
Here's some babka so no one should starve. Where is
everybody, Max?

MIKE
I told you we shouldn't come so early, Vi. They're still eating
supper. You have to rush us so we can interrupt them?
Always in a hurry!

VIOLA
So I'm not related to this family long enough to come
in when they're eating? What'll they think — that I'm a
*schnorrer* or something?

MAX

They're finished anyway. Just having coffee. Go on in.


MIKE

I don't want to interrupt.


MAX
*(ushering VIOLA and MIKE toward the
dining room)*
The Sanhedrin is holding its evening meeting in the dining
room, that's true. But since they have solved all the problems
of the world before you arrived, there's nothing to worry
about. Go on in.
*(then catching himself short)*
Uncle Mike and Aunt Viola, do you know my friends Jules
and Theo?


VIOLA
*(taking Mike's arm)*
We just met on the doorstep. Very good looking boys, your
friends are, Max. What do they do?


MIKE
*(tugging Viola along)*
Come on, Vi. You can talk to Max after we pay our respects
to the rest of the family. Oh, yeah, Max, I'm really sorry
about your old man, but he lived a good life and it's a
blessing to go that way.


MAX

Thanks, I know you cared a lot for my father.


MIKE

Yeah, a lot. C'mon, Vi, let's go.
*(pulling open the dining room doors and
stepping through)*

## Scene 3

SETTING:       The dining room. Seated around the table
               ARLENE, EDDY, PHIL, CHARLOTTE,
               URSULA and ELLEN.

AT RISE        MIKE and VIOLA enter. PHIL'S loud
               voice is heard.

PHIL
*(angrily shouting at CHARLOTTE)*

And you think a rabbi won't eat pork? Even if he had to save
his life?

CHARLOTTE

Not my kind of rabbi!

PHIL

What good is a dead rabbi?

*(All fall silent as they realize that MIKE
and VIOLA are standing in the doorway,
and then there is a chorus of greetings.)*

## Scene 4

SETTING:       The living room.

AT RISE        Closing the doors to the dining room
               behind him, MAX turns to JULES and
               THEO, who have been standing to the side
               chatting.

MAX

Welcome to the house of the dead.

JULES

Such a clever boy. You'll go far, my friend, with the gift of wit unsurpassed by any of your generation.

MAX

Not far enough.

JULES
*(Having been friends since childhood, Jules is sensitive to Max's moods from long exposure.)*
Plunging into the family pool getting to you?

MAX

It's too much like a long family Sunday, or Thanksgiving. By the time the evening comes, you can't wait to get away and wonder why you ever came.

THEO
*(A friend of Max since college, now a psychiatrist, Theo is not tuned to Bergman family dynamics)*
You've got a week of it, I understand. You'd better save your energy.

MAX

I've already passed my quota. I'm pissed off enough for three weeks.

JULES

How bad can it be? They're basically nice people. I wish I had a family.

THEO

We're all so perverse. We want to be left alone until we're left alone. Then we want the company of the same people who always annoyed us, or we want new people who will eventually annoy us as much.

MAX

Ah, the profundity of these Greek philosophers. Dark
tending to light and the reverse. The playground of the
Manichean heresy.
        *(ushering Theo to a seat on the sofa and
        Jules to a nearby chair)*
I just learned today that my father was a radical when he was
younger — a card carrying CP guy.
        *(then sitting down on one of the boxes
        provided by the funeral home)*


JULES

A lot of the older guys were. It was a way of dreaming
together about change, and you could go to meetings and
make noise about things . . .


THEO

        *(cutting in)*
An antidote against alienation, a way of belonging to
something, even if you felt that the society at large excluded
you. You could be active in a smaller, more controllable
context, express your point of view, be listened to even if not
heeded, and be exclusive at the same time.

MAX

        *(interrupting in turn)*
Terrific exclusivity among a group of Yiddish-speaking
garment workers who argued about Karl Marx and the evils
of capitalism!


THEO

It gave them comfort and relief from everyday pain. To that
extent you are right because it is nice to think of how good
the future will be "if only" thus and so happens. It makes the
present more tolerable, a kind of mental survival technique,
called proleptic liberation — living as though the future
you want has already arrived — harmless enough unless you
believe it literally, and important for those who have little of
comfort in everyday life.

JULES

But all fantasy is that. It's a survival technique. Maybe it is for artists too.


MAX

No, the past is more important if you're not dreaming of real revolution, and I suspect it's more important for everybody. You should hear them talking,
> *(motioning toward the dining room doors with his head)*

about the way things used to be, when women were women and men were men and everyone believed in work.


THEO

But there was a lot more role definition then than there is now, and one of the direct results of its loss is that the younger generation doesn't know who and what it is ethically, economically, socially acceptable.


MAX

But to discover that the prejudiced, even bigoted, guy I knew as my father was once an idealistic Communist, that he once believed in a new world order, in a workers' paradise and all that. That blows my mind!


JULES

Why? Because you find out that he was human?


MAX

Maybe.
> *(gnawing his lower lip with his teeth)*

Maybe I need to see him as someone who never changed, someone who started and ended the same way, in order to hold on to my own comfortable generalities about him.


JULES

You didn't really know him, Theo, but I'll tell you, when I was a kid, I always envied Max because of his father.

MAX

*(surprised)*

Envied?


JULES

Yeah, envied. He always looked so dapper when you saw him in the street, and he always had time for you, even for your friends. Then, during the summer Ben used to pile any of Max's friends who were around and could fit into the family car and take us to the beach whenever he could.


MAX

Maybe that happened twice.


JULES

Baloney. It was a lot more than that. And what about when he used to take you up to the Thanksgiving Day Parade and tell you to invite me too? Or when he took us to Prospect Park and taught us both how to row a boat? What are you, kidding? I wish my old man had time for me like that. But not him. He worked in his store twelve, fourteen hours a day, and he was never interested in anything I did, as long as it was quiet when he got home. I don't think he ever took me any place. I don't even think he ever saw my grades from school. I was a biological fact, that was all. My mother brought me up, and she was always sick and *kvetching*. So when I used to see you and Ben, I really was envious. That was what I wanted!


MAX

I never knew that.


JULES

*(angrily)*

You never knew a lot. Now your father dies, you sit here intellectualizing and being amazed that he was a human being at all, and that he really was a *mensch*, and you're surprised to find that he cared enough about the way things were to be politically active.


131

MAX

It didn't last very long, apparently.


JULES

Beside the point. He did something; he believed in
something.


THEO

But you're making too much of it too, my friend. Adopting
an ideology may be unusual in this country, but in Europe
it's very common to find working men and women who are
strongly ideological, mostly on the political left. Max's father
still stood between the European politics of his elders and
the present American generation who don't care about much,
as long as it doesn't affect them directly.


MAX

I don't think that it's any different worldwide. Once people
have enough to eat and can live fairly well — have cars, TVs
and the like — they stop caring passionately about much
except protecting what they have from the next upstart
group that threatens to tread on their turf.


JULES
(raising his voice)
Stop! Why the fuck are we sitting around arguing about
ideas when we should be here to comfort Max, who ought to
be crying his eyes out now that his old man, who was a great
guy and who loved him in the way that a father loves a son
once in a million times, because the man is dead, and we'll
never see his like again.


MAX

Boy, you are a tyrant with other people's emotions.

JULES

What emotions do you have to tyrannize?
 *(leaning back and looking at the ceiling*
 *disgustedly, then letting out his breath*
Whew! Sorry, Max.


THEO

What's with you two? I thought you were friends, not
character assassins.


JULES

I don't like post mortem dissections.


THEO

Necessary to medical science.


MAX

Big soul kind of guy.


JULES

I love you, Max, but you're the biggest *schmuck* sometimes.


## Scene 5

SETTING:     The living room. MAX, THEO and JULES
             are sitting and talking

AT RISE:     The doors from the dining room open and
             PHIL enters followed by CHARLOTTE,
             ARLENE and VIOLA.)


PHIL
 *(insisting to CHARLOTTE who is shaking*
 *her head "no")*
Kasha is *much* more nourishing than potatoes.

CHARLOTTE
*(saying over her shoulder to those behind
her)*
A new maven about health and nourishment.
*( then to PHIL )*
Just because you like it, that makes it good?


PHIL
And just because *you* don't like it, it isn't better? Ask Arlene.
I'll bet she knows. ARLENE!


ARLENE
*(moving away from a hushed conversation
with Viola and entering the living room)*
Yes. Coming, Uncle Philly.
*(demanding as she reaches PHIL
and CHARLOTTE)*
"What's so important?"


PHIL
*(begging for a partisan response)*
"Isn't kasha more nourishing than potatoes?"


CHARLOTTE
*(imploring)*
How could it be?


ARLENE
I think that if you are comparing the raw stuff it's about the
same.


*(PHIL'S face falls.)*


CHARLOTTE
*(needling)*
You see, smart guy? I told you so.

ARLENE
*(continuing)*
But considering that most people boil the hell out of peeled
potatoes, and throw away the water they were boiled in, and
compare that with the way we cook the whole grain kasha
and then eat the entire thing with its absorbed cooking
water, kasha is probably more nourishing."

PHIL
*(beaming in victory)*
What did I tell you?

CHARLOTTE
But what about the baked potatoes?

ARLENE
My guess is that if you eat the skin of the baked potato,
there's not much difference between that and kasha.

PHIL
*(losing some of his grin)*
But kasha's still better for you, if you don't eat the potato
skin, isn't it?

ARLENE
It probably has more iron.

CHARLOTTE
*(in a last ditch defense)*
Well, kasha isn't easy to get in Cincinnati!

PHIL
Can't find iron there? What do Indians and hicks know?

CHARLOTTE
*(raising her voice)*
"INDIANS? HICKS? Now I've heard everything!

PHIL

Said everything, but heard? You don't keep quiet long enough to listen. Even your baseball team is Redskin.

CHARLOTTE
*(starting to cry)*
Why are you always picking on me, Phil? Why do you make me your whipping boy? Ever since we were young, you always got something out of needling me. And I don't like it, and I don't have to take it from you. So I'm not the smartest woman in the world. I know it! But why do you have to be nasty to me, whenever you see me. And thank God that's not too often!"

VIOLA
*(enters from the dining room and begins to cheer on CHARLOTTE)*
Give it to him, baby. I know this little piggy ever since we were kids, and even then he would always try to get a finger in your nooky or cop a feel. He used to pinch my ass and run away. I like to see him get his balls banged together once in a while.

MIKE
*(following VIOLA into living room)*
You always gotta talk like a truck driver, Vi?

VIOLA

Look who I had to learn from! Mr. Pure-as-Snow. Did you ever listen to yourself? You think I spent thirty-five years running that truckers' office for you with my ears closed? Guess again!"

MIKE

Still I don't think . . .

136

VIOLA

Correct! Leave it at that."
>                    (*turning from Mike to Charlotte*)
Atta girl! That's the way you give it to these big-shot, big-
mouth punks. They only respect power, so show 'em who's
got it. Otherwise they'll shit all over you and ask you to
thank 'em!
>                    (*Seating herself on the sofa and patting
>                    the seat next to her with a ring-laden
>                    hand tipped by creamy-white manicured
>                    fingernails*)
Sit down next to me, Charlotte.
>                    (*Speaking to THEO who has been sitting
>                    on the sofa watching the interchange with
>                    quiet amusement*)
Move over a bit Honeyman, will ya?

>                    (*As THEO slides to the end of the couch,
>                    VIOLA moves closer to him, and pulls
>                    CHARLOTTE down next to her. Viola
>                    now has Theo on her right and Charlotte
>                    on her left.*)

MIKE
>                    (*sitting down next to MAX on the box,
>                    claps him on the knee affably*)
Long time no see, Maxie. What's up?


MAX

Working, teaching composition at Juilliard, and writing
music. My opera was going to premiere this week, but may
have to be postponed because of my father's death.


MIKE

The show doesn't go on anyway?


MAX

Usually — but not if the composer and conductor can't be
there at the premiere.

                                MIKE

I don't know about things like that, but I guess we'll see your
name in lights soon, huh? You know your father and me go
back lots of years, but the last few, after your mother died,
we didn't see much of each other, not after the first year.
Wasn't the same without Rita, and Vi moves in to take over
wherever she can. So the old buddies kinda' fell apart, if you
know what I mean."

                                 MAX

I guess.

                                MIKE

Anyway, Max, what's to say? I'm really sorry for your loss.
He'll be missed a lot."
                    *(Then clapping Max on the knee again,
                    Mike rises and walks over to where EDDY
                    is sitting alone, and engages him in conver-
                    sation.)*
How's business?

                    *(People keep coming into the house. Soon
                    there are thirty or forty milling about,
                    talking, smoking, eating, drinking.)*


                                 MAX
                    *(speaking to JULES and THEO)*
This is what always happens. People come to pay their
respects, tell you how sorry they are, and then carry on as
though it was a party.

                                THEO

You sound annoyed.

                                JULES

"When doesn't he?

MAX

Shut the fuck up, Julie! You know what I mean, even aesthetically it doesn't go. Death demands a kind of solemnity, a shared mourning.

JULES

That's your version of it. Tragedy, rending garments, loud laments, crying.

MAX

What should we do, dance?

THEO

Why not? How would you celebrate death?

MAX

Celebrate? What a peculiar choice of words!

THEO

Not at all. Many cultures regard death as a kind of liberation, a goal reached. Look at the send-off in New Orleans with a Dixieland jazz band.

MAX

But that's the infusion of the African into the American culture, a hangover from spiritualism, ancestor worship and all that. The souls of the departed going to heaven, Hallelujah.

JULES

You're mixing up fundamentalist and evangelical Christianity with African culture, about which you know beans.

MAX
*(smiling)*
What's wrong with beans?
>*(Jules was his favorite intellectual adver-*
>*sary, but Max wasn't going to be drawn*
>*away from his feelings into a dispute —*
>*not again.)*

THEO
Nevertheless, while it's natural to lament the passing of a life close to ours, there is also great weight of history and culture that marks the passing as a joyful event — a passing on to higher rewards — an end to the uncertainties of life and so on. Not breast beating and the *mea culpas* of modern man.

MAX
Guilt is a modern invention?

THEO
I think that modern guilt is handmaiden to modern alienation; that's a modern phenomenon!

JULES
What a ridiculous tautology.
>*(JULES is interrupted when Arlene's an-*
>*nounces that the rabbi has arrived and*
>*would lead the evening prayer.)*

MAX
God save us from all this.

THEO
*(murmuring under his breath)*
You won't let Him.

JULES
You both talk too much.

MAX

Join a monastery. A silent order.


THEO
(muttering under his breath)
What fun do monks have?
(MAX and JULES look at Theo and wait
for an answer as he murmurs).
Nun!


MAX
(groaning)
Oohh.


JULES

Minus four.


RABBI
(a short bald man in a shiny black suit
began to intone the Kaddish along with the
few people who were immediate relatives
and who could read the Hebrew)
"Yisgadol v'yiskadash shmay rabo. . .

(MAX followed the English translitera-
tion in the little pamphlets distributed to
the family of the bereaved, "Courtesy of
Goodman and Peretz, Funeral Directors."
JULES prayed from the Hebrew text and
THEO read in English.


THEO
(showing Max the translation of the Kaddish after the rabbi concluded)
Look what it says here. It's a hymn of praise to God,
not a dirge for the departed. There's no mention of grief
or anything associated with morbidity. It's more of a
recognition of the power of God and the ongoing process of
human life.

MAX

So how can you extrapolate from one prayer to prove anything?

THEO

I'm just trying to affirm my point from a moment ago that celebration of living is a legitimate way of recognizing the power of death. Life goes on and you don't bury yourself along with the corpse.

MAX

What does that have to do with anything?

JULES

It has to do, jerko, with the fact that you put down all the people who come to pay respect to the and then proceed to act alive by standing and gossiping, talking about their kids, their lives, business, and what not.

MAX

What I want is high drama played out on a bare stage, like a Greek tragedy, with ominous music and an intensity of mood, the dramatic unities and all that.

JULES

Then you'll have to write it, and get actors to perform it. This is life, not a private vision.

MAX

But it was my father, my grief.

JULES

It was your sister's father too, and Charlotte's brother, Ellen's grandfather, and so on. You don't have an exclusive patent.

THEO

I think he's right.

MAX

Thank you, good friends. What I want is sympathy, not criticism!

JULES

That's my way of being your friend, and if you think I don't feel sympathy for you, you're mistaken. In fact, it's because I do that I'm telling you not to be down on everything and everybody. Let them live. Do what you have to do at the keyboard, on paper, at the podium with a baton in your hand, but live here. You've confused the two!"

◆

Max always felt stifled by the intensity of his family's opinions, and the endless bickering over matters of little consequence seemed to be a substitute for saying anything of consequence. They filled the vacuum with assertions of preferences — such as the cleanliness of potato skins. He could imagine them next arguing about whether babka was better with or without nuts or raisins, or should a true coffee cake be eaten with butter or with cream cheese?

What changed from the time when his father's cousin Meyer believed in something of essence so strongly that he picked himself up and went back to Russia to chase a dream? Was Meyer also running away from arguments about potato skins?

But credit to Ben, his skirmishes with Max were not trivial: they were battles of will and won't.

During Max's second year as an undergraduate, Ben told his son how annoyed he was that he switched his major from pre-med to music.

By then Max moved into the city and was living in one of the NYU dormitories, but he would always go home on Friday nights for Sabbath dinner — an unquestioned tradition in the family.

Ben was always glad to see his son, but they usually couldn't get past the chopped-liver appetizer without conflict, and it was always the same: "Why are you doing this to me and to yourself? Aren't there plenty of doctors who play music, get together and play chamber music, even jazz? Why make life so hard for yourself. Look how many unemployed musicians there are around New York."

On Saturday morning Max would return to the city, hitching a ride as far as Williamsburg with his father, who went to his office for a half day, and then taking the subway to Manhattan. If nothing else got in the way, he would meet Jules and Theo at Charlie's Uncle, their coffee shop hangout on Sullivan Street.

The morning ride alone with his father was often worse than the Friday night argument because Rita wasn't there to smooth things over and say, "Look, it's his life, and we're here to observe *shabbos* together, not to argue, so please!"

In the car there was nobody to run defense, and Ben would adopt a different tactic. He said nothing, but would occasionally snort and shake his head in a frowning gesture of disbelief. And Max knew why. How could he not?

Or they engaged in desultory conversation about the change in neighborhoods that always suggested a conflict underneath that would go something like this:

"Once, you could walk through this entire area almost any time of day or night, and no one would bother you, even if you wore gold and jewels on you," Ben said, as he drove down the exit ramp of the Brooklyn-Queens Expressway, and turned toward his Marcy Avenue office. "It was all nice people here."

"C'mon, Dad, 'all nice people?' That's really carrying it a bit too far. Are you telling me that there was no one in our entire neighborhood who was a crook, who beat his wife? Nothing like that? Yeah, right — they were all just good, middle-class people all of whom had jobs, put money in their savings accounts, paid their rent on time, and made sure that their kids had clean handkerchiefs for school?"

144

"Funny guy, always with the smart-aleck answer," Ben would say. "You know what I mean. They minded their business and were basically honest. They lived in a neighborhood and took some pride in it. You didn't find garbage in the streets or graffiti, or these bums hanging around on the stoops getting drunk on beer and taking drugs. Look at them, they're out already!"

He'd thrust his chin toward the right and Max followed Ben's eye toward a run-down tenement opposite the corner where they waited for a traffic light to change to green. A group of black and Hispanic men were sitting on the front steps, joking and talking, drinking from quart bottles of beer, "Hey, baby"ing at passing women, and pitching pennies against a wall.

"That's what I mean," Ben said. "The salt of the earth."

"They're just hanging out, doing no harm," Max said.

"Drinking already?" Ben asked as he started the car moving again now that the light had changed. "It's only eight-thirty in the morning. Imagine where they'll be by five in the afternoon!"

Max couldn't imagine. "Where?" he asked.

"Out of money, wanting more booze or marijuana, and they'll go and rob a candy store or a grocery or a liquor store, and if the little guy behind the counter tries to hold out on the money he's worked so hard for all day, they'll shoot him or stab him. That's what happens. Don't close your eyes to it like the bleeding hearts who say these guys are victims of the system. Bullshit, I say! If you want to work in this country, there's plenty of jobs, and if you want to be honest, you don't have to drink up what you make or shoot it into your veins, then rob someone else to pay for your own lack of self-control."

"You always used to hang out with your cronies by the candy store in Williamsburg," Max retorted. He re-

145

membered his father going down to the street after supper, especially in the warmer weather, to hang around with other men by the corner candy store to wait for the early editions of the morning papers.

"Oh, sure," Ben said. "Real threats we were, working men from the neighborhood who used to drink an egg cream or a coke, or maybe buy a cigar to smoke out there because our wives didn't like the smell in the house. Real criminal element!"

"What else do these guys have?" Max asked. "Maybe they're desperate. They're marginal to the system." *Second semester. Urban Sociology — The role of marginal minorities.* Use what you learned in college to convince your father he's wrong.

"You want something in this world, you work for it," Ben said. "Except if you're born rich, there's no good fairy with a magic wand."

"But what if the system is built to be exclusionary and no matter what you do, you can't get in?"

"That's more bullshit. Is that what your head is getting stuffed with in college?" Ben asked, brimming with anger and righteous indignation. "What about the other minorities? The Jews, the Italians and the Irish who built this city, and what about the Chinese now? You think that they were handed everything? They weren't automatically included either, but they busted their asses to make a living. Sure there were some bums in all these groups, but let me tell you, nobody got off the boat and right onto the welfare rolls. You worked, you saved, you made sure your kids went to school and learned English so they would have it better than you had. You scraped for every dollar and sent them on to college to become teachers, lawyers, doctors."

He paused and looked at Max with eyes that were caught between anger, hurt and pity, and then continued, "and you organized politically to make your voice heard at the polls. In other words you took part in the system and didn't expect that it owed you anything except certain legal rights. I'm sick and tired of hearing about all these poor, oppressed people who won't get off their asses and do anything for themselves, and the god-damned liberals want everyone to share some kind of guilt while these animals destroy everything that the rest of us work for, because it's coming to them. So they can turn this city into a dangerous pigsty like the ones they came from so that even if you survive getting knifed in the street for a couple of dollars, you wonder why you even want to be on the street when it's so dangerous, disgusting, and filthy."

And you! You ride the subways more than I do, so you know what you find there. It's hard to believe how stupid so-called educated people can be!"

Ben finally pulled into the driveway of the garage where he kept the car — "because you won't find it when you come back if you leave it on the street" — and sat there seething with annoyance.

"Thanks for the lift," Max said when they walked to the entrance to the elevated train near Ben's office.

He didn't answered his father's diatribe because he knew it was futile to do so. Another harangue would be provoked, and Max had no answers, although he felt that Ben wasn't correct in his opinions.

And all the while, during these random outpourings of mixed lament and frustration that Ben indulged in regularly, he never hinted at what Max just learned from Aunt Charlotte: that once upon a time, Ben was a radical who wanted to change the world for the better, for whom the oppression of the poor by the system was a real issue. Max never had a chance to admire his father for that.

# 9

MAX WALKED OVER TO THE LIQUOR CART to pour some scotch-on-ice for himself when he felt Viola pressing up against him. Only one woman in the room wore that perfume and had a bosom that reached you so far in advance of her face.

"How's my little Max doing?" Viola asked. Her arms circled his waist and squeezed.

"I'm okay, Aunt Viola," he said, slipping effortlessly into the form of address he always used with his mother's cousin and closest friend.

She smiled with pleasure. "I'm glad you still think of me that way. So give your old aunt a drink already. What's keeping you? Scotch and a little soda. Don't drown it."

He handed her his drink, added a little soda, and poured another for himself.

"Are you really okay, Max? I mean, what do you think it'll be like not to have your father around?"

"Fewer arguments," he answered, turning and looking down at her. He couldn't keep his eyes from the deep cleavage between her heavy and protruding breasts. When he was a little kid, he used to look forward to seeing Viola and Mike because Aunt Viola would always fondle him and hug him. When he was an adolescent, her hugging caused erections: many an afternoon was spent in the bathroom evoking pictures of Aunt Viola shamelessly removing her clothes, and leading him into her bedroom.

"I can't believe that," Viola said. "He never talked about you or what you were doing without a lot of pride. He loved you, Max."

"Until I decided not to be a doctor."

"He was a little disappointed, I know, but you were all he ever talked about, the apple of his eye. He never complained to nobody else about you!"

"One doctor wasn't enough for him? He never stopped *nudging* me about how I should give up music and go back to medicine."

"Not to hear him talk. It was always 'Max did this' and 'Max won this scholarship' and 'Max is having a piece performed here or there', or 'Max is going to study in Paris with a big professor.'"

"Boulanger."

"Yeah, and always like that. You would have thought that he only had one kid. I used to feel sorry for Arlene."

"But they were very close, Viola — Aunt Viola."

She took a long sip at her drink and toyed with the gold chain hanging around her neck. Then she ran her fingers through her hair, smiling mysteriously from under her long false eyelashes. " He had very old-fashioned ideas about women, Max, what they could or couldn't do. Your mother was always the one who would bring your sister into the conversation."

"But he never was able to upset her, just criticize."

"How could he? Arlene wouldn't let him. She was too independent for him to get at."

"I always thought that I was the independent one."

"Rebellious, yes. Independent, I'm not so sure."

For a moment all the coquettish gestures were gone and she looked hard into his eyes. "If you didn't need him, Max, whatever he said wouldn't have bothered you. But it did, and you always tried to get him to tell you that what you were doing was okay by him."

"And he never would, never, even up to a couple of weeks ago, when I called him to ask him to come to the premiere of my opera."

150

"Oh, he was so proud of that!"

"But he wouldn't give *me* the satisfaction of telling me."

"He told everyone else!"

How did Viola know so much? Max wondered

"He bored the pants off everybody by telling them all about you every chance he got. For a man with a lot of different interests, his conversations were always one sided. Max, and Max, and Max. Beginning, middle, and end."

He looked across the room to where the others were standing in small groups chatting. Arlene on her cardboard box with Charlotte and Phil flanking her on opposite sides of the "L" shaped couch. Mike and Eddy were standing by the liquor cart, talking heatedly and gesturing with their hands. Ellen was smiling into the face of a tall boy with blue jeans and long blond hair, and Jules, Ursula and Theo were talking to three of Arlene's friends, all of whom looked like younger versions of Viola. Everyone was in a conversation.

"Hey, Beethoven, come on back here. Remember me?" Viola asked, with an imitation of petulance on her glossy lips.

"Sorry," Max answered. "I have a tendency to let my mind wander, especially today."

He was apologizing and didn't like it. All day he did and said what he wanted without being sorry, only annoyed at others when they objected to his behavior. Yet Viola compelled some recognition of her own needs, and something in him made him respond, apologize and explain with a plea for sympathy. Recognize the special needs I have, today of all days, he wanted to say. Sympathize with me because my father is dead. He felt cheapened by the ploy, so obvious, yet comforted because it worked.

Viola put her drink on the liquor cart and took his free hand in hers, pressing it warmly. "I loved your father too, Max," she said, wistfully. "I know how you feel. But life goes on. I know that sounds corny, but it's true. We're still alive and have to make the most of it."

He looked at her and nodded his head. What kind of feeling, what kind of ferment brewed behind the platitudes? Was his anger, his agony, the only authentic kind because he avoided clichés of thought, because he was intolerant of others who used ready-made phrases to anoint their feelings and expected everyone to understand? How he yearned for raw tears, strong words, loud screams in the void of a deaf universe. And the utter isolation of knowing that you cried, said, screamed and you got no answer. The indifference of silence was a final empty space.

Cold comfort were the rabbis with their prayers and attempts to place death in the perspective of God's goodness. Children's toys, stuff that fell apart when you pressed it too hard.

There was only the world in its beauty and coarseness, the flesh in its demand for satiation, and the devil you were inspired to eschew or chase after. The trio was driving him mad, and he knew that he could only get it out, express it, with music. That was how he could make the abstract concrete, or else he was constrained to live it, act out a profligacy. No other way to tell people. Because the substance of his thoughts was a form of madness for "normal" people like Arlene and his father and Viola. Their normality bored him although he craved a little, a smidgen of the comfort they enjoyed by staying inside the borders. Rita understood, without words.

"Arlene never liked me," Viola said, oblivious to the ferment in his brain. "She was so jealous of the friendship I had with your mother, like I was taking Rita away from her and had no rights. When she used to come visit Rita toward the end, she never liked to find me there, even though it was I who had the time to spend with Rita during the day, and no one else. Your father was in his office and Arlene was working too. I spent the time with her. Arlene hated me for it. Whenever she would come, I left. Even when she was a kid, she'd get sullen if Rita was with me."

"Why are you telling me this?" Max asked.

"Because now that your father is gone, Max, I'm afraid that we'll all drift apart, and I feel toward the Bergmans like they was family . . . actually, Rita was family. Her mother was my aunt — my father's sister, so Rita was my cousin. We grew up together in the neighborhood, had kids around the same time, and we always saw each other, weekends, other times, and when our sweet Rebecca died, they were there to comfort us. Family and friends. I don't really have any others. Mike's relatives are a bunch of selfish slobs. Now Arlene has no reason to keep the contact, and I don't have anyone else. I feel toward you and Arlene like you was my own, so don't forget me, Max. Your father didn't after Rita died, and I think I helped him too. But your sister didn't like it either. Don't leave me all alone now, Max." She wiped her tears.

He was embarrassed by her crying and desperate clutching of his hand. Only the isolation of his own imagination was clear to him, such as his grandmother Adelle in the insane asylum, lost to hiding from the world. He could transform that into art. Feeling abandoned he would transform into the fuel that propelled his neurosis and his art. But Viola's? Sexy Aunt Viola whom he had known all his life? Whose bulging breasts and sexy affect provided endless fantasy? How could she feel so alone and in so much pain, Viola with the brash mouth, Viola who could tell anyone where to get off, whose life seemed centered around her demand that everything be as she wanted? A bossy woman who always got her own way, insisted that those around her recognize the rightness of what she said and bow to it? How come she felt so lost? Max was always awed by Viola's toughness: take no shit, take no prisoners, and wished he had more of that. Did you have to be brassy as she was to get your way? Now what did it get her?

She began toying with the long gold chain that hung around her neck. It was loosely knotted just below her deep cleavage and hung like a golden waterfall five inches from her midriff. An oval locket of filigreed gold dangled from the end.

"You see this, Max? This has the most important people in my life inside," Viola said, snapping open the locket to show him miniaturized photographs: Rita and Ben on one side, Rebecca opposite. "And the chain was your mother's. Ben gave it to me after she died as a keepsake, a memento, and boy, was Arlene pissed off at him.

She said that Rita's jewelry was hers by right, by tradition. I think that if he had given the chain away to the cleaning woman, Arlene would have been less annoyed. But to me? That was beyond bearing."

Max didn't know what to say. He wasn't going to defend his sister, not knowing all the facts of that story, not wanting to. Nor could he agree with Viola, and risk her using his support in her conflict with his sister; that would be a betrayal. The ghost of Rita whispered, "Don't say anything. Say nothing! Others remember when you complain about your immediate family, even though you forget it the next day."

Maybe his mother and Phil had the same source of instruction. Whatever Nachman was, he must have been discreet to keep so much going at the same time. Perhaps they learned from him, although their lives would be a denial of their father's worth in any respect. Was it of value to learn how to connive or conceal?

"It's nice of you to keep them together like that," Max said.

"Will you remember your Aunt Viola," she asked, "now that both Ben and Rita are gone?"

"Sure I will, Vi."

"Arlene will poison your mind against me."

"Don't be silly. Why should she? When we do talk, it isn't about other people."

"We'll see," Viola said, with a sly smile. "When will I see you again?"

"Do you want to come to the premiere of the opera?"

"I'd love to," she laughed. "I thought you'd never ask."

"I'll send you two tickets. Will Mike come too?"

"I'll break his head if he doesn't."

"I'll put them in the mail tomorrow."

"Max," she asked, then hesitated, pouting her lips, "are you coming out here tomorrow?"

"I suppose so."

"Why don't you drop off the tix at my house, only a few blocks from here, because there's something I'd like to talk to you about."

"Can't we talk here? Won't you be here tomorrow?" he asked.

"No, I can't talk here. We would probably be interrupted, and it'll take a few minutes." She was toying with the chain once again, nervously, opening and closing the locket, looking at the pictures absentmindedly, without seeming to see them.

"Okay," he said. "About four?"

"Make it a bit earlier," Viola said. "Three?"

Max said he'd try.

Viola put an affectionate hand on his cheek. "I'll look forward to it," she said and walked away.

Watching her surprisingly well shaped rear-end gyrate across the room, Max wondered what it was she wanted from him, hoping that it wasn't to reveal another dread family skeleton, yet wishing that there was more and more of this intrigue, because he wanted to see his family from different perspectives, and they were just beginning to open up.

Then he recognized the chain Viola was wearing, the gold chain with the picture locket she'd added, the chain knotted so it fell across her Dolly Parton bosom and emphasized its magnitude.

◆

Max would always remember the day Ben bought the chain for Rita. It was one of those Saturday mornings during his second year of college, when Ben dropped Max in Brooklyn near his office, as usual. The ride was filled with acrimonious silence since five minutes after they set out from Queens. Ben asked his son directly whether he would consider going back into the pre-medical program and Max said flatly, "no."

Ben's response was a punishing silence for the rest of the way. He stared straight ahead and worked at creating the impression that he was alone in the car. Not even a guilt-encouraging sigh left his tightly sealed lips. He stopped at the entrance to the elevated train, bypassing his garage and the usual two-block walk with his son in order to get Max out of his sight.

"Goodbye. Thanks. See you next week," Max said as he stepped onto the sidewalk. Ben turned his head away and stared out of the driver's window until Max slammed the door. Then he drove away without looking back.

Max made a decision, he thought, that would affect only himself, but he knew that it forced Ben to change his spiel to friends and family about "my son, the doctor," just like "my daughter, the doctor." His father was acting as though it was his life Max was changing. Nineteen years of Ben's living hopes were dead. Depressed, Max rode back to his dormitory room in Greenwich Village and was thankful that his roommates were gone for the weekend. He spread a music manuscript on his desk and started to rewrite his setting for Joyce's poem, "Ecce Puer," that his composition teacher had criticized severely as a "sentimental tune."

Shortly after noon, the telephone rang.

"I need your help this afternoon," Ben said, in a gruff voice, "and it won't take too long. I forgot to mention it this morning. You got some time?"

When nothing was said about the morning's silent treatment, as though that happened in another life, Max almost asked if he was in good graces again or merely an expedience, but held his tongue, a rare discipline.

Ben picked Max up in front of the dorm an hour later and headed down Broadway to Canal Street. Where the Bowery crossed Canal there was the "One Hundred Jewelers Exchange" and Irving the Jeweler, a distant relative, indistinguishable from the other ninety-nine, worked at an obscure corner counter.

Irving always gave Ben a "special deal" on everything he bought there. Wrist watches for graduations, Stars of David for Bar or Bat Mitzvahs, and every variety of trinket owned by Ben's branch of the Bergman clan was bought from Irving.

The only problem was that there were no places to park the car near the Exchange, and so this day Max was needed to either drive around the block or sit in a "No Parking" zone with the motor idling until a cop told him to move, while Ben picked up whatever it was he bought for Rita.

Max was waiting in front of the fire hydrant just outside the store when Ben returned. Max moved over to the passenger side because when his father was in the car he wasn't allowed to drive.

"You want to see something beautiful?" Ben asked as he got into the car.

"Your mother will love this," Ben said, taking a long blue leather case from his raincoat pocket and snapping it open. On dark velvet lay a long, heavy gold chain. "She pointed out one just like this on some other woman, and then told me that another lady she met owned one, too. So I figured, why not? It's our anniversary next week anyway, and this'll make her happy." He seemed pleased with himself.

Max examined the closely meshed gold links. It was a weighty chain, probably set his father back a bit, but he wouldn't ask the price. He knew Ben was dying to be asked, and Max decided to be spitefully innocent.

"Irving gave me some deal," Ben coaxed.

But Max wouldn't pick up the bait.

Ben couldn't hold back: "Two hundred dollars he charged me. It's worth at least twice that," he said, secure that he had gotten a bargain, a triumphant victory over the *gonifs* who charged more for the same thing, sorry for the suckers who had no jeweler relatives.

Max nodded his approval, and Ben seemed happy, the gloom of the morning forgotten.

"You eat yet?" Ben asked as he steered the Buick away from the curb into traffic.

Katz's delicatessen on Houston Street was crowded with Saturday-polished Puerto Ricans, suburbanites, taxi drivers, out-of-towners who read of the famous old eatery in the *Guide to New York*, and sentimentalists like Max and Ben, who dropped in now and then for old times' sake, and because Katz's made the thickest, juiciest and least expensive pastrami and corned beef sandwiches in the city. Everyone but the out-of-towners went to the counter and gave their orders to the countermen. The curiosity seekers from beyond the pale watched the sideshow from a row of tables along the wall where waiters served them, patiently explaining that you couldn't order pastrami on white with lettuce and mayo.

Max and Ben reached the counter after a minute's wait.

"You go first," Ben urged.

"Pastrami on rye," Max said to the white-coated, wall-eyed gnome who looked at him with indifference, "and make it lean."

"Left or right?"

"Such a comedian." Max commented.

The man speared a large piece of reddish-gray meat and began to carve thick slices: "By me, a sendvich mit out fat's no sendvich. Dry, got no *tam*, y'know what I mean?"

One eye looked up at Max while the other guided the razor sharp blade as he trimmed the glistening rinds of fat from the edges of the steaming beef slab.

"Don't answer him," Ben whispered in Max's ear. "He's just a trouble maker. Probably his feet hurt."

"Then give him your business card," Max retorted to his father, and then to the gnome in soiled whites he said: "But the fat isn't good for you."

"Oh, yeah?" the gnome asked, looking at both Max and Ben, an eye for each of them. "Who says?"

*Who would impress the sandwich man with the authority of inviolable truth? Einstein, Newton, the Baal Shem Tov? Karl Marx, Adelle Davis?* "My doctor," Max said, appealing to the final authority in New York healthy food culture.

With a gleam in the eye focused on Max, the counterman asked, "So tell me, how much does your doctor charge for a visit? Ten dollars or more?"

Behind the counterman's cockeyed glance, Max thought odds were being calculated and he did not want to admit he knew that such low fees had vanished, as dead and gone as the rump being cut for his pastrami sandwich.

"Five dollars," Max said, pleased with his own thoughtful consideration for not disturbing the wall-eyed gnome's universe.

"So, Mr. Smart Guy," said the counterman, "for five dollars, what do you think he eats?"

"I don't know!" Max answered.

"FAT! Vat den?" The eyes rolled back and forth, he and chortled as he punched the price onto Max's ticket triumphantly and plopped the plate onto the counter top.

Ben smirked as they carried their sandwiches toward an empty table in the rear of the delicatessen. He seemed to enjoy watching Max nonplussed and speechless. "Serves you right. I said not to answer. Those guys have nothing to do but make sandwiches and practice their routines. You're too wet behind the ears for them."

"I was just trying to back up what I said in a way that he would understand."

"In school you're smart, my sonny boy, but street smarts you ain't got yet."

"They come with the territory?" Max asked.

Ben looked puzzled. "Guess so," he answered.

The territory they opened up that day was Ben's past; the atmosphere of Katz's seemed to encourage him. " . . . we used to call him Shmooley the Gonif because he was always taking things from the candy store, from Woolworth's; he would even take money from the *pishke* in his mother's kitchen."

"What did he grow up to be?"

"Dead! A gangster, a goon, a strike breaker. He was killed by the cops during a bank robbery. Probably he was set up because his gang wanted to get rid of him. He looked like that guy, the counterman with the *tz'drehter oigen.*"

"You always hear about the hardworking, oppressed, poor Jews on the Lower East Side who struggled against overwhelming odds to make it in America. Good decent people."

"They were, not bums like these Puerto Ricans," Ben said, pointing over his shoulder.

"Yet you tell me about Shmooley the Gonif. He was a hood, a gangster! Not a decent, hardworking citizen."

"Sure, and there were others like him. But also hardworking gangsters. There still are. Yet they were decent enough to take care of their families, their *landsmen*. Respected the ordinary people in the street. If Meyer Lansky and the goons from Murder Incorporated lived in your neighborhood, it was safe, super-safe. So?"

"Well, it disproves your point," Max said.

"No, it doesn't!" Ben objected, pieces of corned beef spluttering from his mouth. "It only means that there were also bums like with any group of people, and the rest is sentimental bullshit. But what was the proportion of Jews who were no-goods? Check that out, wise guy. Find the statistics in your college courses before you jump to conclusions!"

Max was annoyed to think that his father was probably right. It wasn't as if the naive Ben just didn't know the score. More likely, he was able to come to terms with the Jewish criminals because they weren't alien to him. Whatever they were, they were his people, and he knew the soil in which these bad roots grew. But the jabber of gutter Spanish and the alien cultures of the Puerto Ricans, the blacks and the others, blinded Ben to the similarities. He could only see the differences. Compare and contrast: an essay question for the week, for every week. All Ben needed was a pretext.

"We're a peaceful, hard-working people," Ben went on, "and there's more Jews trying to do good for others, even for those *ver-kakte* muggers and bums, than anybody else."

"Quarrelsome, stiff-necked, obdurate is more like it," Max said. "The old guys had it right. Look at the prayer book. It's all there. They knew it five thousand years ago."

"And that makes the Jews killers, murderers, rapists, muggers, robbers?"

"You admit we have our share!"

"Very small share," Ben said, biting deeply into his corned beef sandwich.

"Because they were afraid of the six thousand rules that the old rabbis, who knew what it would be like without such regulations laid down to keep us in line!" Max said.

Ben chewed, swallowed and smiled triumphantly. "It worked, though, didn't it?"

"From fear of the Almighty's thunderbolts, that's all."

"Who cares why?" Ben retorted. "What works, works. And besides, my fine scholar, there were only six hundred and thirteen Mosaic rules for the conduct of your life."

"And who obeys them today? Only the real orthodox. Not your average Jew."

"The spirit of the law still governs our life, if not the letter," Ben countered.

"It's changing," Max said, trying to conclude the conversation with the victory of an undisputable point, just as he finished his sandwich. "And when the glue of oppression no longer holds Jews together, the authority of all those rabbinical laws will diminish, and their lives will be like anyone else's. Except they'll sentimentalize the old days. And all the suburbanites will read stories about the wonderful times in the shtetl or on the Lower East Side, and pine for 'the good old days.'"

"They were!" Ben said.

"Rose colored glasses!" Max answered and demolished the last wedge of pickle.

Ben turned his attention to the rest of his sandwich and the heap of sauerkraut he took from the relish counter.

"Makes the world go round," he said when they stood outside on Houston Street in front of the delicatessen. Cars were double parked while their drivers ran into Katz's for sandwiches "to go," and Ben and Max had to wait in the car until the owner of a brand new Cadillac came out carrying a brown paper bag so they could pull out of their parking space.

"What does?"

"Different opinions!"

161

"I'm surprised to hear you say it," Max said.

"It must be the corned beef," Ben answered. "C'mon, I want to show you something," he continued as he guided his car out into traffic. "Then I'll drop you at the dormitory."

Max had a glimpse then of the possibility of knowing Ben better, of being able to talk to him, and disagree and even fight, yet to come away from the conflict as father and son, the bond of indissoluble love only covered by mud, but still in place. He smiled at Ben, and Ben reached over with his right hand and gave Max a squeeze on the shoulder.

"'When I was sixteen, I thought my father was a damned fool, but when I was twenty-one, I was amazed to see how much he learned in five years,'" Ben said. "I think that's Mark Twain!" He looked proud of the aptness of his allusion.

"I'm not twenty-one yet," Max said.

"You will be," his father answered.

"What are you showing me?" Max asked, lighting a cigarette.

"Do you have to smoke?" Ben asked.

"I don't have to, but I like a cigarette once in a while. I smoke at least eight a week."

"Eight too many," Ben said, stubbing out his own butt. "You could live without it."

"Look who's talking."

"With me smoking is a lousy habit. That's why I'm telling you not to get hooked. I don't even enjoy it anymore, after the first couple of puffs."

"Teach by example not by precept," Max said. "Smoke your pipe or cigars instead."

"Oy," Ben groaned. "Proves you aren't twenty-one yet. Mark Twain was right!"

"But I'm not sixteen either," Max answered.

Ben drove south on Allen Street and turned onto Grand Street: "Right around the corner here on Division Street is the *shul* where I was bar mitzvahed. I wanted you to see it."

He swung the car to the left, narrowly missing a group of *Hasidim* who were crossing the street against the light, oblivious to man's laws on God's day. "Schmucks," he yelled out of the open window. The Hasids didn't even glance at him.

"They're probably coming from the same shul," Max said.

"Nah, to them it's *goyish*. Ordinary Jews are worse than *goyim* to them, a bunch of fanatics, bigots they are." He drove slowly down the street and stopped the car at the curb in the middle of the block. Opposite them, between two dingy tenements, was a vacant lot covered in rubble and garbage. Some Puerto Rican kids were playing tag. Ben stared straight ahead, tears filling his eyes. He wiped the little rivers away from his cheeks.

"I guess I haven't been here in a long time," he said, shaking his head in disbelief and woe. "You lose touch."

Max put his hand out and touched his father on the shoulder. He felt self-conscious doing so and hesitated, but the need to reach out was stronger than the inertia holding him back. "Everything changes," he said.

Ben stared ahead, blinking his eyes, holding back the tears. Suddenly he forced a smile, looked past Max and turned the car rapidly into the center of the street, with another quick glance at the vacant lot.

"Another chapter is closed," he said and drove on, not breaking the silence until they said goodbye when he stopped in front of Max's NYU dormitory.

Max didn't say anything either, but when he was back in his room he couldn't concentrate on the music manuscript that lay half rewritten on his desk; as his instructor suggested, he was trying now to avoid sentimentality by writing discordant harmonies. Sentiment, but not sentimentality, was the mantra. The morning hassle with unyielding Ben and then the midday adventure with vulnerable Ben kept distracting him.

Why did he ask for Max's company after that morning's argument? Was anything different now? What did he want to say? Certainly it wasn't only to save some money that his father had asked Max to go along him to the jeweler's, because he could have parked the car in a garage for a fraction of what he laid out for lunch. Maybe Ben was like a clever general in a military campaign. Finding that one strategy of attack failed, he chose another, circumscribing his risks and cutting his losses before the campaign had to be given up for lack of manpower.

Max pushed aside the music manuscript, took out some blank writing paper and began to write.

Dear Dad,

When you dropped me off this afternoon I saw how hurt you were. It must have been a helluva day for you with its ups and downs.

When I rode into Brooklyn with you this morning I thought that we had reached a dead end in talking, or at least that was what you made clear, and believe me I was sorry, although at the time I was kind of pissed off and had resolved that I was going to let you take your own sweet time in coming out of your grumpy mood, and then we might talk.

Then you called and we went to Canal Street and, believe me, it was great to see you absorbed in the happiness you felt in buying Mom a present and taking such pleasure in it. First I thought that you just wanted me to sit in the car, a sort of utility man.

But then when you wanted to go for lunch I thought that maybe you wanted to continue our discussion on a more open and adult level. I hope that was what you had in mind, or, if not, that you simply recognized that I was going to pursue my own inclinations for a profession and that you could either approve or disapprove, talk to me or not, and that I was going to do it nevertheless, so we might as well be friends.

Naturally I want your approval and support, and I realize that my change of plans has disappointed you, and, believe me, I even understand why. Okay; so there we are in the deli and what happens? The counterman goofs on me, and you use the situation to teach me an object lesson in the ways of the world: I'm wet behind the ears, you never seem to tire of pointing out, in one way or another. That may be so, but I can't use your towel; I've got to find my own, otherwise I'll never get dry.

Then I felt you were somehow mellowing, and beginning for a little bit to think: "Max is taking a different road from the one I wanted him to, but that's all right too, as long as he gets where he wants to go." That's what your admission that different opinions were what made the world go around was about, I think.

Then came the business about the shul where you were bar mitzvahed, and I saw how deeply that affected you, and I didn't know what to say. It was as though the sight of the empty space between two buildings brought together all those ideas of the past, all those dreams carried forward into the present to mean to you that they have no foundation; the past is gone.

I felt bad for you then and I do now as I write this letter, and I don't really know what I could say that would make any difference except to feel so guilty for disappointing you and for adding to the rubble heap of part of your dreams that I would mend my ways and change courses, and follow the one you had charted for me since way back before I was even born. But I can't do that. I'm also not a building that gets wrecked and changed because the tenants move out. I don't want to be in a position twenty-five or thirty years from now, when I take my own son to see a place that I once thought was important because it was where I dreamed of the future, and say to him, in effect, you should do what circumstances or my own choices prevented me from doing, and if you don't, my life is reduced to a vacant lot of rubble. I don't want to heap upon anyone else the load I can't shoulder, for whatever reason.

Becoming a doctor wasn't my dream; it was yours, and you grafted it onto me before I was even old enough to know what my own dreams were. But now I know them. The greatest pleasure I get in the world is from writing and playing music; that's all I want to do, and I want you to accept this in me, whether or not it's something you really understand or not. I sympathize with your point of view and know what you want. But I hope to be what I want, and I take full responsibility for my success or failure. Whatever I do with my life, it's mine. I want and need your love and support, certainly, but even without it, I'm going ahead in my own way. The history of my life is being written, Dad, and, hard as it is to accept, I'm writing it, not you.

I hope you understand that I had to write this letter and try to set the record straight. I don't want to hurt you, and want you to know that I understand and love you.

Your son, Max

No sooner had Max posted the letter than he regretted it. Did he really need to send this long message to his father, put into writing the muddle and confusion of love, obligation, willfulness, guilt that conditioned and surrounded him days and nights? Even the letter, he knew, was confused, and his English professor could have picked it apart for incomplete thoughts, lack of development, hopelessly mixed metaphors. Yet Max knew deep inside himself that the answer was yes. He had to write it, had to send it. There were things he just couldn't say to Ben face -to-face, because an expression, a frown, a silence when Max wanted an answer, would do him in, prevent him from getting across his idea. Max couldn't confront Ben's disappointment and anger without being thrown back onto his own for defense. In the thrust and counter thrust, the meaning behind the conflict would be lost to the techniques of battle.

◆

Phil was a little drunk as he tottered unsteadily in front of Max, who sat on the far side of the room staring at the clusters of people across the room, near the food and drink. The bursts of laughter, animated conversations, the brightly arrayed women: like a party. Why not? Max thought. Why not celebrate someone's death with reminders of living? Theo said it and it was a good idea, but it still bothered Max.

Rending garments, sackcloth and ashes, sobbing women in black shawls, bearded, sober faced men with white shirts buttoned at the collar but no ties, nervous hands wringing cloth caps as their nervous feet shuffled in the house of the dead. This he wanted to see, the immigrant forebears still in a shtetl of their minds.

And what did he get? Uncle Phil in his cups, smelling of gin and onions. Hiccupping. Swaying from side, he said: "Get me another drink, Maxie, please!" Then he plopping down next to his nephew and held out his glass. "He killed himself," Uncle Phil said, "just ended it all because he couldn't take the mess! Gin and tonic."

"You've had enough, Uncle Phil, don't get yourself sick."

"I'm no kid, Maxie. Just do me the favor. C'mon!" He looked up pleading, his eyes glazed or teary.

Max couldn't tell. He took Phil's glass and went to the bar cart, filled it with ice, squeezed a whole lime into it, and added tonic but no gin. Phil took a sip of the drink and looked at Max quizzically.

"Don't taste right," he said.

"New bottle of gin," Max answered. "Store brand. Must have a lighter taste."

Phil seemed satisfied with the answer. "He did," he said. "He killed himself just as sure as . . . " He looked around, "What the hell!"

"My father killed himself?
Are you serious?"

Uncle Phil looked at him disdainfully. "No, My father killed himself! Nachman copped out on his brief and illustrious career of selfless service to humanity. BLAA . . . EAGH!" he belched.

◆

One evening about a year before his bar mitzvah, after returning home from Hebrew school class, Max was told that Grandpa Nachman was dead and Max wouldn't be going to school the next day. Rita, looking ashen and drawn, but without tears, gave Arlene some money and told them to eat at the dairy restaurant around the corner. She had to go to the funeral home to make arrangements. Ben was coming back from his office soon and he would take Rita by car, and pick up her stepmother, Yetta, on the way.

"Come on, brat," Arlene said, grabbing Max's wrist. "Let's go. I'm hungry and I've got lots of homework."

"Ma, she's pickin' on me," Max protested.

For once, his protest against his sister had no effect on Rita. "Go," she said. "You listen to your sister when I'm not around."

"Get your hands off me, Hitler," he said to Arlene as she dragged him through the front door.

"MAX!" came his mother's raised voice through the half-open door. "Listen to Arlene. No trouble from you. I have enough!"

◆

"MAX!" said Uncle Phil, with the same tone his mother had used years ago when her father had died. "You're not listening. First you ask me questions, then you don't listen to the answers. Nachman hanged himself. In the chapel of the funeral parlor. Can you imagine that? That bastard. He had to make a dramatic thing, a spectacle, a show on the way out so everybody could see what they had driven the poor, persecuted Nachman to do."

"Why did he do it? And how come I never knew he'd done that?" Max remembered the numbed funeral. Rita's glum tears, grief, Yetta's wailing.

"You were a kid," Phil said. "BLAA . . . EAGH!" and gassed Max with the aroma of the contents of his stomach. "And what was the difference how he died to you? We were all so ashamed. It was enough that we knew and had to keep explaining to everybody some cock and bull story. It was in all the god-damned newspapers!"

"Why, then?"

"I told you," Phil said, drinking from his glass. "I like this gin. It's almost like vodka. You sure you didn't put in vodka by mistake?"

"I'm sure," Max affirmed.

"I meant, why'd he do it," Max continued.

"A fitting end to a noble life," Phil said, portentously. "He was embezzling money from the company, robbing his partner Goodman blind."

"How'd they catch him?"

"The bookkeeper got nervous. She was his chippy, and she knew about what he was doin.' After all, he was spending a lot of it on her, the rest on the horses. And then he said he was going to leave Yetta and marry this dame, Bella, so she kept quiet. But Nachman, he couldn't keep his fly closed, and he was messing around with some other woman at the same time. So this Bella, she finds out about the other one, and, to get even, goes and tells Goodman all. He threatens Nachman with the cops unless Nachman pays it all back right away, retires from the business and sells his share to Goodman at way below its value. No *schmegegge*, this Goodman, once he found out he'd been done in. Nachman can't pay, already owes the shys a bundle, and sees no way out but the rope. BLAA . . . EAGH! If he had done what Goodman wanted, the gangsters would have killed him soon after anyway. If he hadn't, and they didn't, he would've gone to the clink!" Phil drained his glass and handed it to Max.

"Make sure it's gin this time," he instructed, leaning his head back on a crushed velvet chair.

Max went back to the bar, and mixed another drink. This time he added the gin. *Phil earned the oblivion.* When he returned to hand his uncle the drink, Phil was snoring.

An hour later Arlene called out her brother's name from the second floor landing where she and Aunt Charlotte were struggling to maneuver an alternately belching and singing Uncle Phil toward one of the guest bedrooms.

"My yiddishe momme, ya da di deedle deedle dee..." he sang and added his own punctuation. "BLAA . . . EAGH!"

"Stop that, you disgusting oaf," nagged Charlotte. "It's sacrilege!"

"QUIET! BOTH OF YOU," Arlene raised her voice. "MAX!"

He walked out of the living room, where he and Ursula were sitting in silence now that all the shiva callers had gone, watching Samantha empty ashtrays and pick up glasses and coffee cups. He peered up the stairway: "What?"

"It's late," Arlene said.

"BLAA...EAGH! Deedle deedle dee," Uncle Phil continued his anti-command performance.

"SHUT UP, YOU LUMMOX," Aunt Charlotte scolded.

Phil lowered the volume, but continued singing, "Somebody loves me, I wonder who . . . "

"Max, take Papa's car from the driveway," Arlene said. "I don't need it and you'll get home quickly with Ursula without having to ride the subway. The keys and registration are on the kitchen counter."

"That's a good idea, Arlene, thanks," Ursula said, springing from her seat in the living room and walking to Max's side in the hallway. She pressed Max's arm with her hand. He knew he'd better acquiesce to the suggestion to avoid repercussions.

Later, as the dark-blue Cadillac Coupe de Ville flattened the bumps on Queens Boulevard from Forest Hills to the Long Island Expressway, Ursula said, "That was a good idea of your sister's."

"This car doesn't suit us," Max said, annoyed and feeling self conscious in the flashy car that marked the apogee of his father's career.

"It's comfortable. It'll get us home without the horror of the subway, and it's not a life commitment, Max. It's just a car. Anyway, I like it!" she said, with a sigh, leaning back on the reclining seat.

"Where the hell am I going to park?"

"There's a garage around the corner from us, so stop fussing." She closed her eyes.

Gliding off the Williamsburg Bridge onto Delancey Street Max said, "I'm hungry."

"There's food at home."

"No, I mean, I feel like a pastrami sandwich at Katz's."

She brightened: "Okay, a great idea. Now you're talking business!"

A few old men sat at a corner table arguing. Some truck drivers whose rigs lined Houston Street sat solitary or by twos and threes eating over-stuffed sandwiches and drinking tap beer from small glasses.

Max walked toward a counterman, a younger one who was about his own age. He looked around for the wall-eyed gnome, but supposed that he was long gone. Probably sound-asleep in Miami Beach. A short, dark woman with a fur hat was talking to the counterman in Russian, and he was responding and nodding his florid, heavy-set face.

"Next," he said, dismissing the woman with a smile.

"You Russian?" Max asked.

"I been here five years. I speak good. No?" he said with a grin.

"Pastrami good tonight?" Max asked.'

"When isn't it? Especially if Leo carves it."

A quick movement of the carving knife and he handed Max a steaming chunk of meat.

"And you want corned beef, right, Miss?" Without waiting for an answer he handed Ursula an even larger slice.

"Delicious," she said. "On rye, please!"

Out of the fullness of his mouth Max said, "Mine on club."

Leo made two sandwiches, one piled high with pastrami and the other with corned beef, and a separate plate filled with sour pickles and green tomatoes, and placed them on the counter. Max handed him the checks to punch, but Leo made the universal motion of rubbing his thumb against his fingers with the palm up, ticket puncher silent.

Max glanced up at the time-honored sign on the wall in foot high letters: TIPPING OF COUNTERMEN IS NOT PERMITTED.

"You know the ropes. You're no greeny," Leo said, waiting.

Max pushed two dollar bills furtively across the glass top, which Leo blithely pocketed, indifferent to managerial eyes, and punched holes in the tickets for less than the posted prices. For two dollars, Max had paid for only one sandwich.

"They never do that," Max said to Ursula as he launched into his sandwich.

She bit into a sour green tomato and said, "Famous first."

"They try to discourage special favors — except for the cops."

"But you love the special favors, and probably the cops eat free. Makes friends," she said, eyeing the huge platters of food the tip bought them.

Max never thought of tipping as a double indemnity.

"Do I look like a soft touch? I guess everything changes," he said through a full mouth.

"Not necessarily for the worse. Forget the philosophy and eat."

"Another chapter is closed," he said, and stopped talking.

Back in Ben's car, Max kissed Ursula and pressed her against him.

Later, he watched her from behind as she climbed the stairs, and when they got back into the studio, he wanted her, but it wasn't anything tender, no need for love or to be close. Just a surge in his groin, a need for an outlet, the kind of lust he used to feel as a teenager. Somewhere out in the muddy river of his life there was this shifting shoal that he ran aground on occasionally. A woman became the object of his desire, a pure "thing" that would receive him, let him thrust and wallow inside her, encouraging the heat and exploding together. Lust out, satisfaction in, no strings.

From the bedroom Ursula announced she needed to shower and wash her hair.

Max kicked off his shoes and stretched out on a sofa. Some music, a cigarette . . . .

# 10

WHEN MAX WAS IN HIGH SCHOOL and still living in Brooklyn, there was a girl he used to see on the train. She had dark hair that she wore long, and she had a full-figured, womanly body. Her olive-skinned face was open and smiling. She would appear where he didn't expect to see her — seated in the subway car, or passing him on a Midtown street. And every time their eyes met for an instant, she'd laugh to herself, but before he could gather himself to speak, she would get off the train or disappear in the crowd. He resolved that one day he would speak to her, find out who she was and why she laughed when he saw her, but that would take the courage to follow, to confront, to say words that he was afraid would be misunderstood, to be rejected. Instead, by the time he was seventeen she replaced Aunt Viola  and became his bathroom fantasy .

One Friday night Max played a gig in Manhattan, a dance in a basement gymnasium of a church school. The group was a pick-up quintet that Max used to jam with. The leader, Larry Lefkowitz, a clarinet and saxophone player, booked a lot of these fifty-dollar-a-man dances and brought in three or four of his friends to play. It was usually fun and good pocket money. They used the standard fake book and took turns improvising choruses. "Larry Lane and

His Lads" said the ornate, spangled script on the cardboard music stands Larry set up on the stage. The "lads" wore blue suits and black bow ties, and they felt like real pros. Larry and Max were even in Local 802, the Musicians' Union, although these jobs were below scale at non-union halls. But no delegates ever came to check out the contracts at a church dance; that was the unwritten law, so the worry was left to Lefkowitz, who got double the salary for his trouble.

In the middle of a cha-cha direct from the borscht belt, which the parochial school girls danced without style and their male companions could hardly follow, Max looked up from the keyboard and saw the girl from the train watching him. Her white blouse fit closely over her headlight breasts, and a tight, dark skirt emphasized the Rubenesque hips Max often saw walking away from him. Standing in the corner of the gym close to the raised bandstand, she swayed back and forth by herself, and she was staring at him.

When she realized he was watching her, she smiled, and suddenly his trousers tightened across his groin and he felt lucky to be the seated piano player and not Larry Lane honking his horn in everyone's plain sight. Comping lightly, Max watched the girl and constructed hot, new scenes for the porn flick of his imagination: Underpants and brassiere fell to the thickly carpeted floor of a bedroom, where the soft light of a dark-shaded lamp glowed on the pink satin headboard and matching plump comforter, ever so slightly pulled back . . ..

" . . . cha-cha cha . . . olay!" sang Sol, the greasy-haired trumpet player, giving a final stamp of the metal tapped heels of his pointy black shoes. He always danced in place as he sang the Spanish lyrics learned by rote, the dance a challenge flung in the blotchy faces of the male preppies, as was the Marlboro he emptied of tobacco and filled with grass that he lit as soon as Larry said, "take a break."

The fantasy girl approached as Max stepped off the low bandstand.

"Hi," she said, "you are really a good piano player."

He imagined that when he answered she'd be overcome with lust, fall on her knees instantly and zip open his fly with a practiced hand. Below the waist he shuddered with apprehension.

"I'm Max Bergman," he said, "the piano player," in case she hadn't noticed.

"Oh, you're not Italian?" She sounded disappointed. And in Max's mind the fly closed itself.

"My mother's mother was Italian," he lied. "From Argentina. Lots of Italians there."

"I didn't know that. I thought they all came from Italy. I'm Angela Battaglia," she said.

"Well, you're Italian, aren't you?"

She smiled at the quickness of his perception. "Yeah."

"And you're from New York? Right?"

More impressed by his razor sharp mind, she said: "So, what's that got to do with it?"

"Well, she was Italian from Argentina!"

"Oh, I get it!"

"Actually, my mother's mother was Italian, her father was German. My parents were born here, but my father's parents came from Russia. So we're very international!"

"Oh, that's very interesting," Angela Battaglia said. "When I seen you looking at me, I recognized you from somewheres, so I thought I would come over and say hello because I don't know nobody else here. My girlfriend who goes to this school told me to meet her here, but she didn't show up, so I was getting ready to go home soon. Then I thought I recognized you."

"Where do you go to school?" Max asked.

"I don't go no more," Angela answered. "I used to go to St. Francis, and I was takin' a commercial course. Then when I got to be sixteen I figured why go on? I ain't smart to go to college, and I don't like school so much, so I would be better off if I get a job."

"How'd your parents like that?"

"I don't know. They died years ago. I live with an old aunt and she don't care. I got a part-time job now and I give her money, so she's happy. Where do I know you from?"

"I always see you on the train, or sometimes in the city."

"Oh, yeah, that's it," said Angela Battaglia, looking pleased. "Then you must live in my neighborhood!"

They compared addresses. She did live a few blocks away, near the next elevated stop, which explained why he always saw her on the train. But those few blocks were a world apart. Where Max lived on Hewes Street, the people were mostly Jewish with a random sprinkling of Italians and a few Irish . . . very few. Four or five blocks down Marcy Avenue, going toward the center of Brooklyn, began the real Irish neighborhood, again with some Italians. There the houses were wood-frame with false-brick shingle covering. The richer Italians preferred the Jews as neighbors and lived in brownstones, or the occasional apartment house. The poorer, he didn't know, except that the rents were supposed to be cheaper further down Marcy, and there were bars on every corner. None in his own area. Max and his friends didn't go down Marcy unless they needed to because someone would always call them "sheeney" or "kike" and pick a fight. Sol, who was really Sal, lived there, and even though he was Italian, he was now disguised for his summer's borscht circuit employment, and his dark skin often earned him verbal abuse and sometimes a bloody nose.

The drummer tested his snare, a signal to the band.

"I gotta go," Max said. "Can I see you later? I mean after the dance. Take you home?"

Angela Battaglia's face opened into the happiest smile he ever saw. "Sure!" And then she was serious: "Would you play another cha-cha?"

"Got a request for another cha-cha, Larry," he said as he sat down at the piano.

"IT'S MAMBO TIME!" shouted Larry into the microphone and as the drummer started the rhythm Larry said "later" to Max and began a repetition riff of what the club date musicians called "the C7th mambo." With only two chords, the C7th and B♭ 7th, it was essentially a rhythmic exercise and an opportunity for Sal and Larry to play screeching high notes and do loud honking. They dived into the lead line enthusiastically and were already making the noises that impressed the untutored, who responded enthusiastically:

"Yeah . . . "

"Go, man, go . . . "

"Hit it, man . . . go . . . " came the shouts from the crowd, who, as usual, artfully gave in to their voices' superiority over their feet while one couple, more graced in the art of Latin dancing, became the focus of attention in the middle of the floor. The others, clapping and shouting what they thought you were supposed to shout to encourage both the musicians' ecstasy and the dancers' fervor, stood around the wriggling twosome in a large circle.

Max, his mind wandering, laid down the chords that required no attention and watched Angela Battaglia on the fringe, again her hips swaying to the music, her clearly defined tits bouncing with each move of her body. It wasn't a dream, and he was going to take her home. His lips were as dry in anticipation as his jockey shorts were wet with perspiration.

Larry shouted "Take it, Max" and pulled him out of his reverie as the band leader moved the microphone over to the old, upright piano. Max eased into his solo by playing up and down the two-chord harmonies in octaves and then thirds echoing the trumpet player's last phrase. Larry and Sol moved forward together, faced the audience and did a dance step in unison, a bit of showmanship they practiced. It would go over well on their Catskill summer job.

Meanwhile Max began to push his solo beyond the restrictions of the chord progression that limited the trumpet and sax players. He thought of the C7$^{th}$ as the dominant in the key of F minor instead of merely as a chord and the B♭7 chord as dominant in E♭ minor. Having established F and E♭ minor as tonal centers he then used the melodic minor scales in each of the keys with the root of the dominant chords as the epicenters. An enormous range of tonalities opened up because he wasn't limited; he was freed of the limits that the chordal playing of the horns' improvisation suggested. Instead he was in a realm of open space. Substituting minor ninth chords at the second step of the scale for the dominants, he expanded the possibilities and soared into a three-chorus improvisation that wove together thematic ideas already established by the horns with the syncopations and melodic phrases that were thrumming in his mind. He tried playing the modal formations his teacher had shown him, and found the mixolydian offering exciting possibilities. He was flying without limits of gravity beyond everyone else. All that confined him was the rhythm of the drummer. The bass player, completely confounded in his attempt to follow Max, decided wisely to lay out. It was free flight, and phrase after phrase linked together as though he were composing a sonata.

"Far out!" Larry shouted after the third chorus and pulled the microphone away from the piano for a last chorus to re-establish the familiarity of the mambo melody, brought to a shrieking loud conclusion by the trumpeter's high notes and the honking saxophone and crashing cymbals, the statute of limitations safely imposed.

"Man, that was incredible," Sol said to Max. "I never even heard playing like that on this tune. All I can do is run up and down the chords. What were you doing?"

"Come on, stop yakking," Larry ordered. "Let's give 'em a slow one," and he held up three fingers to indicate E♭ and started to play "The Nearness of You."

"Sol, do you know the changes on this one?" Max asked the trumpet player.

"Yeah, why?"

"Sit in for me, okay?"

"Where you going?" Larry asked between phrases.

"To dance with a chick, man, my golden opportunity!"

Larry wasn't too happy about Max's decision to walk off the bandstand, but it was within the unwritten law: You could take a couple of dances with someone as long as one of the other musicians would cover for you. Many a time Max led the group so that Larry could dance with a girl he fancied. There was no basis for objection and Max knew it.

Angela Battaglia felt as good to hold as he thought she would, and the pressure of her body against his gave him an erection. But she seemed oblivious to it, and pressed her bosom to his chest so hard that he thought he would walk away dented.

"If I said you had a beautiful body, would you hold it against me?" Max asked Angela, coyly, trying out one of comedian Groucho Marx's corny lines.

"No," she said, and he dropped two rungs on the ladder of his self-esteem. "I like to get compliments," she added, "because hardly no one ever gives me any."

So much for wit, he thought, and turned to other subjects.

"You are some terrific piano player," she said as the dance ended and they made a final dip. "Is that what you're going to do when you grow up?"

"No," Max answered. Wasn't he grown up? What did she mean? "I'm going to be a doctor."

"Ooh, that's great," she said. "I used to want to be a nurse."

Larry was signaling from the bandstand.

"I gotta go back, Angela, but we just have one more set. Then you and I shall go out for ice cream or something and I'll take you home. Okay?"

She agreed.

Tripping over someone because he was looking at her chest rather than where he was walking, Max stumbled up onto the bandstand.

"Look at him," Larry said, "he can hardly walk, he's got such a hard-on."

"You're jealous because you can't get it up," Max responded cleverly.

"She's got some knockers," Sol said.

"And a fat ass," Larry said.

"What do you like, big shot?" Max asked.

"Slim, sophisticated women, not pudgy broads built like brick shithouses," Larry retorted.

"He likes 'em to look like boys because he's a secret gay," Sol said, laughing to show he was teasing.

"That kind's good to look at; this kind's better to fuck," Max said, speaking from his vast bathroom experience.

"You never got your pecker wet except in the shower," Larry said.

"If I found a girl like that one," Sol said, "I'd go for her too. That's the kind that sticks with you, does what you want in bed. Built for comfort, not for speed."

"How the hell do you know?" Larry demanded.

"Italian girls that look like that, or Jewish girls like that, the same thing. That's what you want for a steady, not some skinny fashion plate like you like, Larry."

Max decided that the trumpet player was a man of infinite good judgment, and that Larry was a schmuck, which he knew all along.

"Shut the fuck up and play," Larry said, "or they'll all go home." And he launched into "When The Saints Go Marching In."

◆

"Ya wanna come upstairs?" Angela asked, after ten minutes of necking in the vestibule of her house.

He hesitated.

"My aunt's not home. She's staying over at my cousin's house in Flatbush. But I gotta call her and the phone is upstairs or she'll get worried."

When he seemed uncertain, Angela took Max's hand and pulled him through the inner door.

"Come on, Max, I won't say nothin' about you being here!"

"You sure it's all right?" he asked, standing in the middle of the kitchen. The floor was covered with brittle linoleum washed so many times that most of the pattern had been rubbed off, and there were religious pictures on the walls. Christ with thorns, the Virgin Mary and a couple of saints looked down on him mournfully.

"Sure it is. You ain't no rapist or nothin' like that," Angela said. "Lemme go and call my aunt."

He heard her voice talking on the telephone from another room and then she returned.

"Ya wanna cuppa coffee or some soda or sometin'?"

"Coffee would be great," he answered and watched her at the sink, her hips moved as she let the water run into the percolator and ground some coffee beans in an old hand grinder.

All she would let him do that night was unbutton her blouse and feel her breast, without removing her bra. Large, soft and round, cupped in his hand, but larger than he'd imagined. Other than hold it and squeeze it gently, Max didn't know what to do. They necked, his hands squeezing her, his fingers working their way under the wire and rayon.

"That's a little too far," she whispered in his ear when he touched her nipple.

He wanted her to move her hand down his body and touch his penis, but she didn't do so, and he was afraid to suggest it, so they stood in the saint-decorated kitchen, feet crackling on the old linoleum, pressing hard into each other, perspiring in the confines of their clothes, Max straining in his trousers, thinking he would burst the seams, and trying to hold back the rush of fluid he was afraid would come.

When the coffee was ready they sat opposite each other at the kitchen table and drank it, and he felt that this is what it must be like to be married to a girl like Angela — drinking coffee together every night in the kitchen and then going to bed with her and letting his hands play on her full, soft, round body.

He thought of her legs surrounding him as she made him keep moving, wanting more and more, begging, "Please fuck me again," until they fell asleep exhausted, only to wake up in the morning and do it all over. He would quit school and get a job anywhere if he could have that.

"I don't know anybody who's gonna be a doctor," she said, pouring him another cup of the best, rich, dark coffee he had ever tasted.

"Ever since I was a little kid that's what I wanted to be," he said.

"What about your music playing?"

181

"I'll always do that, just not for a living."

"You play so good," she said. "I never heard anybody play so good in my whole life."

"You want to go to the movies tomorrow?" he asked.

She smiled, happily pleased to say "yes," and he thought of the kinds of jobs he could get.

Another long kiss at the door kept his hands and mouth busy.

"I like you a lot, Max," she said as she closed the door.


Jules let them use his bedroom after the movies because his parents were away visiting relatives in Spring Valley.

She made him say he loved her, and that they would be married someday for the final admission ticket. He had spent a fortune on condoms, but he couldn't allay Angela's fear of getting pregnant. "At least not now," she said.

He went to the bathroom, removed the wrinkled rubber from his now shriveled penis because the evidence of his pleasure was seeping out, flushed it away, washed, and returned to Jules' now dampened bed.

"Wait till we're married next year," she said. "Then we'll have lots of babies. They have to be brought up Catholic, you know," she said, as she leaned over him to tickle his face with her big nipples.

Feeling himself get hard, he answered, "Sure, yeah, I know." Only agreeing with what she said would get him what he wanted: to be inside her again. He didn't even know what it meant to be brought up Catholic, except that you wore a cross, went to church, put those silly pictures on the walls, and had a Christmas tree. Big deal.

Angela kissed her way down his neck and chest until she reached his penis, and then, without hesitation, put her lips on its head and drew it into her mouth almost completely. At the same time she began to massage the area behind his balls with her finger, gently tickling the outer rectal ring. Waves of pleasure flooded through him different from anything he'd ever known. He couldn't locate the sensation in any one place. All of his groin and pelvic area tingled.

"Hey, what are you doing?"

"You like it?" she asked, letting him out of her mouth." I can stop if you don't," lifting her head and facing him.

He felt sudden cold and his penis dropped. "Yeah, stop, I love it."

She shifted herself over his chest, rear end to his face and didn't stop at all. He got hard again.

"Where'd you learn to do that?"

"From a book," she mumbled, hardly pausing in the up and down movement of her head and the massage. A force generated inside him pressing on the outer limit of his skin, a volcanic rumbling beneath the surface. He became agitated, shifted and thrust up and down. Angela picked up the same motion and kept the rhythm, her full breasts bouncing, flopping on his stomach, her large round buttocks slapping his face. Max tried to wedge his hand between her full thighs, but she tightened and pulled away.

"Not now," she said. "I'm busy."

Having made the effort to return the pleasure, he just let himself be carried on Angela's drive. The rumbling increased inside him, and on the Richter scale his tremor slid up to a high point, subsided slightly and then moved up again even higher. Now something new: Angela slid her fingertip into his ass, moved it around and pushed it into him as she sucked his swollen-to-bursting penis. She was fucking him! He groaned, moaned and the earthquake of his loins increased, thundering inside him, the sensations ricocheting from his navel to his knees. And then it was flowing; explosion after explosion rocked his body, pushing his hips forward, thrusting involuntarily out of control. He couldn't stop coming. The shock waves ran through him, again and again, shaking his body with intense pleasure. It was all over him, an almost torturous agitation, a re-arrangement of everything he had ever felt before, from his nose to his toes.

Max couldn't stop pumping his juices into Angela's greedy mouth, and she drank and sucked out more, swallowing the fluid as if it were precious, nourishing. When he thought he could take no more and would die if the coming continued, the contractions began to wane and reduced to small shudders at the base of his penis. And then there was no more, nothing left. He knew the meaning of spent.

Her face red and wet, black hair disheveled, Angela turned and smiled, her lips swollen. "Was that good?"

"Good?" he answered weakly, "it was the greatest. I didn't know there were such sensations in me. You are incredible."

"When we're married," Angela said, "I'll do that for you all the time, and more."

She gave his drooping penis a final kiss and straddled his chest with her fleshy thighs, inching her way back until her wet, dewy crotch was above his mouth.

It was a first for Max and he craned his neck up, then pulled her buttocks down to get closer. The heavy globes of her ass covered his face and he felt himself deliciously smothered by the warm, moist flesh. She pressed her cunt directly against his mouth and he inserted his tongue as far as it could go. The roots strained in his throat, but he plunged in and around without a pause, until she began to moan. His shoulders were imprisoned by the weight of her thighs and all he could do with his hands was to rub her back and her wide hips.

Angela reached back and guided his hand to her breast, placing the thumb and forefinger around the nipple and pressing his fingers gently to show him how she wanted to be massaged. When he moved the other hand to her left breast she began to moan more. "Oh, oh, oh . . . that's so good . . . OOH . . . "

He dove with his tongue deeper and harder, more frenetically. It was sore and hurt, but he kept going while Angela pushed down with her arms and arched her body backward until she was sitting fully on Max's face, all of her weight pressing him down into the pillow, smothering him, locking his nose and mouth inside her. He had to gasp for breath.

"Don't stop," she pleaded when he withdrew his tongue for an instant. "Don't stop," she repeated. "I'm gonna come in a minute."

He hoped it was a short minute because his tongue would fall off if he didn't stop soon.

Angela reached for her clitoris and massaged it while Max's tongue worked its way in and out. She rubbed with two fingers in a circular motion and suddenly Max felt her begin to contract inside. The walls of her cunt crushed on his tongue in sharp spasms and Angela screamed with pleasure.

"Aaaaah . . . aaaah . . . keep going," she gasped.

Max kept plying his tongue, his hands useless at his side now that she had pushed them away from her enlarged and stiffened nipples. Pinned down by her thighs, her legs doubled on his shoulders, her fleshy buttocks over his eyes, Max had little choice but to do as she bid. He thrust his tongue, rolled it around the inner lips of her vagina, while she rubbed and massaged her swollen clitoris. Billow after billow, the waves of her coming flowed down inside Angela while she kept massaging, rubbing herself, polishing her magic lamp to bring out all the genies. A wash of warm sticky fluid descended into Max's mouth, tasting like salty, slightly sour milk. He couldn't turn, he couldn't move his head, and he had to swallow her juices in order to breathe.

"Oh . . . wow . . . oh . . . man . . . that was the best ever . . .," Angela said after her excitement subsided and she lifted her weight from him and lay at his side. "Unbelievable!" she repeated several times.

"Why is it," Max asked after they both caught their breath, "that you came so much like this, but couldn't the regular way?"

"This way I can't get pregnant, can I? And when I can take you in my mouth, I don't have to worry about the bag slipping off or a leak, so I don't mind really going to town."

"I never felt like that in my life," he said, with a twinge in his groin as he recalled how she had drawn every drop out of him, made his body quake and erupt.

"Wait until we can do it all the ways and not worry about anything. That'll really be something," she said, and fell asleep.

Max couldn't wait.

♦

This is what really happened between Max and Angela —

Max did see her on the train or sometimes in the city. He didn't know she lived so near him until the day that he met her at the church dance. But it was Max who spoke first and afterwards he took her to Schraff's for an ice cream soda, and then home. He kissed her chastely in the vestibule of her house and then reached for her breast in the dark until she pushed his hand away.

"Come upstairs for a little while," she said. "My aunt is visiting some relatives and won't be home yet."

Max was hardly able to walk up the stairs because of his erection. Forbidden fruit, that's what he was reaching for, and kissing her soft lips, and a brief touch of her cantaloupe-sized breasts only increased his hunger. Fortunately the weather was cool and he wore a loose fitting raincoat over his blue suit, so his predicament didn't show. But the best laid plans went awry when Angela opened the door to her apartment and they entered the kitchen full of religious pictures. A shuffling noise and a cough in the corridor leading to the rest of the house interrupted their magnetic movement toward each other.

Max froze and his trousers grew instantly more comfortable.

"Angie? That you?" said a short, rotund, middle aged woman who wore a long, striped dressing gown over her large, pear shaped body. She had black hair tied in a single braid behind her head and a dark mustache on her upper lip.

"Angie, is it you?" she repeated, peering into the dimly lit room.

"Yeah, Aunt Theresa, it's me, and this is the boy who brought me home. He lives nearby."

Aunt Theresa rotated toward Max and squinted hard into his face. "You look like a nice boy. What's you name?"

"Max Bergman."

"Bergman. Bergman," she repeated, as though searching her memory for a key she had left somewhere in the dark.

"Any relation to Doctor Bergman . . . the foot doctor?" she

pronounced Ben's title "doctorrey" and rolled the double "r."

"He's my father," Max admitted.

"Oh! I'm a know him verrah well," Aunt Theresa said." I see him every month to take off these tings dat hurts my feets."

"Corns and callouses," Max supplied the information.

"That'sa right. You a smart boy . . . gonna be a doctor, right?"

Max confirmed. Did all his father's patients know this?

Aunt Theresa beamed with her information; "You papa talk about you all the time. He's a nice'a man. Angie know him too. I'm glad my Angie makes nice'a friends." She smiled, her moustache stretching over-widely spaced front teeth, squeezed Angela around the waist, and turned back toward the corridor.

"Welcome to my house," she said, motioning with her head, and then she shuffled to the doorway. "Angie, give the man something to eat, some wine, coffee, whatever he wants'a eat. He looks'a like he's'a hungry, and too skinny."

"Nice to meet you," Max said.

"My Angie, she's a good girl, you know what I mean," Aunt Theresa said, stopping again in the corridor, her head turned to face them. "And I know you papa. Good night!"

"Good night," Max and Angela said at the same time. They sat on opposite sides of the white enamel topped kitchen table and talked for another half hour, nibbling at anise-flavored cookies that Max didn't like and sipping red wine, without touching. When he left Angela gave him a brief and distant kiss.

"You'll call me?" She wrote her number on a scrap of paper.

"Sure, I'll call you, and maybe we'll go someplace next weekend if I don't have a gig."

"I can't wait," she said.

Max lifted his eyes from her bosom to her expectant face and left quickly.

The following Saturday afternoon Max had a piano lesson in the city and a rehearsal of a big band at one of the grimy studios on 48th

Street. He then returned to Brooklyn and went to his father's office to wait for Ben to lock up. Together they walked toward Grandma Bergman's house — Ben's mother, Sarah Leah — where her children and grandchildren visited every Saturday afternoon — a family tradition.

A trolley had broken down on the corner at Marcy Avenue and Division, and the strong smell of ozone floated on the unseasonably warm and hazy air. The passengers were waiting at the curb for the another trolley to continue their journey.

"Jewish girls?" Ben asked, and then hesitated as they crossed the street. "There aren't enough of them in the world for you?" Ben continued when they had passed the crowd at the corner and were walking up Ross Street toward Grandma's house.

"Sure there are!" Max answered with trepidation, knowing that he was being stalked, but not agile enough to outfox the hunter.

"SO WHAT ARE YOU FOOLING AROUND WITH THE ITALIANS FOR?" his father yelled, stopping and facing Max, his face red and apoplectic.

"I'm not!" Max protested, "I'm not!"

Ben's hand moved so fast that Max didn't have time to duck. The open palm caught him on the cheek and stung like a dozen hornets.

"That's for lying to me!" Ben said. "Anything I can forgive, but not a lie."

Max started to walk away, but Ben held fast to his arm with a grip stronger than his slight appearance suggested was possible. Some elderly women sitting in the late sun on wooden folding chairs in front of their apartment house witnessed the slap from the other side of the street, stopped whatever they had been talking about and stared. A free show, the event of the day, Max thought, glaring at the audience. Ben propelled him along the shady sidewalk, away from the *yentas*.

"It's enough embarrassment," he said. "We don't have to give those big mouths something more to talk about. I'm well known around here."

Then silence and the unrelenting grip until they got to Grandma's doorway.

"And speaking of lies," Ben said, stopping and pulling Max around to face him. "Since when is your mother an Italian from Argentina? What are you, crazy? A pathological liar?"

Max was stunned by the information Ben had.

"I thought her mother was from Argentina. Wasn't she?" he pleaded.

"Not Italian! Romanian Jews from Bucharest who emigrated to Buenos Aires, and then came here later. That's all. Don't make up fantasies to embarrass us!"

Max was silent.

"And," his father went on, "what kind of stupidity is it to fool around with Italian girls? What do you want . . . to get in trouble? You're so wet behind the ears! If you get a girl like that pregnant, your goose is cooked."

Max hoped that his cock would be cooked and thought nearly all week about how to get Angela into bed at Jules' house that night while his friend's parents were out of town. His plans were being shredded before his eyes and he was powerless.

"With a Jewish girl it would be bad enough, but at least, something could be arranged, but what do you want to fool around with a *Taliener*?" Ben used the Yiddish for Italian.

"She's just a girl I met the other day, from the neighborhood," Max protested.

"Mrs. Battaglia came into my office today," Ben interrupted, "a nice old woman, been my patient for many years, and began to tell me how she didn't know that your mother was Italian and how nice it was that we had something in common. And I felt like a god-damned fool."

Max smirked, and Ben grew angrier.

"I didn't raise you to see you blow it all away because some little slut gives you a hard-on," Ben yelled, his glasses steaming from the heat in his face.

They stood aside to let an old couple enter the building, returning the greeting, "*Gut Shabbos.*"

"I'm not blowing anything away," Max protested. "Why do you call Angela a slut? She's not."

"You wouldn't know, and you're too naive to know the difference."

He pushed Max into the tiled hallway of the apartment house. It smelled from the weekly Friday afternoon disinfectant washing that mingled with the cooking odors of chicken and onions, and lemons and tea, which Max always remembered as the aromas of old Jewish homes.

"Listen, you never lie to me again or you'll get worse than a slap in the face. Does it hurt?"

"No," Max said. It did, but he wouldn't give Ben the satisfaction of admitting that.

"And you watch yourself with the girls. Only Jewish girls. Clear?"

Max nodded a long frown on his sullen face as he saw a week's dreams of conquest fading into the air he must breathe as his father commanded.

"And even to them you don't do anything. And you're right about one thing: Angela's a nice girl, not a slut, all the more reason to keep your hands off."

"But I'm only human, Pop."

"Then you go to a whore," Ben said, pronouncing the word "hoo-er."

"But don't go sticking your pecker into some nice girl who won't know what to do with it and wind up with a pregnant shiksa on your hands, or even a Jewish girl, which is better, but in some cases could be worse. Not 'til you're finished with your education and you can afford to get married."

Max said that he couldn't believe that his father was telling him to stay away from girls until he was established as a doctor.

"Stay away, I'm not saying," Ben said. "Just don't go too far."

"Never touch a woman until I'm twenty-seven or eight? What are you, nuts?"

190

"Well," Ben weakened, "at least not now. A teen-age *pishiker* shouldn't get mixed up with girls yet. I mean in a serious way."

"Maybe you'd be happier if I was AC/DC! Then you wouldn't have to worry about abortions and all that shit," Max said.

He pulled his arm away and went through the inner doorway into the long dark hallway leading to his grandmother's apartment.

Puffing, Ben hurried after him.

"My God, Maxie, what are you saying? A son of mine, queer? God forbid. What a terrible embarrassment that would be, and where would I get a grandson from?"

"Yeah," Max said, "that'll be better, Pop, and you wouldn't have to worry whether my partner was Jewish or not. What's the difference?" He relished the discomfort he was causing Ben, who seemed agitated and looked worried.

Ben took his glasses off and wiped his face with a handkerchief. "But Max, you're kidding, aren't you? Teasing me, getting even?"

He whirled around and faced the street looking away from Max, who stood at the foot of the marble steps leading to the second floor where Grandma lived. The hall was dark, Pinesol disinfectant pungent in the still air.

"And Jules is bent, and Sol, and all the guys in the band too. And when I tell you I go to rehearsals of the big band I really go to Greenwich Village for an orgy. All the guys in my school are gay — that's the new word — except for a few straight oddballs — that's new too, and all the girls are lesbians. That's why this Angela was a refreshing change. I thought I'd try to see what's it like to be a real guy, but if you don't want me to. . .. "

Ben turned back to face Max, with a half smile, a pressed-up crescent on a background of pain.

"Now I know you're teasing me," Ben said. "Not my Max. Nothing like that for him, huh?" Ben held out his arms in the gesture of a spread embrace toward his son, and Max reluctantly moved toward his father until he was close enough for Ben to grasp him and squeeze him in a bearish hug.

"I'm sorry, Max, if I hurt you. I'm sorry I hit you like that, but I was so upset when that old Mrs. Battaglia told me about her daughter and you. I couldn't stand to see you throw your life away. I want you to be somebody, not just a corn and callous cutter like me."

Max held on to his father for a moment in the dark hallway, and the odors of pipe tobacco and cigars on Ben's jacket replaced the hall smells. He pulled himself away when he could without hurting Ben's feelings. Now there were tears in his own eyes. His father up-close made Max remember when he was younger and Ben held him close more often, when it was acceptable to both men's own idea of the limitations to manly affection.

"People will think that we're gay," Max said.

Ben put his glasses back on and ignored the provocation.

"Did you say Angela was her daughter? Max asked. "I thought she was her niece."

"Nah," Ben said, "the poor kid has no father. Theresa got knocked up by some guy who left her even though he promised to marry her. Disappeared. So Theresa made up the story to save face, about a sister who was killed along with her husband in an accident, and Angela being left to Theresa as the only living relative. She went back to Italy to try and find the guy and had the baby there, so who's to know?"

"How do you know?" Max asked.

"My patients tell me lots of stuff. They trust me. It's a professional relationship and all that. Don't repeat this, ever! Angela doesn't know."

They walked toward the worn marble steps. The lights in the hallway flickered once then came on as Max and Ben climbed. Ben unwrapped a cigar. He could smoke now in Grandma's house because it was officially sundown.

"I also got another patient, a good lookin' woman about thirty. She's a pro . . .."

Max looked at his father, not understanding.

Ben stopped at the landing, found a match for his cigar, and, after he puffed out enough smoke to compete with the other aromas in the hall, he said, "I mean she's a prostitute, a hoo-er. But nice, clean. Good looking too. I could talk to her about maybe seeing you once or twice. Better than knockin' up some little girl who don't know better, and she'll teach you a thing or two also. What do you say? A deal?" Ben stuck out his hand.

Max grasped it, dumbfounded in disbelief at the events of the past fifteen or twenty minutes, of the entire week for that matter. Did Ben really offer to get Max laid? Or maybe he was dreaming? Max pinched his thigh. It hurt.

"Come on," Ben said affably, taking Max by the arm, gently this time. "They'll think that something happened to us. Want a cigar?"

A month later Ben announced that he and Rita had found a new apartment in Forest Hills and would move at the end of June when Max finished the school year.

# 11

"SOMETIMES YOU ARE REALLY grotesque," Ursula said when Max had suggested making love after she returned from her shower. She pulled off her bathrobe and slipped into bed, turning away from him, toward the wall of their sleeping loft at the rear of the huge studio.

"I can't lie here in the dark and look at the ceiling. I keep thinking that I'm in a coffin and the lid is being closed," he replied after a few minutes. He had been listening to her deep breathing for a long time and spoke louder this time to wake her.

Ursula put out her hand and touched his hip. The hand was cool and didn't caress. It lay dormant on his skin.

"So because you have a vivid imagination, I shouldn't go to sleep when I feel exhausted and don't want to say a word, when my body is pulling away from my head. Just because Max wants, I should open my legs and lie still, or worse, pretend that I enjoy being fucked by his lordship. What the hell am I, just another piece of meat, seconds, dessert after the pastrami sandwich?"

"You don't understand, Ursula."

"And I don't want to, Max. Good night!" She pulled the cover over her head, hand withdrawn.

"But . . . " he said.

"Go jerk off," she said, and nothing he could say would get her to respond. He decided against taking her advice; he wasn't going to be manipulated by her. He buried his face in the pillow and, thinking that he wouldn't be able to sleep, soon did, and dreamed . . .

♦

". . . I'm not sure how to voice this, Professor Bergman," the student was saying. Max was sitting at the desk in his Juilliard office, staring out the window at the traffic on Broadway, thinking about Angela Battaglia, whom he had just seen on a train. They made a date. She looked the same and lived alone now. There was no question in his mind about the agenda for the date. In fact she said so.

". . . *I hid from them in the open country / And the reports came from outside . . ." the madwoman sang in my opera. I think that phrasing needs to be altered . . .*

The student's problems with voicing, harmony? Dammit! The last thing in the world he wanted to hear about was somebody else's work. He was too wrapped up in his own problems, in meeting Angela again after all these years.

"I'm trying to create the tension you might feel from too much random energy," the girl went on, oblivious to her teacher's distraction. She was annoying him with her incessant chattering. "You know, Professor Bergman, like the traffic on a city street at rush hour. The energy of all those people who are rushing to different places, but who have to be on the same road, the same bus, the same street for a moment. But I don't want it to be flighty, sentimental, sort of pseudo-French, Paris boulevards. Of course I've never been in Paris myself, but, you know, Professor Bergman, the bustle that Gershwin gets into 'American in Paris.' Nothing cute . . . "

♦

The light from the window was defying the dirty glass skylight and streaming down on Ursula's yellow hair spread all over her pillow. Her eyes, fastened on Max's sleeping face, suddenly woke him. Ursula

196

was saying something, asking him a question: "Getting some?" she asked again, "Who were you dreaming of? Not me! Someone cute?"

He adjusted his eyes. No, not cute, but beautiful. Ursula was beautiful in an open way. Spring, and early summer, not the full-fledged ravage of August heat. He leaned toward her as she watched his face, a puzzled expression clouding her gray eyes grayer.

Max bent over Ursula and kissed her fully on her unadorned morning lips, ran his hand through the silkiness of her hair. He felt her respond, a curious little tongue making forays into the unknown territory.

"Not home yet," he said when he broke away, feeling that she would have continued for as long as he could stay in that position. He also wanted to anticipate any annoyed reaction or response with a good offense.

"Not home yet," he repeated. "I'm not concentrating on you, all engrossed in my own thing. You're too beautiful to look at this minute. I'm absent. Let's reschedule."

Ursula responded by sitting up. She grabbed his face with both hands, and kissed him. This time the tongue wasn't tentative. Then holding Max as though he were a cello, Ursula played him vigorously, coaxing the fullest response from his lower register. Her blond hair and soft body covered him, lay alongside, under, gripping, sweating, straining, urging, pressing, drawing from him every bit of power, until, at last, when he was sated but still firm, she pulled him onto her and, gripping his waist with locked legs, she came with a series of convulsive groans, holding him still with her hands in the small of his back while she writhed with the pleasure of her own orgasms.

Afterwards he lay back, his eyes half closed, his attention wandering from the collection of teddy bears on a shelf above a small worktable that served as Ursula's desk to the framed manuscripts of medieval music on the white walls of the room. An electric keyboard he often used with earphones late at night was hidden in the corner, its top completely covered with music and manuscripts, and above the keyboard a photograph of Mahler, who looked down on the scene benignly. *Was he thinking of Alma when it was taken,* Max wondered? *Where had Mahler been just before the picture was taken?*

"That was great," Ursula said, planting a gentle kiss on his lips and handing him one of the two cigarettes she had just lit.

"What are we doing here?" he asked. "And who are you?"

"You don't know?"

"I'm not a moron," Max said, pulling himself up on one elbow and staring at her. "I meant you look like a Botticelli Venus."

"No, you're not a moron! And I'm not Venus! I'm more than a painting. But you always live in your head, not here on earth. Yeah, at least in looks, I'm your classic, blond shiksa, but my eyes are gray, not blue. So you re-create me as if I'm a character in the novel of your life, endlessly rewritten, probably with blue eyes. That's what you can make believe you're doing here: fucking a good looking Christian or Pagan goddess even though you know she's really a nice suburban Jewish girl, whose parents attend a reform synagogue, and who went to Hebrew school and was Bat Mitzvah at 13. But your imagination trumps reality all the time, and you think that's okay. Well maybe it is for a book or an opera, but not here or at Arlene's or in everyday life. Don't act like a pretentious shit, like the creative genius who floats above it all. Here you live like a regular guy. Me too! Or I'll think that you are just a character, a stereotype, a cliché from a Jewish joke!"

Ursula wasn't angry when she spoke — or she didn't seem so to Max, and he had no one else's energy to build his rage on. He felt it subside.

"What I meant," he said, "is what am I doing, making love, en-joying myself, taking pleasure, and, so on, when my father is dead and not even cold in the ground?"

She blew a smoke ring at the ceiling and didn't answer.

"Huh?" he prodded her with his elbow.

"Oh, so when you were horny last night, that was okay, but now it's wrong because I initiated? What you're doing is being alive. We eat, we drink, we sleep, we fuck, we do our things, your music and my art, for others selling shoes, whatever, making a living. That's what it is. Life. With a capital L. It goes on, no matter who dies. Same thing will be when we go. You want to feel guilty? Have fun in your discomfort, but leave me out."

"Yeah, okay, like I didn't know that," he grumbled.

"You know it in your head," she said, "and when it pleases you, you use it. Otherwise, you want some kind of special dispensation from the concerns in the codes of the rest of the human race, like some kind of fucking prince: Max Bergman, Ph.D., Composer, conductor, Jewish Prince."

"But I'm not the same as everyone else," he protested, grinding out the cigarette in an ashtray Ursula held atop her navel. "I'm an artist; I have a different sensibility."

"So am I, and not by a long shot as accomplished as you, probably never will be. Maybe it's not in the genes, who knows? But I know that I have to pay like everyone else to get on the bus, and I have stop my car for red lights, just as you do."

"What does that prove?" Max asked. He was irritated now and wanted no lectures.

"It proves that everyday reality is there for everyone, including you, and that you can't beat the system, or not for long."

"You know, I thought that I was the abstract one, but I don't understand what the hell you're yakking about," Max said.

But he did. So he lay back on the pillow and stared at the ceiling. Mahler still looked down benignly from his perch over the electric keyboard, and Max thought only of chords, ten-voice clusters marching squarely across the keyboard, Debussy clusters. He sat up, climbed over Ursula's supine body and walked across the room to the piano. She raised herself a bit in curiosity, and a glance in her direction convinced him that she looked like Goya's "La Maja Desnuda," but with blond hair and an ashtray. Maybe he should learn to paint.

He unplugged the earphones, turned up the power and hit the keyboard with a loud augmented 11th chord against which he suspended the natural fourth, raised an octave so that the dissonant effect was painful with the fourth and eleventh adjacent. He moved his hands to another cluster, hinting cadence but not arriving, and went on playing a series of allusive overtones with a dirge-like, but syncopated, momentum. It was the same musical idea that had suggested itself when Max left the cemetery, which he sketched out and then played on Arlene's basement piano. Now he sat naked, playing loudly without fear of infamy, liquids of loving drying to a crackle on his thighs.

"No resolutions, don't you see, Ursula, no resolutions. That is death. This funeral march, never comes to rest, but always goes on. It doesn't end, it just stops."

Max pounded the keyboard, talking, swaying, his voice caught in a moaning, a humming of a haunting *bel canto* over the dissonance of the chords, tears running down his cheeks, dripping onto his chest.

Ursula reached for her dusty cello, daily tuned but rarely played, and drew the bow across the strings, trying to catch the upper voice of the clusters.

"F♯ . . . G♯ . . . F . . . B♭ . . . A . . . B♮ . . .," Max sang to her. "No, no, take it up an octave. Yes! That's it. Repeat half . . . half . . . eighth, eighth, dotted quarter, eighth, half . . . "

He called out the rhythmic values and she leaned into the instrument, her round, high breasts pressing it, her long blond hair hanging around her face, partly concealed; the bow drawing across the strings, with the tones Max called out surging across the room back to his ears. It was for him a transmission from beyond knowable space, and he felt for the moment the breath of immortality in the sounds as the two of them swayed over their instruments, each completely one with the sound, as though the cello and the piano were parts of their bodies. Max felt he was touching Ben and Rita across endless time. This wasn't a memorial. It was a reaching out, a union with what floated in the ether.

He stopped suddenly, exhausted, and hung his head to his hairy, sweating chest. He could go no further. Ursula raised her bow from the strings and looked at him, her face flushed, her eyes searching his when he turned to look at her.

" . . . and the Word became flesh," Max said to no one in particular.

"What's that?"

"In the Beginning was the Word . . . and the Word became flesh," he repeated. "That's what it means. What just happened. Gospel. Saint John. He got it!"

"It wasn't words; it was sounds," she said, looking puzzled.

She lit another cigarette after placing the cello back on its stand, and offered it to Max. He shook his head "no."

"Sound, words, logos, the same thing," he said, "bringing the inchoate into life. The Word became Flesh. Path from God's creation to Jesus. That's what it means. You understand?"

But he saw that she didn't. Only the connection he made with the origins of the music, the personal significance. It was still private, for him, lacking titles and other defining words. Not literature, pure music. It would remain only chord clusters in a stately rhythm somewhere between a dirge and a pavan. Six peacocks, fans extended, paraded across his mental dance floor, but how could she see them? He looked back over his shoulder at the framed picture of Mahler, who had surrendered his own torture for the moment of the photograph and looked serene, calm. What was he hearing in his head as the shutter clicked? The sounds he wanted to put on paper, but might fade before the photographer stopped adjusting the camera? Or was Almas's heaving chest gesturing in silence because she knew that Mahler wanted her and she was just waiting for the man with the black box on a tripod to finish and clear his stuff out of the house so Gustav could bury his face between her breasts again and nourish his genius in the way she knew best?

As though she was reading his mind, Ursula stubbed out her cigarette and walked across the room to where Max sat, and, lifting her breasts with her palms, pressed them around his face. Max sobbed, and then broke, a flood letting itself over the dam into her soft forgetfulness. On the bed again they rolled together from side to side like a lopsided football, hugging, kissing, crying, as Max could not remember happening before. There hadn't been such closeness when they were younger and more constrained by the forms of their adventure. Now it was as if some mold gave way and allowed them to flow outward, not yet annealed, to assume a shape much the same as planned but slightly different. He held her tightly and she gripped him with her arms and legs, forcing his almost limp penis into her, but only to hold him inside, hug him as she was doing with her arms and legs. Something he never felt before in his long, infatuated involvement with her replaced the tension, the raw lust, the hurt of being rebuffed, the anger of a failure to satisfy. A feeling of warmth and safety spread up his body from his toes and Max knew that he didn't just love Ursula as he always repeated to her, to himself, as though to assure each of them, but that he was also in love with her. He wanted only to keep the feeling he had at the moment. It was as close to heaven as he had ever come, and he wanted this to last for an eternity. In his music only would he play with the dark side. There he'd keep the Faustian compact.

"Max, love," Ursula whispered. "Don't leave me for some creature of your imagination, some girl of your dreams, or a ghost of the past!"

"Why do you say that?"

"Because you talked in your sleep all night, saying different names, and that frightened me," Ursula said, holding him tighter. "I'm sorry I was so sharp with you before we went to sleep," she went on, not letting go. "I just was too battered by the whole day, and I needed to get back into myself, not put on an act for your sake. Please allow me the same freedom you demand for yourself," she said as she stifled a sob, "and I'll love you forever."

"'Love is as strong as death,'" Max said.

"Stronger," she whispered quietly.

Max rolled away from her slightly and looked into her tear-shining eyes. The sun in the skylight still touched the trailing wisps of her hair.

Oh, how he did love her, and how little she really demanded in return. Ursula was everything he had ever wanted in a woman, and he had known it inside for all the years since they had met, but couldn't say so. What would have been an ignominious surrender to the values his father wanted to foist upon him now seemed like peacemaking, coming to terms by equals.

"All my thoughts are peopled by the past, and I can't help that," he said softly, turning his finger in the golden ends of her hair. "But they, the ghosts, can't . . . won't hurt you. I promise. Nothing can."

"They can, Max, but we won't let them, will we?" she asked, taking his hand in hers.

He shook his head in an affirming "no."

"Let's get married, Ursula," Max said after a short silence. "Let's get married and have a kid."

"Are you ready to give up what you have? The freedom, the lack of ties, the only limited responsibility to the world?" she asked, her eyes showing how startled she was by Max's statement, although her body was quiet and placid as before. "I hope you're not acting in some way because you think it would please your father. Even up the score, so to speak. Because if that's the reason, then I don't want to do it. Only for us, for you and me, only because we want to make something, a life, between us."

"A work of art? A joint venture?"

"No, my love. A human being. The art is finally just a painting, notes on paper, sounds in the air, a lump of chiseled marble. But a human life is more. There's something too sacred about it to tinker with. And you can't tear up the score if you don't like it, or paint out the blots and start again. You . . . we've got to be sure."

"I do feel that I owe the world a life," he said. "I won't deny that!"

"Okay, but not out of guilt, Max. Only out of love, or else we're sentencing ourselves to death."

"No!" he said, taking her wet face in his hands and kissing her long and softly on both cheeks and then her lips. "No, no!" he repeated. "Only to life."

And could he believe that what he was saying was true? That he wasn't giving himself the endless, rationalized manipulation, a sort of mental onanism? He didn't want to see himself as another Ben, holding a little boy's or little girl's hand while they walked, telling the child that when it grew up it would be . . . whatever? Was he dooming himself to repeat history by not studying it? Yet, there was a core in him where he knew that he had learned something, if only in his own pig-headed, obstreperous way, and that he was ready now to take on the responsibility of making life as well as making art, and that Ursula was the one he wanted to make life with.

He never understood the meaning of the word "mate" before, but it was clear to him that Ben was Rita's mate, and that much of what Ben did was a result of the union. To have made Max into what Ben was never to become was the way his father tried to immortalize himself. The man had tunnel vision. Rita had a broader view and was probably less vain. After all, she didn't have an idol to prove anything to. She only had herself to rely on. And now Max understood the irony of Ben protecting her against the depredations of her nonconformist son and trying to conceal from her the cancer orgy of her own cells. In that moment of the flowing out of himself to Ursula, he knew both the need Ben had to immortalize his dreams and protect his own beloved, and the futile vanity of it all.

"Only to life?" Ursula repeated. There was a puzzled expression on her face.

He just smiled at her and lay his head back on the pillow, watching the motes of dust flit through the sunbeams climbing the wall of the bedroom. "Something wonderful happened today," he said finally," And I want our life to be full of that."

"I hope it can," Ursula said, a bit sadly.

"Do you doubt it, really?"

"I'm worried, Max, about what happens when you come down from the euphoria into one of your long depressions. Can we weather it? Maybe something really happened for us today. Maybe not. Let's see when this awful time is past, when the opera is finally performed.

Then maybe we can get to ourselves and see where we stand. We're not kids anymore who can run off to Paris and live on air."

"Today was wonderful," Max said again, "and it changes things."

"Then thank your music, and not me."

"Modest!"

"Truthful!"

"Anway," Max said, "we won't have to wait long for the opera. Just 'til Friday."

"You're going to do it as scheduled? Despite everything?" Ursula looked alarmed.

"You said so before, love! Life. With a capital L, goes on. And that's mine, and then there's more us, etcetera," he said, feeling a bit embarrassed by how close to the surface his emotions were, how raw and open he felt, and yet, how happy.

Ursula propped an arm under her tangled mass of blond hair, and looked over at him across the tousled bed. A smile radiated out of the now deep gray of her eyes.

"I love you, Max Bergman. You really are an artist, and you're also becoming a mensch. Maybe I am too."

There were suddenly no more words to say.

He slept. An hour later, Max woke from a dreamless sleep to find Ursula sitting up looking at him, a soft smile in her eyes.

"Feel better?"

He nodded "yes" in silence, hugged her quickly, rose and crossed the room to a steaming shower.

# 12

"YOUR FATHER DIED FROM BEING ALIVE," Viola said, taking a long swig of her drink. Max lit the cigarette she dangled from her lips expectantly with the gold Dunhill lighter he picked up from the brass and glass coffee table. The living room of Viola's apartment had wall-to-wall white carpet. They sat facing each other at the corner of a black velvet, modular sofa that stretched around three sides of the room. She wore a black dressing gown to match.

"Sure you won't have anything stronger?" she asked again.

He shook his head, no, and sipped at the club soda.

"Arlene is never going to forgive me," Viola continued, "but I suppose she has already poisoned your mind against me."

"She didn't say anything to me," Max assured Viola.

Arlene muttered something about Aunt Vi, but he wasn't paying attention at the time and chalked it up to the old rivalry between them. The daughter resenting the mother's best friend, competitors for love.

"I'm glad you came to see me right after seeing me just last evening. I wanted to talk to you, Honeybunch, before she could really turn your head and make you dislike me, or even worse, forget me now that poor old Ben is dead." She wiped her eyes on an embroidered handkerchief pulled from the sleeve of her gown.

Uncomfortable in the silence, Max said, "I brought you tickets for the premiere of my opera on Friday night."

Viola stared at him without answering, and he continued talking because it felt better to have the baton in his hand, to originate the sound in himself.

"I thought about what the family would all say, with their 'nice' versus 'not nice' routine where everything you do falls into one category or the other as defined by god knows which rule — probably number 614. But it isn't going to do my father a god-damned bit of good if I delay the premiere, and if I wouldn't change my plans for him while he was alive, why should I when he's dead?"

"You're lucky it doesn't come out on a night when they sit shiva. Otherwise you'd never hear the end of it."

"It'll be a *shonda* anyway because he just died within the week, and it's Shabbos," Max said, feeling he had a sympathetic supporter, a member of a community of outcasts. "Very convenient for those self-righteous put-down artists!"

"I'm sure it'll be wonderful, Maxie," Aunt Viola said, "and everyone will be proud of you. Even your father would have. He was really looking forward to it."

"He what? Looking forward? You've got to be kidding. From the first thing, he didn't want me to use that story of Adelle in the asylum, as though he was protecting someone. Who? My mother? She gave me the diary and even suggested that I should use it. What in hell was Ben trying to prevent? Like it was his own mother. He never even knew Adelle."

Viola shrugged her shoulders, heaving her heavy bosom high with a deep breath.

"He was always afraid of embarrassment," she said. "He didn't want anyone to talk about him or his family in any way that would be embarrassing."

It was at that moment that Max realized why his father was so angry with him for the career change — he was embarrassed to tell his friends that his son, his *Kaddishl* — Rita hated that term —

would rather be a starving musician than a prosperous physician. And that understanding partially explained the polarities that defined the reigning moods of Ben's mind: good/bad, swell/lousy, a little in between.

"Remember the bug?" Max asked.

She shook her large, blond-colored head "no."

"In the bathroom. I must have been ten. I went in and there on the toilet seat was a gigantic roach, a waterbug, and I ran into the living room screaming. You and Uncle Mike were there. It must have been a Sunday. And my father came into the bathroom and killed it. Then he took me into my room and smacked me for embarrassing him in front of other people."

"I don't remember that," Viola said.

Max had been sure that the situation was engraved on everyone's memory, and was disappointed it wasn't, "You sure you don't recall?"

"No, I don't."

"I never knew what it was that embarrassed him," Max said.

"That's easy. The idea that someone else should know that there was bugs in his house. That meant it must have been a slum or something. Your mother was an immaculate housekeeper too."

"So why would a single bug in the bathroom mean anything?"

"It didn't. You embarrassed him in front of friends."

"Except for himself," she added shrewdly. "There he could bend a rule or so, as long as no one found out the secret. So secrecy avoided embarrassment."

"Like what secret?"

"Like being . . . " she lowered her voice, "a Communist . . . back in the '30s."

"Big deal, as though J. Edgar Hoover himself was going to ferret him out."

"You can kid about it, but for Ben it was very serious business, and he thought if anyone in the neighborhood discovered it, he'd lose lots of patients, his livelihood. You didn't live through the 'Red Scare' back in the '50s. You were just a little kid, afraid of bugs."

Viola stubbed out her cigarette and lit another immediately herself, not waiting for Max.

"Well, anyway, I'm going to do the opera on Friday," he said, "and if they don't like it, too bad. The whole thing is a fiction and it's only suggested by the diary my mother gave me."

"She used to cry about that, not about giving it to you, but about really having a mother and never getting to know her, or even to know that she was alive."

Max remembered something that had been tugging at his mind. "How did she find out about Adelle? That she was in that institution?" he asked Viola. "You were there, weren't you?"

Viola nodded her head, left the room for a moment and returned with several sheets of paper, written in a large, flowing childish hand.

"About the time Rita gave you the diary, she returned this to me; maybe she felt that it was time to settle things, ashes to ashes, sort of."

She handed him the slightly tattered papers.

Dear Rita,

I wanted to talk to you, and I stopped at the bakery yesterday, but you had already left for the day. Mama needs me home to help out with supper because Uncle Freddy isn't feeling well and she's got to make special food for him, so I have to cook for Papa and the kids, and so I couldn't go to your house. So I'm writing you this letter to tell you that I found out something the other day when your father came over to see Uncle Freddy after supper.

They were in Freddy's room that is right next to the kitchen and I was cleaning the plates off. Your father asked Uncle Freddy to loan him some money because the sanatorium upstate wrote him to say that Adelle needed an operation and she had no more money left. Uncle said that if your father himself needed an operation he wouldn't lend him any money because your father only knew how to take it, but not to give it back, but that Freddy would do anything for Adelle. He got up and went to his bureau drawer and said that he would lend your father one hundred dollars and he better pay it back soon. Then your father left. Uncle Freddy heard me putting the plates away and called out, "Who's there?" I said it was me. He said, "Come in here." When I went in he asked me if I was in the kitchen when Uncle Nachman was here and did I hear what they said. I told him yes because I can't lie to Uncle Freddy. He asked me if I knew who Adelle was and I said that I thought it was Rita's mother, but I thought that she died years ago, and that Uncle Nachman married Aunt Yetta after that. Uncle Freddy said that Adelle got very sick when you were little, and the doctors said that it was no use because something was bad in her brains, so they put her away in an institution. Nobody went to visit her because she didn't recognize no one anyway, and everybody thought it was better to tell you and Phil that she was dead, because she was just like dead and could never be cured. He asked me to keep this a secret because it wouldn't be good if you knew, it would make no difference. I promised him I wouldn't tell.

The next morning he gave me a letter to mail. It was to the Mountainview Rest Home in White Plains, New York, addressed to a Doctor Simansky. Rita, I know I shouldn't have done it, but when I got to work I asked my boss if I could use the telephone and he could take the money off my pay. He likes me and said yes. I got the operator to find the number in White Plains and called up Dr. Simansky. At first he didn't want to tell me anything but I told him I was Adelle Peretz' niece and I heard she was very sick. He said she was, but how come if I was so concerned I never visited. I told him that I thought she didn't recognize anybody or remember anything. He said that was only true in the first year she was there, but after that she was better. But nobody ever came to see her, and she thought nobody

cared so she stayed on at the home where she liked it, sort
of a helper-out. He said that now she was very sick and
needed an operation. I asked him if she could have visitors
and he said yes.

Now Rita, I don't know if I did right or was maybe
too fresh, but I arranged to see her this coming Saturday.
Dr. Simansky told me how to get there. Rita, here's your
chance. We spoke about this so much, how if only you had
a real mother things would be different. Please come with
me on Saturday. I'll meet you at Bridge Plaza at eight in the
morning. I hope God forgives me for being such a nosey-
body.

Love, your cousin Viola.


Max looked at the blowzy face that had dropped its defenses,
and a rush of sadness choked him. How little he knew about all of
their lives.

"All the more reason for me to have written the opera, and now
to perform it," was all he could say, "a kind of monument to my
mother's pain."

"But she could take it. Ben couldn't. Look at the way they
handled the business of her sickness. She accepted it; he pretended
to her that it wasn't there."

"Except when he wanted to use the situation to gain leverage
with me."

"That's not a very nice thing to say about your father; I thought
you loved him."

"I did, but it doesn't mean I have to gloss over all of his *shtick*
and pretend that he was the most perfect human who ever walked."

"No, that was your mother. If she was a Catholic, she'd be a saint."

"Once I made her into an Italian," Max mumbled.

"What was that?" Viola asked. "I didn't hear you."

"Unimportant."

She paused, and took a long swallow of her drink.

"What you said before, about Ben using situations to gain advantage. You think that was true?"

"A very political man, my father."

"Not after all that Communist stuff in the '30s," Viola interrupted. "I think he just lost interest. Oh, he was a liberal and . . ."

She stopped in the middle of her sentence as Max smiled and shook his head.

"I'm wrong?" Viola asked cautiously, as though she was afraid to be wrong.

"I don't mean political with parties, elections, issues and all that," Max answered, amused by the literal response. "I mean . . ." he continued, annoyed with himself for the feelings of superiority, the intellectual elitism he must have generated toward Viola, givens that should have been accepted and forgotten if there was to be any relationship between himself and the people whose accolades he knew he sought: ". . . I mean that he played the odds, manipulated me, my mother and sister every day, about everything. The whole purpose of it was to get his way, to make things work out the way *he* saw them or wanted to see them."

Viola stood up, heaved a sigh that made her very large bosom rise under the black velvet dressing gown, and carried her empty glass over to the bar in the corner.

"Sure you won't join me?"

She poured another large scotch for herself and added a touch of soda.

Max said he'd stick with the soda water, and rattled the ice in his glass to cover the silence.

"He knew how to live, Ben did," she said, seating herself opposite Max once again, lighting another cigarette, "and he knew what he wanted and went after it, so what's so bad about that?"

"When my mother was dying, day by day, he would keep up the big lie to her and cry to everyone else, and I wondered what for."

"What should he have done?" Viola asked, "kept a stiff upper lip?"

"But she was the one in need of pity, of compassion, not him!"

"You expect too much of people. He was just human, and the life he liked was on the way out along with your mother," she shot back.

"And when I went to Paris for that year to study, he tried to use guilt to make me stay, as though I could have done anything, as though I could have undone the rotten lies he and Arlene told Rita, the false promises, the bullshit cheeriness."

"You did what you had to do and he did what he had to do. That was that! Why look to put blame on anyone else? Enough with the guilt!"

Max mulled and then answered: "Because I can't reconcile myself to the whole damned thing. Because I feel that I'm alone, all alone in the world now. I don't even have him to fight with on the telephone. God knows I didn't like to be needled by him all the time, but better that than nothing, no one."

Viola sipped her drink. "I may be just a dumb broad, but I know self-pity when I hear it. And I don't like it. Not me, Maxie. You sound like he did when your mother died. The apple doesn't fall far from the tree. Anyway, you look just like him. Did anyone ever tell you that?"

"I don't see it."

"I could show you pictures of when he was your age, and then you'd see it. Your beard hides the resemblance some."

"Another time. I couldn't take it right now."

"No, me neither."

◆

After Rita died, Max used to go to see his father about once a week, riding out to Forest Hills on the subway, either to have dinner with Ben in the apartment or at a restaurant. Other nights Ben ate with friends or at Arlene's. Until two years later, when Ben moved into the Tango Palace, as Max thought of Arlene's house, and gave up the apartment, there had been an unspoken truce in their relationship. Ben was absorbed in his own grief too much to focus on the errant behavior of his son. Anyway, Max thought at the time, the Ph.D he'd earned plus the faculty appointment at Juilliard, although it barely paid the bills, reinforced the idea that Max was seriously pursuing a real career.

"So, how's the professor?" was the inevitable greeting when Max came through the door. Ben would mix dry martinis and would toast to a better future.

"Why can't I call you 'Doctor' now?" he asked

"I think it's pretentious outside of the academic world," Max answered.

Ben rolled his eyes, but said nothing.

Ben had retired when Rita weakened too much to be alone by day, and now lived on savings and investments. But Max thought his father was bored. His face had a grayish pallor, and he looked old and worn to Max. The immortality he had bequeathed to his father was wearing thin, like a veneer that has been rubbed with abrasives for too many years.

A couple of months before he'd moved to the Tango Palace, Ben was still unshaven and in his undershirt and when Max arrived in the late afternoon.

"I've been in all day. I'm going out later, so I thought I'd wait to shower and shave," Ben said.

"Where?"

"Oh, um, a meeting . . . Queens County Podiatrists' Association."

Max knew from the smell of gin on his father's breath that Ben had a good head start on their martinis, and for Ben not to be up, shaved, showered, dressed for the day and out in the early morning was unusual. A walk in the street, breakfast in a coffee shop and the morning paper was a ritual beyond time's assaults. Something was wrong.

"Is everything okay, Dad?" he asked. "You don't look so good."

"Sure, sure, fine, fine, just decided to mope around today. Nobody's waiting for me anyhow, so what's the difference?" he said with a shrug.

Max didn't pursue it until he got home and called Arlene.

"What do you expect?" she asked. "That meeting stuff is a lot of baloney. He's probably seeing some woman, and she'll milk him dry. He hasn't got much left, you know." Arlene continued by criticizing Max for letting Ben pick up the check whenever they went out to dinner.

"He won't let me pay. He insists on putting it on his credit card."

"But he doesn't pay the bills, you turkey! I found a whole bunch of them on his desk, and he's being dunned by everyone. I had to sit down with him and pay the bills myself. Be considerate in the future, huh? He has limited resources and he doesn't manage them so well, but he likes to play the big shot."

The next few times Max went to see his father, he brought a steak to broil and salad fixings, and they ate in the apartment.

But Ben finally moved to Arlene's, and Max's visits were fewer. He wasn't comfortable at Arlene's because they were always a word away from a spat. But Ben would not come into the city, and for Max to take his father out of Arlene's house to have dinner in a local restaurant meant his sister would of course be invited, only to refuse. Then Ben would coax her, even if she said no several times, until she relented. The problem with that was it changed the dynamic from just Ben and Max alone together as father and son, but Ben liked the threesome because it made them more of a family together again and it looked nice to the neighbors.

Also, after Ben moved in with Arlene he began to carp at Max anew, and Max blamed Arlene's influence, whether that was the reason or not.

◆

"He wanted me to be what he never could, and never let me forget what a disappointment I was to him for refusing."

"You got it on backwards, kiddo," Viola snapped. "He wanted you to have the security and recognition he never got himself. What do you think, he liked sitting in that office week after week, year after year, cutting off people's corns and calluses? You think that just thrilled him? He just wanted something better for you. For Arlene too, to be fair."

"Only in his own terms," Max rejoined. "It was only his way, and no other way, so that for me to come out and say that I wanted to choose some other way to make my life into something, there had to be a major upheaval."

"Nah," Viola said. "You're making too much of the whole thing. Sure, he wanted you to be a doctor, but then when you decided against it, instead of letting him just cool off and see that you chose what was best for you, *you* insisted that he put the kosher stamp on it. You were like the kid who threatens to run away from home and then asks his mother to walk him to the corner because he can't cross the street by himself!"

Max laughed. Old Viola had something right there. Max had tried to force Ben's approval, had worked for it.

"Yeah, but because I wanted him to see it my way, he never would, perversely, on purpose."

"So you should have had the sense to stop pushing," she retorted, "and he would have come around eventually. To other people, let me tell you, he never stopped boasting about what you were doing. You wrote something that was performed at college? He told everyone. You got a scholarship or an award? We all knew. Ben's weekly news of Max. And when you became a Ph.D. . . . . Oy!"

"That's why Arlene is so antagonistic to me, I think," Max said. "He never gave her proper due, and he should have. She became what he wanted me to be. Wasn't one doctor enough?"

"And what do you think?" She looked at him intently, a smirk on her face. Was there also a sense of superior wisdom on Viola's part? Did she feel like an omniscient goddess bemused by a naive mortal?

"I don't know, why?"

"Because she thought maybe he would love her better if she became what he wanted to be, or wanted for you."

"It didn't do her any good."

"Because your father felt insulted!"

"Insulted? How?"

"A woman could become what he couldn't? Unthinkable. And his own daughter no less? It made him feel small. Also he thought that once women have kids, they should let any career go. So whatever Arlene became, it would be a waste. So when she proved different, he was pissed off at being wrong. Besides, they never got along because they were both too much alike. I don't like to badmouth your flesh and blood, but she is the most petty, jealous, unforgiving person I've ever come across, even though I could never stop loving her. Not that I can agree with your estimate of Ben, but I see that you have a point. In fact, I sometimes used to think he was using me too, but I always got over that soon enough."

It was getting to be last night's talk, redux. They had only changed living rooms. Although Arlene irritated him and he often saw little hope for any real rapport between them, he didn't want to hear Viola recapitulate conflicts with his sister. For better or worse, she was all he had left now, and he would have to maintain a united front for the world.

"When you tell a stranger," he heard Rita's voice in his head, "they never forget."

He began to stand up, and started to give an excuse for having to leave.

"Oh, stay a few minutes," Viola said, looking alarmed by his movement. "I've still got something I want to tell you about."

She stepped around the glass table to the sofa he sat on and holding on to his arm forcefully, sat next to him, breathing heavily, looking tense. He smelled the thickness of her perfume, a deep jasmine, redolent with the mystery of seductive women and tropical gardens at night.

"I was with your father when he died," Viola said.

Max's jaw dropped. This was new.

Viola stared, not at Max, but at the opposite side of the room and continued to speak a rush of words pouring like a torrent through a burst dam:

218

"We had just made love, like we did most afternoons, and then we went downstairs to the living room. And your father said that he felt very good and very happy, and so was I. We had just decided that the whole business was long enough a secret and that we were going to move in together. I would leave Mike like I wanted to for years because there's nothing left there, hasn't been since Rebecca died. Ben went to the Victrola and put on a record. He said he wanted to celebrate and dance, and that neon sign that Arlene has — Ya' know the one?"

Max nodded silently.

"The 'Tango Palace' sign . . . was flashing on and off in the corner and Ben found an old record of tangos that he put on. And then we danced and danced, you should've seen the two of us, like kids we were, so happy. And I thought that at least whatever years were left for both of us we could be happy, because we had always loved each other. Not what you're thinking, not like that, but when Mike treated me like shit I always knew where to go. Oh yeah, well once or twice right after Becky died, when Mike wouldn't come near me, your father gave me comfort, but that was all it was, and then in the later years when there were other men because I had needs, and Mike just refused to have anything sexual with me for all those years, and when your mother was dying, and I was the only one she could talk to, the only one who knew that she knew what she had, she told me to look after Ben, to do what we both needed to do because Rita knew that I had no life with Mike. He had his horses and his whores, and every year he would hire a new little bimbo in the office, and I was supposed to look the other way. Well, I was fed up with that, and your mother knew it. And she knew that your father and I were great friends. I mean really friends, like we could talk to each other, and she wanted us both to be happy. She told me to do it for her, as a favor, because she knew what Ben was like, and that he had these ideas of loyalty so that while she was dying he wouldn't look at another woman. 'But you, Viola', she said, 'you're different. And I'm worried about him having nobody, no relief from this whole rotten thing.' She was also afraid of someone else getting hooks into him, because even though he acted like a *shtarker*, he was very sweet and innocent like underneath. His bark was worse than his bite."

Max said nothing, but continued to nod his head, amazed, and yet, somehow he wasn't that surprised at what he was hearing. Somewhere inside of him he had known about this, but he didn't know that he knew until just now when Viola shocked him with the announcement.

"Anyway, we were dancing around Arlene's living room like relics of a Fred Astaire movie, and we were talking about where we were going to get an apartment, or if we were going to move down to Florida, and having a good time. Your father was some good dancer, and such a handsome man, Max. I know I sound like a fool and a terrible, immoral woman, but we were so happy, and who was being hurt? Rita would have wanted just that, and we both knew it. And Mike? That son of a bitch would have welcomed me moving out. Sure he'd make a stink and threaten and all that, but I didn't care anymore because I had my shares in the business and he could make all the noises he wanted. All those years when he was screwing anything that had tits, that was all right! But for me, no. I had to go home and wash his socks, and manage the office, too. Well, the hell with that!"

"So we're dancing around the room. He could really do the tango, your father. When there was a wedding or bar mitzvah he would always do that with me because he liked to make a show of how good he was at it, and your mother was embarrassed, but not me. I love to shake my fat ass around on a dance floor. So then we were tired. Ben sat down in his chair and I went into the kitchen to make us some tea, and when I came back," she sobbed, drew a difficult breath, ". . . he was sitting there, just sitting, staring at the ceiling with his head laid back on the cushion. And I shook him, I tried breathing into his mouth, and then I called the 911 emergency number and then Arlene. She got there first."

Viola's stiff blonde hair shook with the sobbing that exploded from the depths of her body, and her face was streaked with the black smudges of her mascara.

Max held his arms open, and Viola lunged forward, hugging him convulsively, gripping her short, soft arms around his waist, pressing him against her heaving chest. They swayed back and forth, both weeping. And the flow from his eyes broke something in him, something brittle and hard that had been waiting to crack to pieces for a long time, held in place by the glue of obstinacy.

Max was used to turning all his feelings into sound so music became his laughter and tears. But for once he couldn't do that. The picture in his imagination was enough. Ben and Viola dancing around Arlene's over-decorated living room, sweeping around the plush carpets to the tango rhythm, while the sign blinked on and off. Courtship and happiness were real, and their lives then had something more than hiding in the embarrassment of what others would say. "It isn't nice!" didn't count. Whatever else would be, they had been happy with each other, and alive in that moment with everything to live for in front of them. How to cross that line between living as you wanted to and living as others thought you ought to? Well, maybe Ben had discovered that courage at the penultimate moment. Maybe he would never have been able to overcome the weight of the past, and it was just an intermission. Maybe, to fulfill the dream, Ben had to die.

◆

Rita had to die, too.

Max knew that when he left her to go to Paris that September, and knew all his rationales were false. Sure, he wanted to study with Boulanger; he had wangled a grant to do it. But underlying it all, the prospect of being with Ursula, whose MFA graduation present from her doting parents was a year in France, including rental of an atelier near the Boul' Miche, and tuition money for studio classes at the Ecole des Beaux Arts. Ursula was not a scholarship student, either in need or talent, but she was good enough for an indulgent father, and talented enough to benefit from the experience.

And Max? He wanted to be young and in love and a composer and in Paris all at once, and this was his opportunity. Rita's slow dying had gotten in the way.

Paris had what he knew he'd find because he wanted to: yellow light filtering through the gray of the old city and reflecting on the twisting cobbled streets, falling through the windows of the atelier onto a bowl of fruit and some objects Ursula set on a table near the balcony. Curtains stirring in the faint wind as they lay naked on the couch in the studio, love-worn and spent, looking across the verdigris copper roofs, toward Montmartre, the dome of Sacre-Coeur ablaze in the light. Satie's "Gymnopédie" played on the phonograph. The life of eternal art, an aesthetic spell . . ..

And then there were the walks: the treading in the famous footsteps of the past, a city redolent of everything Max wanted from his life, where Stravinsky had been egged at the premiere of *Rite of Spring*, where Debussy mused in the Tuileries, where Ravel refused to teach Gershwin saying he didn't want to spoil him, the cafes where Hemingway sat, the house where Camus lived, the noisy boulevards Pissarro painted. Beyond, in the countryside there were the rivers of Monet, the fields of Corot, the coast of Normandy: Honfleur where everyone had painted, and Deauville where Proust and Flaubert had walked. And finally there was the bleakness of that coast — Omaha, Juno and Sword beaches, where so many Americans had died in the invasion.

And then he would think of his mother, the cancer-invaded image of her emaciated body came stabbing into his mind, as she lay in her bed helpless, day after day, all the while he was living and feeling the tingling of every sense.

He studied with the famous teacher, and exercise after exercise tumbled out of him, out of the rickety spinet in the studio onto the heavy, staved manuscript paper, and the exercises turned themselves into fully rounded compositions as he moved from song settings to a sonata for clarinet and piano, to a string quartet, a fugue for full orchestra, and finally the opera's germ, with Boulanger's blessing of the conception and what she called the "sacred truth" of its story.

And Rita's looming death was always there, hovering vulture-like behind his left shoulder, waiting to pounce the moment Max's almost complete absorption in his own life nodded. It came barging in while he was walking, talking, making love with Ursula, sitting in a cafe . . . there it was.

Home for visits for Thanksgiving, Christmas, and Easter, he sat by Rita's bed and told her about France and watched her glow with delight as he described the sights and smells that had rooted in his consciousness. Arlene and his father, all smiles in the sickroom were all frowns and remonstrations outside. "As soon as she's a little stronger we'll come and visit you," became "here is where you belong," or "at least somebody is having a good time."

One hot afternoon, Max was sitting at the piano while Ursula sketched on the balcony. The telephone rang.

"Max," his father's voice gurgled under three-thousand miles of water and land, "Maxie, please come home right away. She won't last more than another day or two. The doctor was just here."

He heard the quiet desperation in Ben's voice, the edge of tears that his father was holding back, and said he'd be on the first plane he could get.

"Let us know which flight. Arlene will come for you."

"I'll take a cab," Max said and put the phone down.

He opened the front door with his own key and dropped his carry-on in the foyer. Arlene, Eddy and Viola sat in the living room. The women were wiping their eyes. Eddy got up, gripped Max's hand, and smiled glumly.

"She's gone, ten minutes ago. Your father's with her."

Viola looked at him with sadness, Arlene with anger.

Max stepped into the bedroom, not speaking. His father cradled what had been Rita in his arms, rocking back and forth. Her arms dangled like a broken marionette, thin and emaciated as a victim of Auschwitz, the ravaged face sunken to thin, bluish skin covering the protruding cheekbones and jaw of Death's timeless skull. A night-gown from earlier days, draped plentifully over the body, mocking with its abundant folds of excess fabric.

"Don't leave me. Don't leave me. My Rita, my love, my Rita, my love. Don't leave me," Ben crooned, moaning as he rocked.

"Daddy," Max said, stepping closer and shutting the door, "I'm here."

Ben hesitated at the sound of his son's voice and turned around to look at him, still holding his wife's body in his arms. His was not so much a face Max saw, not the familiar jowly squareness, but an image of all the agony of irrevocable loss molded into a single lump of drying clay, neither stern nor frowning, but as though everything had melted, dripped downward.

"Max," his father reached one arm toward him, "come say goodbye to your mother."

Ben pulled Max over to hold and hug the broken doll that had been his mother. Not daring to withdraw, although it frightened him to touch the corpse and feel the rapidly cooling flesh, he joined in the last embrace and let his own tears flow and mingle with his father's, dripping onto the pale blue silk of Rita's gown. Smelling Ben's familiar tobacco breath, feeling his scratchy beard, reminded Max of the times Ben rocking him to sleep when he was a small boy sick in bed. Despite the pain and the sobbing that convulsed his own thin frame, he felt wholly welcome, unquestionably loved by the living and the dead.

Ben let Rita's body down gently, brushing the lank, dark hair, grayer than Max recalled and thinned to half its former volume by the drugs and radiation treatments, smoothing it away from the closed eyes. Rita's mouth was formed into either a smile or a grimace.

"I was sitting in the living room reading the paper," Ben said.

Max stood and now hovered over him sitting on the edge of the bed and Rita lying back on the pillows as though asleep.

Ben wiped his eyes with the back of his hand, fished a crumpled handkerchief from his pocket and blew his nose.

"And she was napping after lunch, and I heard her call, 'Ben, come help me' and I ran in here and she was sitting up, stark upright in the middle of the bed, with her eyes popping out of her head and her mouth wide, wide open. You could see that her body was being ripped apart with the pain. I grabbed her and held her tightly and she was much colder than usual and I felt death in her body pulling her away from me, stronger than me, and I hated it. I wanted to kill it! 'The pills,' I said. 'I'll get the pain pills.'"

"'No', she said, 'there's no use. Just hold me like always.'"

"I held her. Her arms were so weak she couldn't even lift them, and she pressed her face against mine. 'Aaaaaaoohh,' she groaned and it almost sounded like she was relieved. 'It's over,' she said. 'Rita,' I said. 'No, no! Thank you for loving me,' she whispered, and there was nothing left. The others came in a few minutes later. But I told them to leave us alone. I just wanted to hold her until you got here."

Ben's sobs burst up from his body like a volcano exploding, and he began to cry again, sitting on the edge of the bed, with Rita's stick figure stretched out behind him. Max stepped forward, put his hands on Ben's heaving shoulders and then pressed the gray, grizzled-lion head against his chest, feeling the hot tears run into his shirt, etching like acid into his body of memory. The orchestra in his mind played the final chord of *La Boheme*, and all Max could think of saying to his father was "Corragio," but he didn't.

Knocking on the bedroom door and opening it at the same time, Arlene said, "Daddy, the men from Riverside Chapel are here."

Max helped Ben to his feet and led him away from Rita, and past the professional gloom of the undertakers' pick-up detail into the living room.

◆

Max stood, helping Viola up with him, and she hugged him closer still, her voluptuously soft body against him while his impulses

225

ping-ponged between the benign comfort he was supposed to be bringing her as the healer, the visionary, the carrier-on of the family name, and the malignancy of wanting her body, wanting to thrust his hands beneath the black velvet robe and possess her, as his father must have done so many times. That too was tradition.

*Was there something about unmarried brothers having to marry their widowed sisters-in-law? This could be an updated version, for wasn't he his father's brother in a way?*

Viola must have felt something like that too, although her body was miles ahead of her need for saying anything, even thinking it, and she pressed against him firmly, lightly moving her pelvis against him.

Max was sure that she was naked beneath the robe, and with the beauty parlor smell of her dyed hair heavy in his nostrils he knew that it would be all too easy to realize the fantasy of his youth and fuck Viola, Aunt Viola, right here amidst the plush baroque of her daily life. "How do you like that, Ben?" The impulse made his arms feel leaden and his cheeks bristle. The numbing tingle of his nose felt the same way when he had a few drinks, and his penis stirred in the prison of his jockey shorts.

But to act would be to yield to a life force that wasn't his. It belonged to others around and beyond him. He could only know and then transfigure what he knew into another form: that was his life, and he had to live it. There wasn't really a choice, except to be true to what he knew or betray it and pay the price.

"Courage," he said to Viola, and giving her a final squeeze, he left the apartment.

A crash on the cymbal, a shimmering sizzle in the aftermath of reverberation, and then a quickened silence under the skilled fingers of the percussionist.

# 13

MAX MANEUVERED BEN'S CADILLAC into Arlene's two-car garage and then waited by the side-door of the house until she let him in.

"The car's in the garage. Here's the keys," he said, placing the keys and registration on the kitchen counter where he had found them last night.

"Where's Ursula?" she asked.

"She had something to do. She'll come out a little later."

Arlene was wearing a simple, but very expensive, black Chanel suit; she resembled their mother more each day: the eyes, the way she did her hair, the shape of her body. She also was starting to act like his mother, he realized, when she looked at Max's chinos and open collared shirt, frowned, and delivered a Rita line: "Would it have killed you to put on a tie and jacket?"

"For what?"

"To show respect for your father and for the people who will visit us here, for them too there should be a sense of dignity."

"I should have worn white tie and tails, as if I was conducting," Max said.

"Oh, for that kind of occasion you understand what's required, but for this you have to remain a rebellious adolescent!"

"When are you going to get off my back, Arlene? That monkey suit that conductors wear is a uniform, that's all. It doesn't distract the audience's focus from the music. To sit shiva there's no prescription. Maybe sackcloth and ashes, and I don't notice them on you either!"

"Just as a suit or a blazer and tie stands for decorum. Shiva is not about you! There a plenty of Daddy's jackets and ties upstairs, nice ones, and you 're about the same size. Why don't you go try some on. You can have them, anyway. Better than giving everything away. His watches and rings and links are yours too, by rights. Think about it.

Max didn't answer.

"You can also have the car if you want," Arlene said, changing the subject. "He didn't owe any money on it, and I don't need it, so if you want, just take it. I'll find the title, and we'll get some kind of transfer papers and it's yours."

Max was surprised by his sister's offer. She was usually not that generous.

"No, but thanks…seriously. I don't need a car more than a couple of times a year, and then I'd rather rent one. Who needs the headache of a car in Manhattan? Besides, I'd have to park in an expensive garage where I live. No thanks. It's too much trouble."

"You could just leave it parked out here and come get it when you want it?"

"That's a good idea. I'll think about it. But why don't you let Ellen take it to school? Maybe she'd like to have it."

"I don't want her driving around up there. She's flaky enough without giving her the ready means to avoid the work she has to do by zooming around Dutchess County every night."

"Then give it to Phil or Charlotte. I don't know. Sell it and use the money. Or give me the money. That I can use."

"I don't think that either Phil or Charlotte wants or needs our father's car. If you want to sell it and keep the money, that's your choice, but don't ask me to do it."

"Then sell it and pay for the funeral with the money. Yeah, that's a good idea."

"You think I can't afford to pay for the funeral? And what made you think that I was going to do it alone? You have some responsibility in all this. It isn't like years ago when Mom died and you were a student."

"I would have contributed something back then. I offered, but Dad said no . . ."

She cut in sharply: "Wasn't that always the way? He constantly protected you. Sure, why should you have to pay anything? Weren't you noble enough to come home when he called you? And by then too late to even see her alive for the last time. God forbid that anything should tear the new Beethoven away from his studies abroad. Your father never shut up about how great you were going to be, how you were studying with the world's most famous teacher, and how you would be teaching at Juilliard and would also get a Ph.D. I could have found a cure for cancer and he would have said 'that's nice' and have done with it. But if you lit a match, that was a great accomplishment."

"Where's Aunt Charlotte?" Max asked, hoping he could change the subject and avoid the embarrassment of anyone overhearing his squabbling with Arlene.

"She was getting on my nerves so I asked her to go to Waldbaum's to buy some fruit and vegetables. Uncle Phil got here early too, so he drove her over there. Let's go in and sit down in the living room."

Arlene led the way.

"Are you hungry?" she asked, glancing over her shoulder.

"No, thanks."

"You want something to drink? Coffee, soda, beer?"

"Nothing. I'm fine, Maybe later, when the others get here. Where's Ellen?"

"Upstairs in her room, lost to the world with earphones on. I told her that she couldn't play the stereo this week so that's her way out. She said it was a stupid rule and had nothing to do with her feelings about her grandfather."

"She's right," Max said, sitting down on a chair.

"Ellen is wrong," Arlene retorted, sitting down opposite him, "and she's just like you in that regard. She thinks that the whole world revolves around her and that its customs and rules were made for other people, not her."

"The serpent within," he said. "There's a wild gene loose in this family and you are wasting your energy trying to fight the chemistry!"

He looked around the room. Everything was the same as always, but Arlene had draped a cloth over the "Tango Palace" sign for the shiva. It stood in the corner like a veiled monument, a silent witness to Ben's last dance. Ironic, Max thought, that he'd bought it for his sister as a house gift, a "conversation piece." Thank God it couldn't talk.

"I don't need you to tell me how to raise my daughter."

"I never have."

"Well, don't start now."

"And I don't need you to tell me how to live my life. It's mine, not yours, and I'm not doing so badly at it."

"Oh yeah, wonderful. You're a big success and you're so happy you could bust."

"Maybe I will be after Friday night!"

Arlene looked confused. Then she realized what Max was saying.

"You're going ahead with the opera? You didn't cancel the performance? postpone? What kind of thing is that? How can you be so heartless, and show no respect for the man who loved you more than anyone or anything else in the world?"

Her face flushed red with anger, and hatred leaped from her eyes as she went on: "First you run away when your mother is dying, then you use information that she kept hidden all of her life and make it public, advertise to the world what shamed your parents. And your father, who would have laid down his life for you — you don't deserve it, God knows — he tried to discourage you from using that story. But no, there is no other story you can use for your god-damned opera than the shame in your family history. So when your father is dead, what do you do? You piss on his grave, and you don't even have the simple, basic decency to postpone the date. You have to do it during the week of shiva to rub your independence in the whole family's faces. You really are a rotten, spoiled brat. Even though you're tall enough to be an adult."

Max didn't want to yell. He wanted to avoid this fight, hide from it, but there was nowhere to run.

"Maybe it's my memorial to him — to them. What the hell does all this hocus-pocus mean?" he asked. "You repeat prayers you couldn't give a shit about, you — the observant synagogue goer? You don't see a shul between Yom Kippurs, except for someone's wedding or bar mitzvah. But for sitting shiva you cover the mirrors and have everyone come by to stuff their faces, drink your booze and make a cocktail party? And then some twerp rabbi who didn't even know Papa conducts a service and does P.R. for his temple? This is religion by you? This is respect for the dead? I think it's a swamp of bullshit that you're wallowing in for convenience and you try to drag me into the muck in the hope of inundating me in the same way. Well, close, but no cigar! You missed again."

She looked and sounded almost apologetic: "Maybe I just wanted to say to the world, 'we're a family after all; we honor our parents and have respect for the traditions that make us a people'. And this is the way Jewish people the world over deal with the loss of loved ones. But what would that mean to you? At least I go to shul on Yom Kippur, and other times as well, FYI. You haven't been near one since your bar mitzvah."

"That only proves that I'm less of a hypocrite than you are. I act as I believe."

"You sound so self-righteous," Arlene said. "As you believe? What the hell do you believe? In Max Bergman and what he wants, nothing else!"

He didn't want to fall into that trap. "In some very ordinary things, Arlene, some very ordinary things: I lost my father, and his death upsets me, and because I was never able to make my peace with him as you did, apparently. That is going to bother me for a very long time, if not forever. Also, there's just the ordinary feeling of him not being there, not going on as a constant, even though he never let me get to know him better in these last few years."

"You wouldn't have liked it so much. Besides, you stayed away, hardly came out to see him."

"Because I didn't want to see you at the same time. Whenever you were there he attacked me to show you that he wasn't favoring me."

"So why didn't you come out in the afternoon, sometimes, when I wasn't here, and sit and talk to him, drink a cup of tea with him, be of some comfort to him. But what would you know about that, about anyone else's loneliness? You talk about 'ordinary' feelings? You don't know what ordinary feelings are! You only respond to what you see on paper, not what other people go through in their lives! Once it's in the high realm of 'Art' you can deal with the whole thing abstractly. Then you don't have to step in the shit, the everyday ordinary shit most people's lives are filled with. But what would you know of that? It's too ordinary for a great artist like you. A new Mahler! With your little Alma to look after you. What else do you need? Certainly not your ordinary, everyday father and, oh, God knows, not your pedestrian sister and her family. You have a niece who adores you and you don't even know her, although maybe it's better, because you'd be a model of misbehavior to her, and that would be a total disaster."

"What do you know about Alma Mahler? And how can you compare her to Ursula?"

Max knew that focusing on the barb would irritate Arlene.

"You must think that I'm a total nincompoop, and that I never read anything, and that I don't know anything except about my profession. A dull, uninformed, Queens housewife who happens to be a doctor! But certainly no more than a technologist of medicine, a kind of classy plumber. Is that about right?"

She couldn't have been more accurate, but Max couldn't say he agreed because that would only enrage her more, and what he wanted was to end the argument, not continue it.

"So I didn't spend as much time with Papa as I could have; you're right, but mostly because he always used to get on my case about what I should be doing. He would never accept me for what I had chosen, as a career, as a life style, and what I was doing well by all accounts. He'd have to bug me about something. If it wasn't the opera, then it was when I was going to marry Ursula and give him a grandson. You notice that he never even considered that I could have a daughter?"

"No, that was for me to disappoint him with." Arlene laughed in the midst of her anger. "And then, when he came to live here with us he doted on her more in a few years than he ever even talked to me all my life."

"Or," Max went on, avoiding the possible detour, "he would tell me that I should move out of the city where it was very bad to live, and he knew because he himself had lived on the Lower East Side sixty years ago, and that was, after all, only a stone's throw from where I lived, and he knew how unsafe it was. Always something."

"Yeah, but were you aware that he had no friends as he got older, and he used to spend most of his days alone?"

"What about Aunt Viola . . . and Uncle Mike?"

Arlene looked at him suspiciously and grimaced.

"What do you mean?" she said, and Max knew that she was fishing for information.

"I mean, I know about him and Viola."

Silence covered them like an ominous cloud that suddenly darkens the summer sky, makes the birds stop singing or flee for safety, and brings a halt to insects' buzzing .

"What do you know? . . . who told you?"

"She did."

"When?"

"Today, this afternoon just before I got here."

"That bitch! That no good, scheming whore," Arlene screamed. "It wasn't enough that she killed him and that . . . that I have to keep their dirty little secret. No! She has to advertise the whole thing.

233

Next she'll take out an ad in the paper. I wonder how many other people she's told."

"I don't think she told anybody. She just felt I should know."

"Know that your father was betraying your mother with her best friend . . . and cousin, no less! Do you know how many years that was going on?"

"Since right after Ma died."

"Don't be so naive. You believe everything? While she was sick too, and even years ago, when they were all younger. Everybody knew about it, about what a whore Viola was, still is, and what a fool your father used to make of himself whenever she was around. That's why Mike is always so crabby, and stayed away from Ben in the last few years. Only Rita never knew. She was always oblivious of everything like that."

Max was incredulous. He couldn't believe that Arlene accepted such mythologies. Rita knew everything. She just chose not to pay attention to things she couldn't do anything about. Whose lies were worse? Arlene's telling her mother that she was going to get well, or Ben and Viola keeping themselves alive by giving each other the little physical pleasure that they took in each other's company, in and out of bed, and keeping it a secret?

"Rita sanctioned it, Max said. "She told Vi to 'take care of Ben because he was lonely.' She knew. It was her will."

"LIAR," Arlene screamed. "Why would she do such a thing when she knew that your father made such a fool of himself with that whore anyway? What was she, his pimp? How dare you?"

"Viola told me that, and I believe her. Why should she lie?"

"To protect herself, and to use you as she has used everyone else. As she used your mother for so many years as a way just to be near Ben. It must have been the longest ongoing affair in history. She's a whore and a liar, and she's spent a lifetime using people to get what she wanted. So god-damned brazen, too. You know that she used to see Ben almost every day since Mama died. She wouldn't leave him alone because she's insatiable, a nymphomaniac. I'm surprised she didn't pull your pants off when you were with her. When I saw her with you last night, I knew she was on the make."

"She was lonely, upset. She just wanted to talk," Max said.

Under the fury there were some vestiges of truth in Arlene's accusations, but he knew that these were distorted by her need to lay blame, to find culprits so that she could keep the memory of her mother holy and unsullied. Saint Rita. Why should he cloud her illusions? Was that his job, his vocation?

"She killed him, Max. She killed him. If she had let him alone to live out his old age in peace with me, he'd still be alive today. You think a man of his age can take that kind of sex life, and dancing, no less? What kind of monster is that woman? And you believe her? You're a bigger fool!"

"Bigger than whom?"

"Than your father, always living on his dreams."

"And they were such bad dreams?"

"He never was what he wanted to be, Max, never, and he tried to make you into what he could have been."

"But you filled that role!"

"I wasn't good enough. I wasn't his son. I was only a girl and no matter what he said, he had no respect for women. They were inferior creatures. Okay to cook, clean and make babies, but if they did anything real, it was a freak show, like a seal balancing a ball on its nose. A circus act."

"Why do we have to fight all the time, Arlene? Why do you have to pick on me?" Max asked. "Is it my fault that he doted on me? I didn't do anything to curry special favor. The opposite. So why in hell do you blame me? For being born? I didn't want to upstage you. It just happened. But I feel the loss of him too, and perhaps the fact that I could never please him makes it worse."

"Well, don't ask me to pity you," she said haughtily. "You are self-centered, just as he was, and you think that the sun rises and sets with what you do. So now you feel some remorse? Big deal! It's too late."

235

"Too late for what? To prove something to you? I don't have to do that."

"You lost all your opportunities as far as I'm concerned. When you went away while Mama was dying, when you went against everyone's wishes and used that diary she gave you, and now, when despite everything, you are going to dishonor both of your parents and shame the family by not only going ahead with the opera, but you don't even have the simple decency to postpone it. No, not Max. He won't wait. What's a father's death after all? Just another event."

"I miss him as much as you do, just differently, maybe more abstractly."

"What kind of shit is that, 'abstractly'? You turn everything into some kind of aesthetic crap. I live with the everyday: the sick and dying at work. But more mundane, do you have to come across his reading glasses in the bathroom, or a cigar butt in the ashtray, or a pipe that he left with some tobacco still in it, or some notes he made to himself on the telephone pad? Do you have to live with the smell of him around the house and be reminded as you walk from room to room that there was a human being there. No, it's all some kind of abstraction that you can deal with by writing some music. But what the hell can I do?"

"You can stop hating everything and everybody who doesn't fit into your ideas of the way things should be. You're just like Ben that way, and you can stop thinking that you score points by only coloring inside the lines," Max shouted.

"What do you mean? Just like him? How dare you! I try to model myself on Rita. She knew what to do, and so she did it. You think she had an easy life? But she pulled up her socks and went on. She never asked for anyone's pity for her hurt. She kept it all in."

"So she let it eat her up, and she got cancer?" Max interrupted.

"Look," Arlene said with disdain, "don't talk to me about mystical, half-baked, psychobabble hypotheses concerning medicine, and I won't discuss musical harmonies with you. Okay?"

He laughed at her grudging admission of his competence, at least.

"The only thing she ever let out was that diary of her mother's, and she expected me to use it. That was her intent."

"Are you mad? Do you think she wanted to shame and embarrass the family?

"I think that she wanted me to understand that there is a real past that determines the present, not just the nice convenience of death, of forgetting everything. What might she have done with the story if she had the talent and training? But she wasn't dealt that hand. It was her assignment for me to carry out, and she knew it."

"What a twisted, self-aggrandizing statement," Arlene said, her voice rising in pitch and volume once again. "How you manage to justify doing whatever you want is amazing. It's a major talent."

"And there was never anything that Rita said to you, nothing that she said to set the record straight?" Max asked.

Arlene didn't answer him. She looked away, stood and walked over to the covered "Tango Palace" sign and fingered the cloth, then lifted it a bit, then let it drop back into place. Max went to her, put his hands on her shoulders and made her look at him. There were tears of anger and frustration in her eyes.

"What good is it to bury all the past like that?" he asked imploringly. "That's what I mean when I say that you're like Ben. He spent a lifetime concealing that he was a communist in the thirties, as though anyone cared, and that the bottom dropped out of his life when cousin Meyer returned to Russia to follow his own dream. Ben didn't have the courage to do what he wanted to do openly, and he tried like hell to prevent you and me from getting out of line, with me, especially, as though he could secretly redeem himself within the system if I became a replica of his fantasy. And look where it all got him."

"He was a happy man, Max. He had a good life, and don't you think different!"

"He was an angry man, frustrated, and he made everything into a deep secret. Come on. Don't be the same way. What did Rita tell you?"

Arlene shook his hands off her shoulders and backed away a pace, looking like a cornered cat. A wild energy flashed from her eyes, and Max was afraid that she would claw at his face.

"She knew what a philanderer he was," Arlene hissed in his face, "so don't you come around with the bullshit that fucking whore Viola hands you because you're innocent enough to believe it. She took care of him? Looked after him when your mother was sick? At Rita's own request? What a lie!"

"What did she tell you? What are you talking about?" He pressed, wanting to back off, but knowing that he couldn't, not now, not having pushed so far.

Arlene took a deep breath, closed her eyes, and, looking as though opening her mouth caused great pain, screamed: "NOTHING, NO-THING, NOTHING AT ALL! She never told me anything, never confided in me the way a mother ought to talk to a daughter, never let me in. It was like she was some kind of monument rather than a mother!"

She noticed the surprise and alarm on Max's face: "Oh, don't worry. She took care of me well enough, always dressed me like a little doll, even when they had very little money in the early years, and I got ballet lessons and lots of toys and all that. But I don't remember her ever hugging me, — just hugging me because I was her kid and she wanted to. She wasn't built for it, I guess, because she never had a real mother. That was for Papa to do, when I was little, until you came along, you little brat."

Then, realizing how silly the last phrase sounded, she snickered.

"Welcome to the human race. You were jealous," Max said.

"Sure I was, what four-year-old wouldn't be? But then you did add fuel to the fire by being such a rotten kid."

"Rita used to say that if you want to beat a dog, you can always find a stick," Max said, vaguely remembering the Yiddish proverb, one of his mother's favorites.

"I always had a stick," Arlene said. "I just wanted her to love me, to be a pal to me, the way Papa was to you. But it didn't happen.

Everything was done properly, by the book, and I was such a good girl. I did what I was told. I even became a doctor, and I thought that it would please them."

"But it did!" Max said.

"Not enough," she said, her voice harsh again with bitterness. "Ben even used to complain how much the medical school tuition cost him. Can you imagine how that made me feel?"

Max nodded his silent sympathy.

"So what was the business about his being a philanderer and that she knew. How can you say that if she never confided in you?" he asked.

"I don't know," she said, holding back.

He put his hand out and took her arm. "You do," he said. "So tell me, please!"

Her face drained pale and she stared past him saying quietly, "I made it up. I made it up! When you and Viola and Mike's daughter Becky were little and you used to play with each other all the time I would watch Ben chortling and fussing over the two of you, picking you both up, one in each arm and being happy and so full of love for both of you. I hated Becky for that. I guess I already hated you, and I used to think or pretend that she was really his daughter, and that I was adopted or something, you know, maybe Rita really had twins and gave one away to Mike and Viola because they didn't have any kids, all that kind of fantasy. I used to wish . . ."

Arlene stopped talking and started to cry uncontrollably.

Max felt helpless once again. This was the third time that day he found himself dealing with crying women, calming their anger and grief. Awkward with such face offs, he preferred to control emotions by imagining and re-creating them in music or libretto, and thereby be able to turn feelings on or off like a water tap. He withdrew his hand from her arm and sat staring at his fingers, then fished a handkerchief from his trouser pocket and gave it to her. Lucky it was clean.

She blew her nose and wiped her reddened eyes.

"I used to wish," she said, calmer now, "that Viola was my mother too, so that I could be loved in the way Becky was, so that I could be kissed and held and coddled. And when Becky died, I hate to admit it, I was secretly glad. 'May she rot in hell along with her whore of a mother.' I used to think that, wish it! And you know what? In some ways, I still do. There, are you satisfied? Now you know it all. You know why."

Arlene turned away from him and began to cry again, her entire body in convulsions of deep sobs coming out of the most inaccessible of burial grounds. Max was stunned. He had tipped back the tombstone and seen the great worm feeding. It made such a frightful mess. Exposed, would it now waste away?

He waited until Arlene's sobbing subsided and asked, "Why do you have to carry out some kind of vendetta, against Ben, and Aunt Vi, and Becky, who was innocent, after all? And what about Rita, who unconsciously condoned the very thing that hurt you?"

Arlene turned, her face contorted by the hatred, red and swollen now with tears and fury. "Your mother was too pure. A saint, a marble statue, and she never suspected any motives other than decent ones. She never understood *her* bastard of a father, and she spent a life trying to be perfect to make up for what her horrible, crazy mother did to her by abandoning her. Highly polished stone. She was the textbook mother to me, and all her feelings were underground, dead."

Max didn't want to contradict his sister because he realized that there was no point in it. There was no final truth to be uncovered here. The worm had done its work well. There were only fragments left, and they could certainly only be identified by the need to see them in your own way.

"Well then, aside from everything else," he asked, "why do you continue to hate Becky and Viola, if you know that so much of your feeling is based on a childhood fantasy?" And as he spoke he realized that it was the wrong question to ask, but too late to retrieve.

"Because they took my father from me! How stupid can you be?" Arlene screamed in his face, spittle flying from her mouth. "He used to talk about how cute Becky was all the time, and me? He hardly gave me the time of day. And I thought that maybe after Mother died, maybe he'd come to value me, to see how important I really was to him. But no. Then there was that fucking Viola to take him away. Me? I was a convenience, or an inconvenience. That's all!"

"And you never stopped trying to win him back from them?" Max said. "Why do you have to any more? Arlene, it's all over."

"I don't know. I don't know." Arlene said.

Max put out his hand to her, but she got up and stepped away towards the covered sign.

"That rotten bastard. THAT ROTTEN BASTARD . . . and his fucking whore!" she screamed. "Dance, did they? Dance on my mother's grave, dance on my life? I'll hate them all forever, cheap shits. They weren't fit to be in the same room as Rita, let alone live with her, get her love."

She ripped the cloth off the "Tango Palace" sign, catching the cover on the switch. The neon starter buzzed and the letters began to flame on and off, on and off, green and purple: TANGO PALACE . . .TANGO PALACE!

"I'll teach them to dance!" she screamed, and kicked out with her foot, knocking the sign to the floor, where she stamped her foot on the broken bits of glass, again and again.

Max tried to stop her, but she pushed him back in fury.

"MA! WHAT ARE YOU DOING?" Ellen shouted from the foyer near the front door. "What are you doing?" She looked horrified at this education away from school.

Arlene stopped. "How long have you been there?" she demanded.

"A long time," Ellen answered, without averting her eyes.

The front doorbell rang.

"It's Uncle Phil and Aunt Charlotte. I'll get it," and Ellen stepped quickly to the door.

"What happened here?" Charlotte asked. She was clutching two brown supermarket bags. "Phil went back to the car for more bags," she said, to assure them that they wouldn't starve.

"Nothing," Arlene said, "a little accident, that's all . . . a little accident."

"Oh, I'm glad," Charlotte said, smiling relief. "You should see what we got."

Arlene stepped away from Max and the broken glass.

"Sit down," she ordered him. "I'll get a dustpan and brush."

How they had wronged each other, he thought, for half a lifetime. Could it change now?

A strong ozone smell filled the air.

# CODA

FOR ONCE MAX WAS GLAD that he needed glasses for distance. When he walked onto the podium and turned to bow to the audience before the tap of his baton brought *Number Our Days* to life, he could only make out a blur in the row of seats he had reserved for his family and friends. The gleaming dome of Uncle Phil's head winked like a beacon in the darkened hall and the rest of the row was a blur. Were some of the seats empty?

"I am dedicating this work to the memory of my father," he announced to the blurred darkness, "who died this week and could not bear witness." Turning his back to the murmur, Max struck the baton, and the curtains lifted on the long one and only act.

He was caught then in the spectacle and sound he created: the ominous threading of double basses carried him down to hell. The soaring arias of the soprano lifted him to heaven. The clairvoyance of the threatening tympani and the false lulling of the woodwinds served as a prelude to the bittersweet mockery of the soprano saxophone as the mad heroine sought refuge from the wind, which would always find her because it blew across her barren mind. All the light and darkness of the words from his grandmother's nightmare vision lifting above the abyss, the swelling waves of the orchestra, and he made it all. He soared with it and was lifted out and beyond himself to a place where no one else traveled. He knew then, confirmed for always, that this was what he lived for. If he created acceptable fictions from unacceptable facts, so be it. Such was his mission; he was dedicated to serve it by the force that sprang to life at his birth. Above and around him, leaping from his baton, transforming the notations on the page into life, was the God he sought, the only deity he could serve.

Max's act of worship was the end and the beginning, nothing and everything. When the laser projection on the backlit screen enlarged the family picture until it exploded in brilliant fragments and dispersed into the audience, and the tympani pounded the world into utter darkness and silence, Max stood on the podium as though suspended in space completely alone.

Another few seconds of complete silence and darkness, then light, and shouts of "*Bravissimo*" and he turned to face the crowd that stood, clapping, whistling, stamping their feet. The concert hall was alive with the recognition he had demanded and won.

Now, with his eyeglasses on, he saw that the row he reserved for family and friends was filled, standing, cheering, applauding: Eddy and Ellen, Jules, Theo, Viola and Mike, Charlotte, Phil, Gertie, and Ursula wiping her eyes. And next to her, Arlene, hands raised high above her head flailing at each other like crashing birds. And next to her, an empty seat Max could fill with visions.

The worst and best had happened, but the world was still here. In the morning, he'd wake up and get on with it. Unguarded, nothing between him and eternity.

◆　◆　◆

# ACKNOWLEDGMENTS

The help and support of the following people made this book possible:

Agent (and wife) Joan Brandt (Schwartz), "a woman of valor";

Editor and designer Marian Haley Beil, extraordinary talent;

Writer John Coyne, friend, litmus test, advisor;

Attorney Harvey Sigelbaum, best man, my amen corner;

Daughters Nancie, Erica, Jennifer and Anna, my best work;

Niece Jill Fishbane Mayer, M.D., asked great questions;

Nephew Bruce Fishbane, M.D., read the manuscript with pride and pleasure, but did not live to see it published.

CPSIA information can be obtained
at www.ICGtesting.com
Printed in the USA
LVOW10s1910141216
517264LV00001B/65/P